THE AUSTRALIAN CLASSICS LIBRARY

The Workingman's Paradise

'John Miller' (William Lane)

Introduction by Andrew McCann

General editors

Bruce Bennett, University of New South Wales

Robert Dixon, University of Sydney

SYDNEY UNIVERSITY PRESS

Published 2009 by Sydney University Press

SYDNEY UNIVERSITY PRESS
Fisher Library, University of Sydney
www.sup.usyd.edu.au

First published in 1892 by Edwards, Dunlop & Co. and Worker Board of Trustees, Brisbane

This, the Australian Classics Library text of *The Workingman's Paradise*, is a repaging of text files on SETIS, themselves input from the 1892 edition published by Edwards, Dunlop & Co. and Worker Board of Trustees, Brisbane

The publication of this book is part of the University of Sydney Library's Australian Studies electronic texts initiative. Further details are available at www.sup.usyd.edu.au/oztexts/

Front cover image: portrait of William Lane, Cosme Colony Collection. Courtesy of the Rare Books and Special Collections, University of Sydney Library

ISBN   978-1-920899-00-4

Designed in Australia at the University Publishing Service, University of Sydney

Contents

Introduction

William Lane arrived in Brisbane in 1885. True to an itinerant life that had already taken him from Bristol to Canada, the United States, and back, he did not remain there long either. In 1893 he left Australia together with 220 other 'settlers,' for Paraguay, where he envisioned a utopian community, a 'New Australia,' based on socialist principles of cooperation. Lane's importance to Australia's cultural and political history is striking given the amount of time he actually spent in the country. One need only glance at those seminal histories of the 1890s to see this. Works as diverse as Vance Palmer's celebratory *The Legend of the Nineties* (1954) and Bruce Scates's circumspect and scholarly *A New Australia* (1997) include chapters largely devoted to him; John Docker's *The Nervous Nineties* (1991) includes two. In a matter of half-a-dozen years, it seems, Lane had become representative of a kind of working-class militancy that would subsequently be seen as central to a developing Australian identity. By the same token, it is the ultra-conservative, even proto-fascist, underpinnings of this militancy that new-left voices—such as Humphrey McQueen's in his enormously influential *A New Britannia* (1970)—have pointed out, making Lane also central to debates about the political legacy of the period he now seems to represent.

Lane's journalistic output in Australia was significant. He co-founded the *Boomerang* in 1887, founded *The Worker* three years later, and published extensively on labour issues, particularly on the role and treatment of women under industrial capitalism. Our sense of his centrality to the interface between literature and working-class radicalism, however, rests largely on his 1892 novel, *The Workingman's Paradise*, which he published under the *nom de plume* John Miller in response to the bitter Queensland shearers' strike of 1891.

It is an extraordinary, and troublingly paranoid novel. In it Lane's vision of Australia ravaged by the twin evils of exploitative capitalism and Chinese immigration consolidates the particularly xenophobic brand of socialism he had practised in the *Boomerang*. And yet, for all its concern with the striking shearers, it is an overwhelmingly urban novel that explores the material culture of late-nineteenth-century Sydney with a drama seldom seen before in an Australian narrative. Much of the novel is structured in a way that evokes the urban ethnographies and physiologies that were a mainstay of nineteenth-century journalism. Nellie, the novel's heroine, leads her Darling Downs suitor, Ned, on a tour of the 'real Sydney.' What she reveals is a world of squalid slums and commercial degradation driven by acute racial anxieties in which a debilitated proletariat, and especially its women, confront the promise of a new world—the optimism that Lane no doubt inherited from Charles Kingsley's *Alton Locke*—with a mounting sense of irony, bitterness and outrage. Along the way we get stunning descriptions of Sydney's class divide, a tour through the commercial squalor of Paddy's Market on a Saturday night, and are introduced to a circle of bohemian intellectuals, at whose centre stands the radical philosopher Geisner, a charismatic itinerant with distinctly Carlylean overtones. But it is Nellie who is the real focus of the novel: she is an object of both intellectual and, implicitly, erotic infatuation for the men who cluster around her. At one point, as she watches a child of the slums struggle with death, she embarks on a long interior monologue that couches Lane's radical worldview in a thoroughly mythic, racial and disturbingly violent idiom: 'Oh, for the days when our race was young, when its women slew themselves rather than be shamed and when its men, trampling a rotten empire down, feared neither God nor man and held each other brothers and hated, each one, the tyrant as the common foe of all!' (152–53) The passage goes on to evoke a world of Teutonic aggression in which 'communists and conquerors' burst from 'the forests and the steppes,' forming a 'a fierce avalanche of daring men and lusty women who beat and battered Rome down like Odin's hammer that they were!' Nellie dreams of the 'heathen virtues and the wild pagan fury for freedom and for the passion and purity that Frega taught to the daughters of the barbarian!' In this respect she is clearly presented as the guardian of a particular racialised consciousness. The evocation of Norse myth in this passage is powerfully suggestive of the sort of worldview Lane ultimately fosters. The solution to the ills of modernity is a return to a sort of primal being: racially pure and uncorrupted. Part of the novel's interest for a contemporary reader is that it embodies the conceptual and aesthetic framework that allowed a settler society to imagine itself in terms of this fantasy of a primitive communism that also underwrote visions of a white Australia.

The passage brings us face to face with the most troubling aspect of Lane's work, and one that should occasion a good deal of unease in discussions that assume his canonical status. Lane was a key voice in the articulation of anti-Chinese sentiment in the late 1880s and early 1890s. His first novel, serialised in the *Boomerang* in 1888, was *White or Yellow? A Story of the Race War of A.D. 1908*. It is an invasion-scare novel that reflects the fundamental xenophobia informing the unionist milieu of the period, a xenophobia that found an extreme manifestation in the formation of anti-Chinese leagues. Here Lane fixates on the sexual threat that Chinese men pose to white women, includes a speculative evocation of an Asianised Brisbane and concludes with apocalyptic levels of retributive violence as the invaders get their just deserts.

It is hard to find a clearer example of proto-fascist tendencies in Australian literature. When we read *The Workingman's Paradise*, and especially when we read it under the curatorial imprimatur of the 'Australian classic,' it is important to remember that the book shares these tendencies. That Lane would ultimately try to realise his dream of a racially pure Australia in South America is powerfully suggestive of the fantasy-element in the fascist imaginary. *The Workingman's Paradise* opens up a window into this worldview. It is important that we understand it, and understand it critically, not lest because contemporary

Australia, wrestling with the politics of globalisation, still seems caught up in many of the cultural and political anxieties so evident in Lane's work. As our recent history has shown us, it would be naive to think that Australia has outgrown these uglier aspects of its political formation.

Andrew McCann

Dartmouth College

References

Souter, Gavin. *A Peculiar People: The Australians in Paraguay.* St Lucia, Queensland: University of Queensland Press, 1991.

Whitehead, Anne. *Paradise Mislaid: In Search of the Australian Tribe of Paraguay.* St Lucia, Queensland: University of Queensland Press, 1997.

THE

WORKINGMAN'S PARADISE:

AN AUSTRALIAN LABOUR NOVEL.

BY JOHN MILLER.

EDWARDS, DUNLOP & CO., SYDNEY, BRISBANE AND LONDON.
WORKER BOARD OF TRUSTEES, BRISBANE.
1892.

[Facsimile of first edition titlepage]

PREFACE

THE naming and writing of *The Workingman's Paradise* were both done hurriedly, although delay has since arisen in its publishing. The scene is laid in Sydney because it was not thought desirable, for various reasons, to aggravate by a local plot the soreness existing in Queensland.

While characters, incidents and speakings had necessarily to be adapted to the thread of the plot upon which they are strung, and are not put forward as actual photographs or phonographs, yet many will recognise enough in this book to understand how, throughout, shreds and patches of reality have been pieced together. The first part is laid during the summer of 1888–89 and covers two days; the second at the commencement of the Queensland bush strike excitement in 1891, covering a somewhat shorter time. The intention of the plot, at first, was to adapt the old old legend of Paradise and the fall of man from innocence to the much-prated-of 'workingman's paradise'—Australia. Ned was to be Adam, Nellie to be Eve, Geisner to be the eternal Rebel inciting world-wide agitation, the Stratton home to be presented in contrast with the slum-life as a reason for challenging the tyranny which makes Australia what it really is; and so on. This plot got very considerably mixed and there was no opportunity to properly re-arrange it. After reading the MSS. one friend wrote advising an additional chapter making Ned, immediately upon his being sentenced for 'conspiracy' under George IV., 6, hear that Nellie has died of a broken heart. My wife, on the contrary, wants Ned and Nellie to come to an understanding and live happily ever after in the good old-fashioned style. This being left in abeyance, readers can take their choice until the matter is finally settled in another book.

Whatever the failings of this book are it may nevertheless serve the double purpose for which it was written: (1) to assist the fund being raised for Ned's mates now in prison in Queensland, and (2) to explain unionism a little to those outside it and Socialism a little to all who care to read or hear, whether unionists or not. These friends of ours in prison will need all we can do for them when they are released, be that soon or late; and there are too few, even in the ranks of unionism, who really understand Socialism.

To understand Socialism is to endeavour to lead a better life, to regret the vileness of our present ways, to seek ill for none, to desire truth and purity and honesty, to despise this selfish civilisation and to comprehend what living might be. Understanding Socialism will not make people at once what men and women should be but it will fill them with hatred for the unfitting surroundings that damn us all and with passionate love for the ideals that are lifting us upwards and with an earnest endeavour to be themselves somewhat as they feel Humanity is struggling to be.

All that any religion has been to the highest thoughts of any people Socialism is, and more, to those who conceive it aright. Without blinding us to our own weaknesses and wickednesses, without offering to us any sophistry or cajoling us with any fallacy, it enthrones Love above the universe, gives us Hope for all who are downtrodden and restores to us Faith in the eternal fitness of things. Socialism is indeed a religion— demanding deeds as well as words. Not until professing socialists understand this will the world at large see Socialism as it really is.

If this book assists the Union Prisoners Assistance Fund in any way or if it brings to a single man or woman a clearer conception of the Religion of Socialism it will have done its work. Should it fail to do either it will not be because the Cause is bad, for the Cause is great enough to rise above the weakness of those who serve it.

J.M.

FROM A LETTER

On the Flinders.

In a western billabong, with a stretch of plain around, a dirty waterhole beside me, I sat and read the WORKER. Maxwellton Station was handy; and sick with a fever on me I crawled off my horse to the shed on a Sunday. They invited me to supper; I was too ill. One gave me medicine, another the WORKER, the cook gave me milk and soup. If this in Unionism, God bless it! This is the moleskin charity, not the squatter's dole. The manager gave me quinine, and this is a Union station. I read 'Nellie's Sister' (from THE WORKINGMAN'S PARADISE) in your last. A woman's tenderness pervades it. Its fiction is truth. Although my feelings are blunted by a bush life, I dropped a tear on that page of the WORKER.

—From a letter.

PART I

THE WOMAN TEMPTED HIM

Ah thy people, thy children, thy chosen,
Marked cross from the womb and perverse!
They have found out the secret to cozen
The gods that constrain us and curse;
They alone, they are wise, and none other;
Give me place, even me, in their train,
O my sister, my spouse, and my mother,
Our Lady of Pain.

—Swinburne

CHAPTER I

WHY NELLIE SHOWS NED ROUND

NELLIE was waiting for Ned, not in the best of humours.

'I suppose he'll get drunk to celebrate it,' she was saying, energetically drying the last cup with a corner of the damp cloth. 'And I suppose she feels as though it's something to be very glad and proud about.'

'Well, Nellie,' answered the woman who had been rinsing the breakfast things, ignoring the first supposition. 'One doesn't want them to come, but when they do come one can't help feeling glad.'

'Glad!' said Nellie, scornfully.

'If Joe was in steady work, I wouldn't mind how often it was. It's when he loses his job and work so hard to get—' Here the speaker subsided in tears.

'It's no use worrying,' comforted Nellie, kindly. 'He'll get another job soon, I hope. He generally has pretty fair luck, you know.'

'Yes, Joe has had pretty fair luck, so far. But nobody knows how long it'll last. There's my brother wasn't out of work for fifteen years, and now he hasn't done a stroke for twenty-three weeks come Tuesday. He's going out of his mind.'

'He'll get used to it,' answered Nellie, grimly. 'How you do talk, Nellie!' said the other. 'To hear you sometimes one would think you hadn't any heart.' 'I haven't any patience.' 'That's true, my young gamecock!' exclaimed a somewhat discordant voice. Nellie looked round, brightening suddenly.

A large slatternly woman stood in the back doorway, a woman who might possibly have been a pretty girl once but whose passing charms had long been utterly sponged out. A perceptible growth of hair lent a somewhat repulsive appearance to a face which at best had a great deal of the virago in it. Yet there was, in spite of her furrowed skin and faded eyes and drab dress, an air of good-heartedness about her, made somewhat ferocious by the muscularity of the arms that fell akimbo upon her great hips, and by the strong teeth, white as those of a dog, that flashed suddenly from between her colourless lips when she laughed.

'That's true, my young gamecock!' she shouted, in a deep voice, strangely cracked. 'And so you're at your old tricks again, are you? Talking sedition I'll be bound. I've half a mind to turn informer and have the law on you. The dear lamb!' she added, to the other woman.

'Good morning, Mrs. Macanany,' said Nellie, laughing. 'We haven't got yet so that we can't say what we like, here.'

'I'm not so sure about that. Wait till you hear what I came to tell you, hearing from little Jimmy that you were at home and going to have a holiday with a young man from the country. We'll sherrivvery them if he takes her away from us, Mrs. Phillips, the only one that does sore eyes good to see in the whole blessed neighbourhood! You needn't blush, my dear, for I had a young man myself once, though you wouldn't imagine it to look at me. And if I was a young man myself it's her'—pointing Nellie out to Mrs. Phillips—'that I'd go sweethearting with and not with the empty headed chits that—'

'Look here, Mrs. Macanany!' interrupted Nellie. 'You didn't come in to make fun of me.'

'Making fun! There, have your joke with the old woman! You didn't hear that my Tom got the run yesterday, did you?'

'Did he? What a pity! I'm very sorry,' said Nellie.

'Everybody'll be out of work and then what'll we all do?' said Mrs. Philips, evidently cheered, nevertheless, by companionship in misfortune.

'What'll we all do! There'd never be anybody at all out of work if everybody was like me and Nellie there,' answered the amazon.

'What did he get the run for?' asked Nellie.

'What can we women do?' queried Mrs. Phillips, doleful still.

'Wait a minute till I can tell you! You don't give a body time to begin before you worry them with questions about things you'd hear all about it if you'd just hold your tongues a minute. You're like two blessed babies! It was this way, Mrs. Phillips, as sure as I'm standing here. Tom got trying to persuade the other men in the yard—poor sticks of men they are!—to have a union. I've been goading him to it, may the Lord forgive me, ever since Miss Nellie there came round one night and persuaded my Tessie to join. 'Tom,' says I to him that very night, 'I'll have to be lending you one of my old petticoats, the way the poor weak girls are beginning to stand up for their rights, and you not even daring to be a union man. I never thought I'd live to be ashamed of the father of my children!' says I. And yesterday noon Tom came home with a face on him as long as my arm, and told me that he'd been sacked for talking union to the men.

'It's a man you are again, Tom,' says I. 'We've lived short before and we can live it again, please God, and it's myself would starve with you a hundred times over rather than be ashamed of you,' says I. 'Who was it that sacked you?' I asked him.

'The foreman,' says Tom. 'He told me they didn't want any agitators about.'

'May he live to suffer for it,' says I. 'I'll go down and see the boss himself.'

'So down I went, and as luck would have it the boy in the front office wasn't educated enough to say I was an old image, I suppose, for would you believe it I actually heard him say that there was a lady, if you please, wanting to see Mister Paritt very particularly on personal business, as I'd told him. So of course I was shown in directly, the very minute, and the door was closed on me before the old villain, who's a great man at church on Sundays, saw that he'd made a little mistake.

11

'What do you want, my good woman?' says he, snappish like. 'Very sorry,' says he, when I'd told him that I'd eleven children and that Tom had worked for him for four years and worked well, too. 'Very sorry,' says he, my good woman, 'but your husband should have thought of that before. It's against my principles,' says he, 'to have any unionists about the place. I'm told he's been making the other men discontented. I can't take him back. You must blame him, not me,' says he.

'I could feel the temper in me, just as though he'd given me a couple of stiff nobblers of real old whisky. 'So you won't take Tom back,' says I, 'not for the sake of his eleven children when it's their poor heart-broken mother that asks you?'

'No,' says he, short, getting up from his chair. 'I can't. You've bothered me long enough,' says he.

'So then I decided it was time to tell the old villain just what I thought of his grinding men down to the last penny and insulting every decent girl that ever worked for him. He got as black in the face as if he was smoking already on the fiery furnace that's waiting for him below, please God, and called the shrimp of an office boy to throw me out. 'Leave the place, you disgraceful creature, or I'll send for the police,' says he. But I left when I got ready to leave and just what I said to him, the dirty wretch, I'll tell to you, Mrs. Phillips, some time when she'—nodding at Nellie—'isn't about. She's getting so like a blessed saint that one feels as if one's in church when she's about, bless her heart!'

'You're getting very particular all at once, Mrs. Macanany,' observed Nellie.

'It's a wonder he didn't send for a policeman,' commented Mrs. Phillips.

'Send for a policeman! And pretty he'd look with the holy bible in his hand repeating what I said to him, wouldn't he now?' enquired Mrs. Macanany, once more placing her great arms on her hips and glaring with her watery eyes at her audience.

'Did you hear that Mrs. Hobbs had a son this morning?' questioned Mrs. Phillips, suddenly recollecting that she also might have an item of news.

'What! Mrs. Hobbs, so soon! How would I be hearing when I just came through the back, and Tom only just gone out to wear his feet off, looking for work? A boy again! The Lord preserve us all! It's the devil's own luck the dear creature has, isn't it now? Why didn't you tell me before, and me here gossiping when the dear woman will be expecting me round to see her and the dear baby and wondering what I've got against her for not coming? I must be off, now, and tidy myself a bit and go and cheer the poor creature up for I know very well how one wants cheering at such times. Was it a hard time she had with it? And who is it like the little angel that came straight frem heaven this blessed day? The dear woman! 1 must be off, so I'll say good-day to you, Mrs. Phillips, and may the sun shine on you and your sweetheart, Nellie, even if he does take you away from us all, and may you have a houseful of babies with faces as sweet as your own and never miss a neighbour to cheer you a bit when the trouble's on you. The Lord be with us all!'

Nellie laughed as the rough-voiced, kind-hearted woman took herself off, to cross the broken dividing wall to the row of houses that backed closely on the open kitchen door. Then she shrugged her shoulders.

'It's always the way,' she remarked, as she turned away to the other door that led along a little, narrow passage to the street. 'What's going to become of the innocent little baby? Nobody thinks of that.'

Mrs. Phillips did not answer. She was tidying up in a wearied way. Besides, she was used to Nellie, and had a dim perception that what that young woman said was right, only one had to work, especially on Saturdays when the smallest children could be safely turned into the street to play with the elder ones, the baby nursed by pressed nurses, who by dint of scolding and coaxing and smacking and promising were persuaded to keep it out of the house, even though they did not keep it altogether quiet.

Mrs. Phillips 'tidied up' in a wearied way, without energy, working stolidly all the time as if she were on a tread-mill. She had a weary look, the expression of one who is tired always, who gets up tired and goes to bed tired, and who never by any accident gets a good rest, who even when dead is not permitted to lie quietly like other people but gets buried the same day in a cheap coffin that hardly keeps the earth up and is doomed to be soon dug up to make room for some other tired body in that economical way instituted by the noble philanthropists who unite a keen appreciation of the sacredness of burial with a still keener appreciation of the value of grave-lots. She might have been a pretty girl once or she might not. Nobody would ever have thought of physical attractiveness as having anything to do with her. Mrs. Macanany was distinctly ugly. Mrs. Phillips was neither ugly nor pretty nor anything else. She was a poor thin draggled woman, who tried to be clean but who had long ago given up in despair any attempt at looking natty and had now no ambition for herself but to have something 'decent' to go out in. Once it was her ambition also to have a 'room.' She had scraped and saved and pared in dull times for this 'room' and when once Joe had a long run of steady work she had launched out into what those who know how workingmen's wives *should* live would have denounced as the wildest extravagance. A gilt framed mirror and a sofa, four spidery chairs and a round table, a wonderful display of wax apples under a glass shade, a sideboard and a pair of white lace curtains hanging from a pole, with various ornaments and pictures of noticeable appearance, also linoleum for the floor, had finally been gathered together and were treasured for a time as household gods indeed. In those days there was hardly a commandment in the decalogue that Mephistopheles might not have induced Mrs. Phillips to commit by judicious praise of her 'room.' Her occasional 'visitors' were ushered into it with an air of pride that was alone enough to illuminate the dingy, musty little place. Between herself and those of her neighbours who had 'rooms' there was a fierce rivalry, while those of inferior grade—and they were in the majority—regarded her with an envy not unmixed with dislike.

But those times were gone for poor Mrs. Phillips. We all know how they go, excepting those who do not want to know. Work gradually became more uncertain, wages fell and rents kept up. They had one room of the small five-roomed house let already. They let another—'they' being her and Joe. Finally, they had to let *the* room. The chairs, the round table and the sofa were bartered at a second-hand store for bedroom furniture. The mirror and the sideboard were brought out into the kitchen, and on the sideboard the wax fruit still stood like the lingering shrine of a departed faith.

The 'room' was now the lodging of two single men, as the good old ship-phrase goes. Upstairs, in the room over the kitchen, the Phillips family slept, six in all. There would have been seven, only the eldest girl, a child of ten, slept with Nellie in the little front room over the door, an arrangement which was not in the bond but was volunteered by the single woman in one of her fits of indignation against pigging together. The other front room was also rented by a single man when they could get him. Just now it was tenantless, an additional cause of sorrow to Mrs. Phillips, whose stock card, 'Furnished Lodgings for a Single Man,' was now displayed at the front window, making the house in that respect very similar to half the houses in the street, or in this part of the town for that matter. Yet with all this crowding and renting of rooms Mrs. Phillips did not grow rich. She was always getting into debt or getting out of it, this depending in inverse ratio upon Joe being in work or out.

When the rooms were all let they barely paid the rent and were always getting empty. The five children—they had one dead and another coming—ate so much and made so much work. There were boots and clothes and groceries to pay for, not to mention bread. And though Joe was not like many a woman's husband yet he did get on the spree occasionally, a little fact which in the opinion of the pious will account for all Mrs. Phillips' weariness and all the poverty of this crowded house. But however that may be she was a weary hopeless faded woman, who would not cause passers-by to turn, pity-stricken, and watch her when she hurried along on her semi-occasional escapes from her prison-house only because such women are so common that it is those who do not look hopeless and weary whom we turn to watch if by some strange chance one passes. The Phillips' kitchen was a cheerless place, in spite of the mirror that was installed in state over the side-board and the wax flowers.

Its one window looked upon a diminutive back yard, a low broken wall and another row of similar two-storied houses. On the plastered walls were some shelves bearing a limited supply of crockery. Over the grated fireplace was a long high shelf whereon stood various pots and bottles. There were some chairs and a table and a Chinese-made safe. On the boarded floor was a remnant of linoleum. Against one wall was a narrow staircase.

It was the breakfast things that Nellie had been helping to wash up. The little American clock on the sideboard indicated quarter past nine.

Nellie went to the front door, opened it, and stood looking out. The view was a limited one, a short narrow side street, blinded at one end by a high bare stone wall, bounded at the other by the almost as narrow by-thoroughfare this side street branched from. The houses in the thoroughfare were three-storied, and a number were used as shops of the huckstering variety, mainly by Chinese. The houses in the side street were two-storied, dingy, jammed tightly together, each one exactly like the next. The pavement was of stone, the roadway of some composite, hard as iron; roadway and pavement were overrun with children. At the corner by a dead wall was a lamp-post. Nearly opposite Nellie a group of excited women were standing in an open doorway. They talked loudly, two or three at a time, addressing each other indiscriminately. The children screamed and swore, quarrelled and played and fought, while a shrill-voiced mother occasionally took a hand in the diversion of the moment, usually to scold or cull some luckless offender. The sunshine radiated that sickly heat which precedes rain.

Nellie stood there and waited for Ned. She was twenty or so, tall and slender but well-formed, every curve of her figure giving promise of more luxurious development. She was dressed in a severely plain dress of black stuff, above which a faint line of white collar could be seen clasping the round throat. Her ears had been bored, but she wore no earrings. Her brown hair was drawn away from her forehead and bound in a heavy braid on the back of her neck. But it was her face that attracted one, a pale sad face that was stamped on every feature with the impress of a determined will and of an intense womanliness. From the pronounced jaw that melted its squareness of profile in the oval of the full face to the dark brown eyes that rarely veiled themselves beneath their long-lashed lids, everything told that the girl possessed the indefinable something we call character. And if there was in the drooping corners of her red lips a sternness generally unassociated with conceptions of feminine loveliness one forgot it usually in contemplating the soft attractiveness of the shapely forehead, dashed beneath by straight eyebrows, and of the pronounced cheekbones that crossed the symmetry of a Saxon face. Mrs. Phillips was a drooping wearied woman but there was nothing drooping about Nellie and never could be. She might be torn down like one of the blue gums under which she had drawn in the fresh air of her girlhood, but she could no more bend than can the tree which must stand erect in the fiercest storm or must go down altogether. Pale she was, from the close air of the close street and close rooms, but proud she was as woman can be, standing erect in the door-way amid all this pandemonium of cries, waiting for Ned. Ned was her old playmate, a Darling Downs boy, five years older to be sure, but her playmate in the old days, nevertheless, as lads who have no sisters are apt to be with admiring little girls who have no brothers. Selectors' children, both of them, from neighbouring farms, born above the frost line under the smelting Queensland sun, drifted hither and thither by the fitful gusts of Fate as are the paper-sailed ships that boys launch on flood water pools, meeting here in Sydney after long years of separation. Now, Nellie was a dressmaker in a big city shop, and Ned a sun-burnt shearer to whom the great trackless West was home. She thought of the old home sadly as she stood there waiting for him.

It had not been a happy home altogether and yet, and yet—it was better than this. There was pure air there, at least, and grass up to the door, and trees rustling over-head; and the little children were brown and sturdy and played with merry shouts, not with these vile words she heard jabbered in the wretched street. Her heart grew sick within her—a habit it had, that heart of Nellie's—and a passion of wild revolt against her surroundings made her bite her lips and press her nails against her palms.

She looked across at the group opposite. More children being born! Week in and week out they seemed to come in spite of all the talk of not having any more. She could have cried over this holocaust of the innocents, and yet she shrank with an unreasoning shrinking from the barrenness that was coming to be regarded as the most comfortable state and being sought after, as she knew well, by the younger married women. What were they all coming to? Were they all to go on like this without a struggle until they vanished altogether as a people, perhaps to make room for the round-cheeked, bland-faced Chinaman who stood in the doorway of his shop in the crossing thorough-fare, gazing expressionlessly at her? She loathed that Chinaman. He always seemed to be watching her, to be waiting for something. She would dream of him sometimes as creeping upon her from behind, always with that bland round face. Yet he never spoke to her, never insulted her, only he seemed to be always watching her, always waiting. And it would come to her sometimes like a cold chill, that this yellow man and such men as he were watching them all slowly going down lower and lower, were waiting to leap upon them in their last helplessness and enslave them all as white girls were sometimes enslaved, even already, in those filthy opium joints whose stench nauseated the hurrying passers-by. Perhaps under all their meekness these Chinese were braver, more stubborn, more vigorous, and it was doomed that they should conquer at last and rule in the land where they had been treated as outcasts and intruders. She thought of this—and, just then, Ned turned the corner by the lamp.

Ned was a Down's native, every inch of him. He stood five feet eleven in his bare feet yet was so broad and strong that he hardly looked over the medium height. He had blue eyes and a heavy moustache just tinged with red. His hair was close-cut and dark; his forehead, nose and chin wore large and strong; his lips were strangely like a woman's. He walked with short jerky steps, swinging himself awkwardly as men do who have been much in the saddle. He wore a white shirt, as being holiday-making, but had not managed a collar; his pants were dark-blue, slightly belled; his coat, dark-brown; his boots wore highly polished; round his neck was a silk handkerchief; round his vestless waist, a discoloured leather belt; above all, a wide-brimmed cabbage tree hat, encircled by a narrow leather strap. He swung himself along rapidly, unabashed by the stares of the women or the impudent comment of the children. Nellie, suddenly, felt all her ill-humour turn against him. He was so satisfied with himself. He had talked unionism to her when she met him two weeks before, on his way to visit a brother who had taken up a selection in the Hawkesbury district. He had laughed when she hinted at the possibilities of the unionism he championed so fanatically. 'We only want what's fair,' he said. 'We're not going to do anything wild. As long as we get £1 a hundred and rations at a fair figure we're satisfied.' And then he had inconsistently proceeded to describe how the squatters treated the men out West, and how the union would make them civil, and how the said squatters were mostly selfish brutes who preferred Chinese to their own colour and would stop at no trick to beat the men out of a few shillings. She had said nothing at the time, being so pleased to see him, though she determined to have it out with him sometime during this holiday they had planned. But somehow, as he stepped carelessly along, a dashing manliness in every motion, a breath of the great plains coming with his sunburnt face and belted waist, he and his self-conceit jarred to her against this sordid court and these children's desolate lives. How dared he talk as he did about only wanting what was fair, she thought! How had he the heart to care only for himself and his mates while in these city slums such misery brooded! And then it shot through her that he did not know. With a rapidity, characteristic of herself, she made up her mind to teach him.

'Well, Nellie,' he cried, cheerily, coming up to her. 'And how are you again?'

'Hello, Ned,' she answered, cordially, shaking hands. 'You look as though you were rounding-up.'

'Do I?' he questioned, seriously, looking down at himself. 'Shirt and all? Well, if I am it's only you I came to round up. Are you ready? Did you think I wasn't coming?'

'It won't take me a minute,' she replied. 'I was pretty sure you'd come. I took a holiday on the strength of it, anyway, and made an engagement for you to-night. Come in a minute, Ned. You must see Mrs. Phillips while I get my hat. You'll have to sleep here to night. It'll be so late when we get back. Unless you'd sooner go to a hotel.'

'I'm not particular,' said Ned, looking round curiously, as he followed her in. 'I'd never have found the place, Nellie, if it hadn't been for that pub. near the corner, where we saw that row on the other night.'

The women opposite had suspended their debate upon Mrs. Hobbs' latest, a debate fortified by manifold reminiscences of the past and possibilities of the future. It was known in the little street that Nellie Lawton intended taking a holiday with an individual who was universally accepted as her 'young man,' and Ned's appearance upon the stage naturally made him a subject for discussion which temporarily over-shadowed even Mrs. Hobbs' baby.

'I'm told he's a sort of a farmer,' said one.

'He's a shearer; I had it from Mrs. Phillips herself,' said another.

'He's a strapping man, whatever he is,' commented a third.

'Well, she's a big lump of a girl, too,' contributed a fourth.

'Yes, and a vixen with her tongue when she gets started, for all her prim looks,' added a fifth.

'She has tricky ways that get over the men-folks. Mine won't hear a word against her.' This from the third speaker, eager to be with the tide, evidently setting towards unfavourable criticism.

'I don't know,' objected the second, timidly. 'She sat up all night with my Maggie once, when she had the fever, and Nellie had to work next day, too.'

'Oh, she's got her good side,' retorted the fifth, opening her dress to feed her nursing baby with absolute indifference for all onlookers. 'But she knows a great deal too much for a girl of her age. When she gets married will be time enough to talk as she does sometimes.' The chorus of approving murmurs showed that Nellie had spoken plainly enough on some subjects to displease some of these slatternly matrons.

'She stays out till all hours, I'm told,' one slanderer said.

'She's a union girl, at any rate,' hazarded Nellie's timid defender. There was an awkward pause at this. It was an apple of discord with the women, evidently. A tall form turning the corner afforded further reason for changing the subject.

'Here's Mrs. Macanany,' announced one. 'You'd better not say anything against Nellie Lawton when she's about.' So they talked again of Mrs. Hobbs' baby, making it the excuse to leave undone for a few minutes the endless work of the poor man's wife.

And sad to tell when, a few minutes afterwards, Ned and Nellie came out again and walked off together, the group of gossipers unanimously endorsed Mrs. Macanany's extravagant praises, and agreed entirely with her declaration that if all the women in Sydney would only stand by Nellie, as Mrs. Macanany herself would, there would be such a doing and such an upsetting and such a righting of things that ever after every man would be his own master and every woman would only work eight hours and get well paid for it. Yet it was something that of six women there were two who wouldn't slander a girl like Nellie behind her back.

CHAPTER II

SWEATING IN THE SYDNEY SLUMS

'WELL! Where shall we go, Nellie?' began Ned jauntily, as they walked away together. To tell the truth he was eager to get away from this poor neighbourhood. It had saddened him, made him feel unhappy, caused in him a longing to be back again in the bush, on his horse, a hundred miles from everybody. 'Shall we go to Manly or Bondi or Watson's Bay, or do you know of a better place?' He had been reading the newspaper advertisements and had made enquiries of the waitress, as he ate his breakfast, concerning the spot which the waitress would prefer were a young man going to take her out for the day. He felt pleased with himself now, for not only did he like Nellie very much but she was attractive to behold, and he felt very certain that every man they passed envied him. She had put on a little round straw hat, black, trimmed with dark purple velvet; in her hands, enclosed in black gloves, she carried a parasol of the same colour.

'Where would you like to go, Ned?' she answered, colouring a little as she heard her name in Mrs. Macanany's hoarse voice, being told thereby that she and Ned were the topic of conversation among the jury of matrons assembled opposite.

'Anywhere you like, Nellie.'

'Don't you think, Ned, that you might see a little bit of real Sydney? Strangers come here for a few days and go on the steamers and through the gardens and along George-street and then go away with a notion of the place that isn't the true one. If I were you, Ned, right from the bush and knowing nothing of towns, I'd like to see a bit of the real side and not only the show side that everybody sees. We don't all go picnicking all the time and we don't all live by the harbour or alongside the Domain.'

'Do just whatever you like, Nellie,' cried Ned, hardly understanding but perfectly satisfied, 'you know best where to take a fellow.'

'But they're not pleasant places, Ned.'

'I don't mind,' answered Ned, lightly, though he had been looking forward, rather, to the quiet enjoyment of a trip on a harbour steamer, or at least to the delight of a long ramble along some beach where he thought he and Nellie might pick up shells. 'Besides, I fancy it's going to rain before night,' he added, looking up at the sky, of which a long narrow slice showed between the tall rows of houses.

There were no clouds visible. Only there was a deepening grey in the hard blueness above them, and the breathless heat, even at this time of day, was stifling.

'I don't know that you'd call this a pleasant place,' he commented, adding with the frankness of an old friend: 'Why do you live here, Nellie?' She shrugged her shoulders. The gesture meant anything and everything.

'You needn't have bothered sending me that money back,' said Ned, in reply to the shrug.

'It isn't that,' explained Nellie. 'I've got a pretty good billet. A pound a week and not much lost time! But I went to room there when I was pretty hard up. It's a small room and was cheap. Then, after, I took to boarding there as well. That was pretty cheap and suited me and helped them. I suppose I might get a better place but they're very kind, and I come and go as I like, and—' she hesitated. 'After all,' she went on, 'there's not much left out of a pound.'

'I shouldn't think so,' remarked Ned, looking at her and thinking that she was very nicely dressed.

'Oh! You needn't look,' laughed Nellie. 'I make my own dresses and trim my own hats. A woman wouldn't think much of the stuff either.'

'I want to tell you how obliged I was for that money, Ned,' continued Nellie, an expression of pain on her face. 'There was no one else I could ask, and I needed it so. It was very kind—'

'Ugh! That's nothing,' interrupted Ned, hiding his bashfulness under a burst of boisterousness. 'Why, Nellie, I'd like you to be sending to me regular. It might just as well come to you as go any other way. If you ever do want a few pounds again, Nellie,'—he added, seriously, 'I can generally manage it. I've got plenty just now—far more than I'll ever need.' This with wild exaggeration. 'You might as well have it as not. I've got nobody.'

'Thanks, just the same, Ned! When I do want it I'll ask you. I'm afraid I'll never have any money to lend you if you need it, but if I ever do you know where to come.'

'It's a bargain, Nellie,' said Ned. Then, eager to change the subject, feeling awkward at discussing money matters because he would have been so willing to have given his last penny to anybody he felt friends with, much less to the girl by his side:

'But where are we going?'

'To see Sydney!' said Nellie.

They had turned several times since they started but the neighbourhood remained much the same. The streets, some wider, some narrower, all told of sordid struggling. The shops were greasy, fusty, grimy. The groceries exposed in their windows damaged specimens of bankrupt stocks, discoloured tinned goods, grey sugars, mouldy dried fruits; at their doors, flitches of fat bacon, cut and dusty. The meat with which the butchers' shops overflowed was not from show-beasts, as Ned could see, but the cheaper flesh of over-travelled cattle, ancient oxen, ewes too aged for bearing; all these lean scraggy flabby-fleshed carcasses surrounded and blackened by buzzing swarms of flies that invaded the foot-path outside in clouds. The draperies had tickets, proclaiming unparalleled bargains, on every piece; the whole stock seemed displayed outside and in the doorway. The fruiterers seemed not to be succeeding in their rivalry with each other and with the Chinese hawkers. The Chinese shops were dotted everywhere, dingier than any other, surviving and succeeding, evidently, by sheer force of cheapness. The roadways everywhere were hard and bare, reflecting the rays of the ascending sun until the streets seemed to be Turkish baths, conducted on a new and gigantic method. There was no green anywhere, only unlovely rows of houses, now gasping with open doors and windows for air.

Air! That was what everything clamoured for, the very stones, the dogs, the shops, the dwellings, the people. If it was like this soon after ten, what would it be at noon?

Already the smaller children were beginning to weary of play. In narrow courts they lolled along on the flags, exhausted. In wider streets, they sat quietly on door-steps or the kerb, or announced their discomfort in peevish wailings. The elder children quarrelled still and swore from their playground, the gutter, but they avoided now the sun and instinctively sought the shade and it is pretty hot when a child minds the sun. At shop doors, shopmen, sometimes shopwomen, came to wipe their warm faces and examine the sky with anxious eyes. The day grew hotter and hotter. Ned could feel the rising heat, as though he were in an oven with a fire on underneath. Only the Chinese looked cool.

Nellie led the way, sauntering along, without hurrying. Several times she turned down passages that Ned would hardly have noticed, and brought him out in courts closed in on all sides, from which every breath of air seemed purposely excluded. Through open doors and windows he could see the inside of wretched homes, could catch glimpses of stifling bedrooms and close, crowded little kitchens. Often one of the denizens came to door or window to stare at Nellie and him; sometimes they were accosted with impudent chaff, once or twice with pitiful obscenity.

The first thing that impressed him was the abandonment that thrust itself upon him in the more crowded of these courts and alley-ways and back-streets, the despairing abandonment there of the decencies of living. The thin dwarfed children kicked and tumbled with naked limbs on the ground; many women leaned half-dressed and much unbuttoned from ground floor windows, or came out into the passage-ways slatternly. In one court two unkempt vile-tongued women of the town wrangled and abused each other to the amusement of the neighbourhood, where the working poor were huddled together with those who live by shame. The children played close by as heedlessly as if such quarrels were common events, cursing themselves at each other with nimble filthy tongues.

'There's a friend of mine lives here,' said Nellie, turning into one of these narrow alleys that led, as they could see, into a busier and bustling street. 'If you don't mind we'll go up and I can help her a bit, and you can see how one sort of sweating is done. I worked at it for a spell once, when dressmaking was slack. In the same house, too.'

She stopped at the doorway of one of a row of three-storied houses. On the doorstep were a group of little children, all barefooted and more or less ragged in spite of evident attempts to keep some of them patched into neatness. They looked familiarly at Nellie and curiously at Ned.

'How's mother, Johnny?' asked Nellie of one of them, a small pinched little fellow of six or seven, who nursed a baby of a year or so old, an ill-nourished baby that seemed wilting in the heat.

'She's working,' answered the little fellow, looking anxiously at Nellie as she felt in her pocket.

'There's a penny for you,' said Nellie, 'and here's a penny for Dicky,' patting a little five-year-old on the head, 'and here's one to buy some milk for the baby.'

Johnny rose with glad eagerness, the baby in his arms and the pennies in his hand.

'I shall buy "specks" with mine,' he cried joyfully.

'What's "specks"?' asked Ned, puzzled, as the children went off, the elder staggering under his burden.

'"Specks"! Damaged fruit, half rotten. The garbage of the rich sold as a feast to these poor little ones?' cried Nellie, a hot anger in her face and voice that made Ned dumb.

She entered the doorway. Ned followed her through a room where a man and a couple of boys were hammering away at some boots, reaching thereby a narrow, creaking stairway, hot as a chimney, almost pitch dark, being lighted only by an occasional half-opened door, up which he stumbled clumsily. Through one of these open doors he caught a glimpse of a couple of girls sewing; through another of a woman with a baby in arms tidying-up a bare floored room, which seemed to be bedroom, kitchen and dining room in one; from behind a closed door came the sound of voices, one shrilly laughing. Unused to stairways his knees ached before they reached the top. He was glad enough when Nellie knocked loudly at a door through which came the whirring of a sewing machine. The noise stopped for a moment while a sharp voice called them to 'come in,' then started again. Nellie opened the door.

At the open window of a small room, barely furnished with a broken iron bedstead, some case boards knocked together for a table and fixed against the wall, a couple of shaky chairs and a box, a sharp featured woman sat working a machine, as if for dear life. The heat of the room was made hotter by the little grate in which a fire had recently been burning and on which still stood the teapot. Some cups and a plate or two, with a cut loaf of bread and a jam tin of sugar, littered the table. The scanty bed was unmade. The woman wore a limp cotton dress of uncertain colour, rolled up at the sleeves and opened at the neck for greater coolness. She was thin and sharp; she was so busy you understood that she had no time to be clean and tidy. She seemed pleased to see Nellie and totally indifferent at seeing Ned, but kept on working after nodding to them.

Nellie motioned Ned to sit down, which he did on the edge of the bed, not caring to trust the shaky chairs. She went to the side of the sharp-featured woman, and sitting down on the foot of the bed by the machine watched her working without a word. Ned could see on the ground, in a paper parcel, a heap of cloth of various colours, and on the bed some new coats folded and piled up. On the machine was another coat, being sewn.

It was ten minutes before the machine stopped, ten minutes for Ned to look about and think in. He knew without being told that this miserable room was the home of the three children to whom Nellie had given the pennies, and that here their mother worked to feed them. Their feeding he could see on the table. Their home he could see. The work that gave it to them he could see. For the first time in his life he felt ashamed of being an Australian.

Finally the machine stopped. The sharp-faced woman took the coat up, bit a thread with her teeth, and laying it on her knee began to unpick the tackings.

'Let me!' said Nellie, pulling off her gloves and taking off her hat. 'We came to see you, Ned and I,' she went on with honest truthfulness, 'because he's just down from the bush, and I wanted him to see what Sydney was like. Ned, this is Mrs. Somerville.'

Mrs. Somerville nodded at Ned. 'You're right to come here,' she remarked, grimly, getting up while Nellie took her place as if she often did it. 'You know just what it is, Nellie, and I do, too, worse luck. Perhaps it's good for us. When we're better off we don't care for those who're down. We've got to get down ourselves to get properly disgusted with it.'

She spoke with the accent of an educated woman, moving to the make-shift table and beginning to 'tidy-up.' As she passed between him and the light Ned could see that the cotton dress was her only covering.

'How are the children?' asked Nellie.

'How can you expect them to be?' retorted the other.

'You ought to wean the baby,' insisted Nellie, as though it was one of their habitual topics.

'Wean the baby! That's all very well for those who can buy plenty of milk. It's a pity it's ever got to be weaned.'

'Plenty of work this week?' asked Nellie, changing the subject.

'Yes; plenty of work this week. You know what that means. No work at all when they get a stock ahead, so as to prevent us feeling too independent I suppose.' She paused, then added: 'That girl downstairs says she isn't going to work any more. I talked to her a little but she says one might just as well die one way as another, and that she'll have some pleasure first. I couldn't blame her much. She's got a good heart. She's been very kind to the children.'

Nellie did not answer; she did not even look up.

'They're going to reduce prices at the shop,' went on Mrs. Somerville. 'They told me last time I went that after this lot they shouldn't pay as much because they could easily get the things done for less. I asked what they'd pay, and they said they didn't know but they'd give me as good a show for work as ever if I cared to take the new prices, because they felt sorry for the children. I suppose I ought to feel thankful to them.'

Nellie looked up now—her face flushed. 'Reduce, prices again!' she cried. 'How can they?'

'I don't know how they can, but they can,' answered Mrs. Somerville. 'I suppose we can be thankful so long as they don't want to be paid for letting us work for them. Old Church's daughter got married to some officer of the fleet last week, I'm told, and I suppose we've got to help give her a send-off.'

'It's shameful,' exclaimed Nellie. 'What they paid two years ago hardly kept one alive, and they've reduced twice since then. Oh! They'll all pay for it some day.'

'Let's hope so,' said Mrs. Somerville. 'Only we'll have to pay them for it pretty soon, Nellie, or there won't be enough strength left in us to pay them with. I've got beyond minding anything much, but I would like to get even with old Church.'

They had talked away, the two women, ignoring Ned. He listened. He understood that from the misery of this woman was drawn the pomp and pride, the silks and gold and glitter of the society belle, and he thought with a cruel satisfaction of what might happen to that society belle if this half-starved woman got hold of her. Measure for measure, pang for pang, what torture, what insults, what degradation, could atone for the life that was suffered in this miserable room? And for the life of 'that girl downstairs' who had given up in despair?

'How about a union now?' asked Nellie, turning with the first pieces of another coat to the machine.

'Work's too dull,' was the answer. 'Wait for a few months till the busy season comes and then I wouldn't wonder if you could get one. The women were all feeling hurt about the reduction, and one girl did start talking strike, but what's the use now? I couldn't say anything, you know, but I'll find out where the others live and you can go round and talk to them after a while. If there was a paper that would show old Church up it might do good, but there isn't.'

Then the rattle of the machine began again, Nellie working with an adeptness that showed her to be an old hand. Ned could see now that the coats were of cheap coarse stuff and that the sewing in them was not fine tailoring. The cut material in Nellie's hands fairly flew into shape as she rapidly moved it to and fro under the hurrying needle with her slim fingers. Her foot moved unceasingly on the treadle. Ned watching her, saw the great beads of perspiration slowly gather on her forehead and then trickle down her nose and cheeks to fall upon the work before her.

'My word! But it's hot!' exclaimed Nellie at last, as the noise stopped for a moment while she changed the position of her work. 'Why don't you open the door?'

'I don't care to before the place is tidy,' answered Mrs. Somerville, who had washed her cups and plates in a pan and had just put Ned on one of the shaky chairs while she shook and arranged the meagre coverings of the bed.

'Is he still carrying on?' enquired Nellie, nodding her head at the partition and evidently alluding to someone on the other side.

'Of course, drink, drink, drink, whenever he gets a chance, and that seems pretty well always. She helps him sometimes, and sometimes she keeps sober and abuses him. He kicked her down stairs the other night, and the children all screaming, and her shrieking, and him swearing. It was a nice time.'

Once more the machining interrupted the conversation, which thus was renewed from time to time in the pauses of the noise. The room being 'tidied,' Mrs. Somerville sat down on the bed and taking up some pieces of cloth began to tack them together with needle and thread, ready for the machine. It never seemed to occur to her to rest even for a moment.

'Nellie's a quick one,' she remarked to Ned. 'At the shop they always tell those who grumble what she earned one week. Twenty-four and six, wasn't it, Nellie? But they don't say she worked eighteen hours a day for it.'

Nellie flushed uneasily and Ned felt uncomfortable. Both thought of the repayment of the latter's friendly loan. The girl made her machine rattle still more hurriedly to prevent any further remarks trending in that direction. At last Mrs. Somerville, her tacking finished, got up and took the work from Nellie's hands.

'I'm not going to take your whole morning,' she said. 'You don't get many friends from the bush to see you, so just go away and I'll get on. I'm much obliged to you as it is, Nellie.'

Nellie did not object. After wiping her hands, face and neck with her handkerchief she put on her gloves and hat. The sharp-faced woman was already at the machine and amid the din, which drowned their good-byes, they departed as they came. Ned felt more at ease when his feet felt the first step of the narrow creaking stairway. It is hardly a pleasant sensation for a man to be in the room of a stranger who, without any unfriendliness, does not seem particularly aware that he is there. They left the door open. Far down the stifling stairs Ned could hear the ceaseless whirring of the machine driven by the woman who slaved ceaselessly for her children's bread in this Sydney sink. He looked around for the children when they got to the alley again but could not see them among the urchins who lolled about half-suffocated now. The sun was almost overhead for they had been upstairs for an hour. The heat in this mere canyon path between cliffs of houses was terrible. Ned himself began to feel queerly.

'Let's get out of this, Nellie,' he said.

'How would you like never to be able to get out of it?' she answered, as they turned towards the bustling street, opposite to the way they had previously come.

'Who's that Mrs. Somerville?' he asked, not answering.

'I got to know her when I lived there,' replied Nellie. 'Her husband used to be well off, I fancy, but had bad luck and got down pretty low. There was a strike on at some building and he went on as a labourer, blacklegging. The pickets followed him to the house, abusing him, and made him stubborn, but I got her alone that night and talked to her and explained things a bit and she talked to him and next day he joined the union. Then he got working about as a labourer, and one day some rotten scaffolding broke, and he came down with it. The union got a few pounds for her, but the boss was a regular swindler who was always beating men out of their wages and doing anything to get contracts and running everything cheap, so there was nothing to be got out of him.'

'Did her husband die?'

'Yes, next day. She had three children and another came seven months after. One died last summer just before the baby was born. She's had a pretty hard time of it, but she works all the time and she generally has work.'

'It seems quite a favour to get work here,' observed Ned.

'If you were a girl you'd soon find out what a favour it is sometimes,' answered Nellie quietly, as they came out into the street.

CHAPTER III
SHORN LIKE SHEEP

'HOW many hours do you work?' asked Nellie of the waitress.

'About thirteen,' answered the girl, glancing round to see if the manager was watching her talking. 'But it's not the hours so much. It's the standing.'

'You're not doing any good standing now,' put in Ned. 'Why don't you sit down and have a rest?'

'They don't let us,' answered the waitress, cautiously.

'What do they pay?' asked Nellie, sipping her tea and joining in the waitress' look-out for the manager.

'Fifteen! But they're taking girls on at twelve. Of course there's meals. But you've got to room yourself, and then there's washing, clean aprons and caps and cuffs and collars. You've got to dress, too. There's nothing left. We ought to get a pound.'

'What—'

'S-s-s!' warned the waitress, straightening herself up as the manager appeared.

*   *   *

They were in a fashionable Sydney restaurant, on George-street, a large, painted, gilded, veneered, electro-plated place, full of mirrors and gas-fittings and white-clothed tables. It was not busy, the hour being somewhat late and the day Saturday, and so against the walls, on either side the long halls, were ranged sentinel rows of white-aproned, white-capped, blackdressed waitresses.

They were dawdling over their tea—Ned and Nellie were, not the waitresses—having dined exceedingly well on soup and fish and flesh and pudding. For Ned, crushed by more sight-seeing and revived by a stroll to the Domain and a rest by a fountain under shady trees, further revived by a thunderstorm that suddenly rolled up and burst upon them almost before they could reach the shelter of an awning, had insisted on treating Nellie to 'a good dinner,' telling her that afterwards she could take him anywhere she liked but that meanwhile they would have something to cheer them up. And Nellie agreed, nothing loth, for she too longed for the momentary jollity of a mild dissipation, not to mention that this would be a favourable opportunity to see if the restaurant girls could not be organised. So they had 'a good dinner.'

'This reminds me,' said Nellie, as she ate her fish, 'of a friend of mine, a young fellow who is always getting hard up and always raising a cheque, as he calls it. He was very hard up a while ago, and met a friend whom he told about it. Then he invited his friend to go and have some lunch. They came here and he ordered chicken and that, and a bottle of good wine. It took his last half-sovereign. When he got the ticket the other man looked at him. 'Well,' he said, 'if you live like this when you're hard up, how on earth do you live when you've got money?'

'What did he say?' asked Ned, laughing, wondering at the same time how Nellie came to know people who drank wine and spent half-sovereigns on chicken lunches.

'Oh! He didn't say anything much, he told me. He couldn't manage to explain, he thought, that when he was at work and easy in his mind he didn't care what he had to eat but that when he didn't know what he'd do by the end of the week he felt like having a good meal if he never had another. He thought that made the half-sovereign go furthest. He's funny in some things.'

'I should think he was, a little. How did you know him?'

'I met him where we're going tonight. He's working on some newspaper in Melbourne now. I haven't seen him or heard of for months.'

She chatted on, rather feverishly.

'Did you ever read *David Copperfield*?'

Ned nodded, his mouth being full.

'Do you recollect how he used to stand outside the cookshops? It's quite natural. I used to. It's pretty bad to be hungry and it's just about as bad not to have enough. I know a woman who has a couple of children, a boy and a girl. They were starving once. She said she'd sooner starve than beg or ask anybody to help them, and the little girl said she would too. But the boy said he wasn't going to starve for anybody, and he wasn't going to beg either; he'd steal. And sure enough he slipped out and came back with two loaves that he'd taken from a shop. They lived on that for nearly a week.' Nellie laughed forcedly.

'What did they do then?' asked Ned seriously.

'Oh! She had been doing work but couldn't get paid. She got paid.'

'Where was her husband?'

'Don't husbands die like other people?' she answered, pointedly. 'Not that all husbands are much good when they can't get work or will always work when they can get it,' she added.

'Are many people as hard up as that in Sydney, Nellie?' enquired Ned, putting down his knife and fork.

'Some,' she answered. 'You don't suppose a lot of the people we saw this morning get over well fed, do you? Oh, you can go on eating, Ned! It's not being sentimental that will help them. They want fair play and a chance to work, and your going hungry won't get that for them. There's lots for them and for us if they only knew enough to stop people like that getting too much.'

By lifting her eyebrows she drew his attention to a stout coarse loudly jewelled man, wearing a tall silk hat and white waistcoat, who had stopped near them on his way to the door. He was speaking in a loud dictatorial wheezy voice. His hands were thrust into his trouser pockets, wherein he jingled coins by taking them up and letting them fall again. The chink of sovereigns seemed sweet music to him. He stared contemptuously at Ned's clothes as that young man looked round; then stared with insolent admiration at Nellie. Ned became crimson with suppressed rage, but said nothing until the man had passed them.

'Who is that brute?' he asked then.

'That brute! Why, he's a famous man. He owns hundreds of houses, and has been mayor and goodness knows what. He'll be knighted and made a duke or something. He owns the block where Mrs. Somerville lives. You ought to speak respectfully of your betters, Ned. He's been my landlord, though he doesn't know it, I suppose. He gets four shillings a week from Mrs. Somerville. The place isn't worth a shilling, only it's handy for her taking her work in, and she's got to pay him for it being handy. That's her money he's got in his pocket, only if you knocked him down and took it out for her you'd be a thief. At least, they'd say you were and send you to prison.'

'Who's the other, I wonder?' said Ned. 'He looks more like a man.'

The other was a shrewd-looking, keen-faced, sparely-built man, with somewhat aquiline nose and straight narrow forehead, not at all bad-looking or evil-looking and with an air of strong determination; in short, what one calls a masterful man. He was dressed well but quietly. A gold-bound hair watch guard that crossed his high-buttoned waistcoat was his only adornment; his slender hands, unlike the fat man's podgy fingers, were bare of rings. He was sitting alone, and after the fat man left him returned again to the reading of an afternoon paper while he lunched.

'His name's Strong,' said. Nellie, turning to Ned with a peculiar smile. 'That fat man has robbed me and this lean man has robbed you, I suppose. As he looks more like a man it won't be as bad though, will it?'

'What are you getting at, Nellie?' asked Ned, not understanding but looking at the shrewd man intently, nevertheless.

'Don't you know the name? Of course you don't though. Well, he's managing director of the Great Southern Mortgage Agency, a big concern that owns hundreds and hundreds of stations. At least, the squatters own the stations and the Agency owns the squatters, and he as good as owns the Agency. You're pretty sure to have worked for him many a time without knowing it, Ned.'

Ned's eyes flashed. Nellie had to kick his foot under the table for fear he would say or do something that would attract the attention of the unsuspecting lean man.

'Don't be foolish, Ned,' urged Nellie, in a whisper. 'What's the good of spluttering?'

'Why, it was one of their stations on the Wilkes Downs that started cutting wages two years ago. Whenever a manager is particularly mean he always puts it down to the Agency. The Victorian fellows say it was this same concern that first cut wages down their way. And the New Zealanders too. I'd just like to perform on him for about five minutes.'

Ned uttered his wish so seriously that Nellie laughed out loud, at which Ned laughed too.

'So he's the man who does all the mischief, is he?' remarked Ned, again glaring at his industrial enemy. 'Who'd think it to look at him? He doesn't look a bad sort, does he?'

'He looks a determined man, I think,' said Nellie. 'Mr. Stratton says he's the shrewdest capitalist in Australia and that he'll give the unions a big fight for it one of these days. He says he has a terrible hatred of unionism and thinks that there's no half-way between smashing them up and letting them smash the employers up. His company pays twenty-five per cent. regularly every year on its shares and will pay fifty before he gets through with it.'

'How?'

'How! Out of fellows like you, Ned, who think themselves so mighty independent and can't see that they're being shorn like sheep, in the same way, though not as much yet, as Mrs. Somerville is by old Church and the fat brute, as you call him. But then you rather like it I should think. Anyway, you told me you didn't want to do anything "wild", only to keep up wages. You'll have to do something "wild" to keep up wages before he finishes.'

'That's all right to talk, Nellie, but what can we do?' asked Ned, pulling his moustache.

'Hire him instead of letting him hire you,' answered Nellie, oracularly. 'Those fat men are only good to put in museums, but these lean men are all right so long as you keep them in their place. They are our worst enemies when they're against us but our best friends when they're for us. They say Mr. Strong isn't like most of the swell set. He is straight to his wife and good to his children and generous to his friends and when he says a thing he sticks to it. Only he sees everything from the other side and doesn't understand that all men have got the same coloured blood.'

'How can we hire him?' said Ned, after a pause. 'They own everything.'

Nellie shrugged her shoulders.

'You think we might take it,' said Ned.

Nellie shrugged her shoulders again.

'I don't see how it can be done,' he concluded.

'That's just it. You can't see how it can be done, and so nothing's done. Some men get drunk, and some men get religious, and others get enthusiastic for a pound a hundred. You haven't got votes up in Queensland, and if you had you'd probably give them to a lot of ignorant politicians. Men don't know, and they don't seem to want to know much, and they've got to be squeezed by men like him'—she nodded at Strong— 'before they take any interest in themselves or in those who belong to them. For those who have an ounce of heart, though, I should think there'd been squeezing enough already.'

She looked at Ned angrily. The scenes of the morning rose before him and tied his tongue.

'How do you know all these jokers, Nellie?' he asked. He had been going to put the question a dozen times before but it had slipped him in the interest of conversation.

'I only know them by sight. Mrs. Stratton takes me to the theatre with her sometimes and tells me who people are and all about them.'

'Who's Mrs. Stratton? You were talking of Mr. Stratton, too, just now, weren't you?'

'Yes. The Strattons are very nice people, They're interested in the Labour movement, and I said I'd bring you round when I go to-night. I generally go on Saturday nights. They're not early birds, and we don't want to get there till half-past ten or so.'

'Half-past ten! That's queer time.'

'Yes, isn't it? Only—'

At that moment a waitress who had been arranging the next table came and took her place against the wall close behind Nellie. Such an opportunity to talk unionism was not to be lost, so Nellie unceremoniously dropped her conversation with Ned and enquired, as before stated, into the becapped girl's hours. The waitress was tall and well-featured, but sallow of skin and growing haggard, though barely twenty, if that. Below her eyes were bluish hollows. She suffered plainly from the disorders caused by constant standing and carrying, and at this end of her long week was in evident pain.

*   *   *

'You're not allowed to talk either?' she asked the waitress, when the manager had disappeared.

'No. They're very strict. You get fined if you're seen chatting to customers and if you're caught resting. And you get fined if you break anything, too. One girl was fined six shillings last week.'

'Why do you stand it? If you were up in our part of the world we'd soon bring 'em down a notch or two.' This from Ned.

'Out in the bush it may be different,' said the girl, identifying his part of the world by his dress and sunburnt face. 'But in towns you've got to stand it.'

'Couldn't you girls form a union?' asked Nellie.

'What's the use, there's plenty to take our places.'

'But if you were all in a union there wouldn't be enough.'

'Oh, we can't trust a lot of girls. Those who live at home and just work to dress themselves are the worst of the lot. They'd work for ten shillings or five.'

'But they'd be ashamed to blackleg if once they were got into the union,' persisted Nellie. 'It's worth trying, to get a rise in wages and to stop fining and have shorter hours and seats while you're waiting.'

'Yes, it's worth trying if there was any chance. But there are so many girls. You're lucky if you get work at all now and just have to put up with anything. If we all struck they could get others to-morrow.'

'But not waitresses. How'd they look here, trying to serve dinner with a lot of green hands?' argued Nellie. 'Besides, if you had a union, you could get a lot without striking at all. They know now you can't strike, so they do just exactly as they like.'

'They'd do what they—' began the waitress. Then she broke off with another 's-s-s' as the manager crossed the room again.

'They'd do what they like, anyway,' she began once more. 'One of our girls was in the union the Melbourne waitresses started. They had a strike at one of the big restaurants over the manager insulting one of the girls. They complained to the boss and wanted the manager to apologise, but the boss wouldn't listen and said they were getting very nice. So at dinner time, when the bell rang, they all marched off and put on their hats. The customers were all waiting for dinner and the girls were all on strike and the boss nearly went mad. He was going to have them all arrested, but when the gentlemen heard what it was about they said the girls were right and if the manager didn't apologise they'd go to some other restaurant always. So the manager went to the girl and apologised.'

'By gum!' interjected Ned. 'Those girls were hummers.'

'I suppose the boss victimised afterwards?' asked Nellie, wiser in such matters.

'That's just it,' said the girl, in a disheartened tone. 'In two or three weeks every girl who'd had anything to do with stirring the others up was bounced for something or other. The manager did what he liked afterwards.'

'Just talk to the other girls about a union, will you?' asked Nellie. 'It's no use giving right in, you know.'

'I'll see what some of them say, but there's a lot I wouldn't open my mouth to,' answered the waitress.

'What time do you get away on Thursdays?'

'Next Thursday I'm on till half-past ten.'

'Well, I'll meet you then, outside, to see what they say,' said Nellie. 'My name's Nellie Lawton and some of us are trying to start a women's union. You'll be sure to be there?'

'All right,' answered the waitress, a little dubiously. Then she added more cordially, as she wrote out the pay ticket:

'My name's Susan Finch. I'll see what I can do.'

So Ned and Nellie got up and, the former having paid at the counter, walked out into the street together. It was nearly three. The rain had stopped, though the sky was still cloudy and threatening. The damp afternoon was chilly after the sultry broiling morning. Neither of them felt in the mood for walking so at Nellie's suggestion they put in the afternoon in riding, on trams and 'busses, hither and thither through the mazy wilderness of the streets that make up Sydney.

Intuitively, both avoided talking of the topics that before had engaged them and that still engrossed their thoughts. For a while they chatted on indifferent matters, but gradually relapsed into silence, rarely broken. The impression of the morning walk, of Mrs. Somerville's poor room, of

Nellie's stuffy street, came with full force to Ned's mind. What he saw only stamped it deeper and deeper.

When, in a bus, they rode through the suburbs of the wealthy, past shrubberied mansions and showy villas, along roads where liveried carriages, drawn by high-stepping horses, dashed by them, he felt himself in the presence of the fat man who jingled sovereigns, of the lean man whose slender fingers reached north to the Peak Downs and south to the Murray, filching everywhere from the worker's hard-earned wage. When in the tram they were carried with clanging and jangling through endless rows of houses great and small, along main thoroughfares on either side of which crowded side-streets extended like fish-bones, over less crowded districts where the cottages were generally detached or semi-detached and where pleasant homely houses were thickly sprinkled, oven here he wondered how near those who lived in happier state were to the life of the slum, wondered what struggling and pinching and scraping was going on behind the half-drawn blinds that made homes look so cosy.

What started him on this idea particularly was that, in one train, a grey-bearded propertied-looking man who sat beside him was grumbling to a spruce little man opposite about the increasing number of empty houses.

'You can't wonder at it,' answered the spruce little man. 'When the working classes aren't prospering everybody feels it but the exporters. Wages are going down and people are living two families in a house where they used to live one in a house, or living in smaller houses.'

'Oh! Wages are just as high. There's been too much building. You building society men have overdone the thing.'

'My dear sir!' declared the spruce little man. 'I'm talking from facts. My society and every other building society is finding it out. When men can't get as regular work it's the same thing to them as if wages were coming down. The number of surrenders we have now is something appalling. Working men have built expecting to be able to pay from 6s. to 10s. and 12s. a week to the building societies, and every year more and more are finding out they can't do it. As many as can are renting rooms, letting part of their house and so struggling along. As many more are giving up and renting these rooms or smaller houses. And apparently well-to-do people are often in as bad a fix. It's against my interest to have things this way, but it's so, and there's no getting over it. If it keeps on, pretty well every workingman's house about Sydney will be a rented house soon. The building societies can't stop that unless men have regular work and fair wages.'

'It's the unions that upset trade,' asserted the propertied-looking man.

'It's the land law that's wrong,' contended the spruce man. 'If all taxes were put on unimproved land values it would be cheaper to live and there would be more work because it wouldn't pay to keep land out of use. With cheap living and plenty of work the workingman would have money and business would be brisk all round.'

'Nonsense!' exclaimed the propertied man, brusquely.

'It's so,' answered the spruce little man, getting down as the tram stopped, 'There's no getting away from facts and that's fact.'

So even out here, Ned thought, looking at the rows of cottages with little gardens in front which they were passing, the squeeze was coming. Then, watching the passengers, he thought how worried they all seemed, how rarely a pleasant face wag to be met with in the dress of the people. And then, suddenly a shining, swaying, coachman-driven brougham whirled by. Ned, with his keen bushman's eyes, saw in it a stout heavy-jawed dame, large of arm and huge of bust, decked out in all the fashion, and insolent of face as one replete with that which others craved. And by her side, reclining at ease, was a later edition of the same volume, a girl of seventeen or so, already fleshed and heavy-jawed, in her mimic pride looking for all the world like a well-fed human animal, careless and soulless.

Opposite Nellie a thin-faced woman, of whose front teeth had gone, patiently dandled a peevish baby, while by her side another child clutched her dingy dust-cloak. This woman's nose was peaked and her chin receded. In her bonnet some gaudy imitation flowers nodded a vigorous accompaniment. She did not seem ever to have had pleasure or to have been young, and yet in the child by her side her patient joyless sordid life had produced its kind.

They had some tea and buttered scones in a cheaper café, where Nellie tried to 'organise' another waitress. They lingered over the meal, both moody. They hardly spoke till Ned asked Nellie:

'I don't see what men can get to do but can't single women always get servants' places?'

'Some might who don't, though all women who want work couldn't be domestic servants, that's plain,' answered Nellie. 'But by the number of girls that are always looking for places and the way the registry offices are able to bleed them, I should imagine there were any amount of servant girls already. The thing is there are so many girls that mistresses can afford to be particular. They want a girl with all the virtues to be a sort of house-slave, and they're always grumbling because they can't get it. So they're always changing, and the girls are always changing, and that makes the girls appear independent.'

'But they have good board and lodging, as well as wages, don't they?'

'In swell houses, where they keep two or three or more girls, they usually have good board and decent rooms, I think, but they don't in most places. Any hole or corner is considered good, enough for a servant girl to sleep in, and any scraps are often considered good enough for a servant girl to eat. You look as though you don't believe it, Ned. I'm talking about what I know. The average domestic servant is treated like a trained dog.'

'Did you ever try it?'

'I went to work in a hotel as chamber maid, once. I worked from about six in the morning till after ten at night. Then four of us girls slept in two beds in a kind of box under the verandah stairs in the back yard. We had to leave the window open to get air, and in the middle of the first night a light woke me up and a man was staring through the window at us with a match in his hand. I wanted the twelve shillings so I stood it for a week and, then got another place.'

'What sort was that?'

'Oh! A respectable place, you know. Kept up appearances and locked up the butter. The woman said to me, when I'd brought my box, 'I'm going to call you Mary, I always call my girls Mary.' I slept in a dark close den off the kitchen, full of cockroaches that frightened the wits out of me. I was afraid to eat as much as I wanted because she looked at me so. I couldn't rest a minute but she was hunting me up to see what I was doing. I hadn't anybody to talk with or eat with and my one night out I had to be in by ten. I was so miserable that I went back to slop-work. That's what Mrs. Somerville is doing.'

'It isn't all honey, then. I thought town servant girls had a fair time of it.'

'An occasional one does, though they all earn their money, but most have a hard time of it. I don't mean all places are like mine were, but there's no liberty. A working girl's liberty is scanty enough, goodness knows'—she spoke scornfully—'but at least she mixes with her own kind and is on an equality with most she meets. When her work is over, however long it is, she can do just exactly as she likes until it starts again. A servant girl hasn't society or that liberty. For my part I'd rather live on bread again than be at the orders of any woman who despised me and not be able to call a single minute of time my own. They're so ignorant, most of these women who have servants, they don't know how to treat a girl any more than most of their husbands know how to treat a horse.'

The naïve bush simile pleased Ned a little and he laughed, but soon relapsed again into silence. Then Nellie spoke of 'Paddy's Market,' one of the sights of Sydney, which she would like him to see. Accordingly they strolled to his hotel, where he put on a clean shirt and a collar and a waistcoat, while she waited, looking into the shops near by; then they strolled slowly Haymarketwards, amid the thronging Saturday night crowds that overflowed the George-street pavement into the roadway.

CHAPTER IV
SATURDAY NIGHT IN PADDY'S MARKET

PADDY'S Market was in its glory, the weekly glory of a Sydney Saturday night, of the one day in the week when the poor man's wife has a few shillings and when the poor caterer for the poor man's wants gleans in the profit field after the stray ears of corn that escape the machine-reaping of retail capitalism. It was filled by a crushing, hustling, pushing mass of humans, some buying, more bartering, most swept aimlessly along in the living currents that moved ceaselessly to and fro. In one of these currents Ned found himself caught, with Nellie. He struggled for a short time, with elbows and shoulders, to make for himself and her a path through the press; experience soon taught him to forego attempting the impossible and simply to drift, as everybody else did, on the stream setting the way they would go.

He found himself, looking around as he drifted, in a long low arcade, brilliant with great flaring lights. Above was the sparkle of glass roofing, on either hand a walling of rough stalls, back and forward a vista of roofing and stalls stretching through distant arches, which were gateways, into outer darkness, which was the streets. On the stalls, as he could see, were thousands of things, all cheap and most nasty.

What were there? What were not there? Boots and bootlaces, fish and china ornaments, fruit, old clothes and new clothes, flowers and plants and lollies, meat and tripe and cheese and butter and bacon! Cheap music-sheets and cheap jewellery! Stockings and pie-dishes and bottles of ink! Everything that the common people buy! Anything by which a penny could be turned by those of small capital and little credit in barter with those who had less.

One old man's face transfixed him for a moment, clung to his memory afterwards, the face of an old man, wan and white, greybearded and hollow-eyed, that was thrust through some hosiery hanging on a rod at the back of a stall. Nobody was buying there, nobody even looked to buy as Ned watched for a minute; the stream swept past and the grizzled face stared on. It had no body, no hands even, it was as if hung there, a trunkless head. It was the face of a generation grown old, useless and unloved, which lived by the crumbs that fall from Demos' table and waited wearily to be gone. It expressed nothing, that was the pain in it. It was haggard and grizzled and worn out, that was all. It knew itself no good to anybody, knew that labouring was a pain and thinking a weariness, and hope the delusion of fools, and life a vain mockery. It asked none to buy. It did not move. It only hung there amid the dark draping of its poor stock and waited.

Would he himself ever be like that, Ned wondered. And yet! And yet!

All around were like this. All! All! All! Everyone in this swarming multitude of working Sydney. On the faces of all was misery written. Buyers and sellers and passers-by alike were hateful of life. And if by chance he saw now and then a fat dame at a stall or a lusty huckster pushing his wares or a young couple, curious and loving, laughing and joking as they hustled along arm in arm, he seemed to see on their faces the dawning lines that in the future would stamp them also with the brand of despair.

The women, the poor women, they were most wretched of all; the poor housewives in their pathetic shabbiness, their faces drawn with child-bearing, their features shrunken with the struggling toil that never ceases nor stays; the young girls in their sallow youth that was not youth, with their hollow mirth and their empty faces, and their sharp angles or their unnatural busts; the wizened children that served at the stalls, precocious in infancy, with the wisdom of the Jew and the impudence of the witless babe; the old crones that crawled along—the mothers of a nation haggling for pennies as if they had haggled all their lives long. They bore baskets, most of the girls and housewives and crones; with some were husbands, who sometimes carried the basket but not always; some even carried children in their arms, unable even for an hour to escape the poor housewife's old-man of-the-seas.

The men were absorbed, hidden away, in the flood of wearied women. There were men, of course, in the crowd, among the stallkeepers— hundreds. And when one noticed them they were wearied also, or sharp like ferrets; oppressed, overborne, or cunning, with the cunning of those who must be cunning to live; imbruted often with the brutishness of apathy, consciousless of the dignity of manhood, only dully patient or viciously keen as the ox is or the hawk. Many sottish-looking, or if not sottish with the beery texture of those whose only recreation is to be bestially merry at the drink-shop. This was the impression in which the few who strode with the free air of the ideal Australian workman were lost, as the few comfortable—seeming women were lost in the general weariness of their weary sex.

Jollity there was none to speak of. There was an eager huckling for bargains, or a stolid calculation of values, or a loud commendation of wares, or an oppressive indifference. Where was the 'fair' to which of old the people swarmed, glad-hearted? Where was even the relaxed caution of the shopping-day? Where was the gay chaffering, the boisterous bandying of wit? Gone, all gone, and nothing left but care and sadness and a careful counting of hard-grudged silver and pence.

Ned turned his head once or twice to steal a glance at Nellie. He could not tell what she thought. Her face gave no sign of her feeling. Only it came home to him that there were none like her there, at least none like her to him. She was sad with a stern sadness, as she had been all day, and in that stern sadness of hers was a dignity, a majesty, that he had not appreciated until now, when she jostled without rudeness in this jostling crowd. This dark background of submissive yielding, of hopeless patience, threw into full light the unbending resolution carved in every line of her passionate face and lithesome figure. Yet he noticed now on her forehead two faint wrinkles showing, and in the corners of her mouth an overhanging fold; and this he saw as if reflected in a thousand ill-made mirrors around, distorted and exaggerated and grotesqued indeed but nevertheless the self-same marks of constant pain and struggle.

They reached the end of the first alley and passed out to the pavement, slippery with trodden mud. There was a little knot gathered there, a human eddy in the centre of the pressing throng. Looking over the heads of the loiterers, he could see in the centre of the eddy, on the kerb, by the light that came from the gateway, a girl whose eyes were closed. She was of an uncertain age—she might be twelve or seventeen. Beside her was a younger child. Just then she began to sing. He and Nellie waited. He knew without being told that the singer was blind.

It was a hymn she sang, an old-fashioned hymn that has in its music the glad rhythm of the 'revival,' the melodious echoing of the Methodist day. He recollected hearing it long years before, when he went to the occasional services held in the old bush schoolhouse by some itinerant preacher. He recalled at once the gathering of the saints at the river; mechanically he softly hummed the tune. It was hardly the tune the blind girl sang though. She had little knowledge of tune, apparently. Her cracked discordant voice was unspeakably saddening.

This blind girl was the natural sequence to the sphinx-like head that he had seen amid the black stockings. Her face was large and flat, youthless, ageless, crowned with an ugly black hat, poorly ribboned; her hands were clasped clumsily on the skirt of her poor cotton dress, ill-fitting. There was no expression in her singing, no effort to express, no instinctive conception of the idea. The people only listened because she was blind and they were poor, and so they pitied her. The beautiful river of her hymn meant nothing, to her or to them. It might be; it might not be; it was not in question. She cried to them that she was blind and that the blind poor must eat if they would live and that they desire to live despite the city by-laws. She begged, this blind girl, standing with rent shoes in the sloppy mud. In Sydney, in 1889, in the workingman's paradise, she stood on the kerb, this blind girl, and begged—begged from her own people. And in their poverty, their weariness, their brutishness, they pitied her. None mocked, and many paused, and some gave.

They never thought of her being an impostor. They did not pass her on to the hateful charity that paid parasites dole out for the rich. They did not think that she made a fortune out of her pitifulness and hunt her with canting harshness as a nuisance and a cheat. Her harsh voice did not jar on them. Her discords did not shock their supersensitive ears. They only knew that they, blinded in her stead, must beg for bread and shelter while good Christians glut themselves and while fat law-makers whitewash the unpleasant from the sight of the well-to-do. In her helplessness they saw, unknowing it, their own helplessness, saw in her Humanity wronged and suffering and in need. Those who gave gave to themselves, gave as an impulsive offering to the divine impulse which drives the weak together and aids them to survive.

Ned wanted to give the blind girl something but he felt ashamed to give before Nellie. He fingered a half-crown in his pocket, with a bushman's careless generosity. By skilful manoeuvring and convenient yielding to the pressure of the crowd he managed to get near the blind girl as she finished her hymn. Nellie turned round, looking away—he thought afterwards: was it intentionally?—and he slipped his offering into the singer' fingers like a culprit. Then he walked off hastily with his companion, as red and confused as though he had committed some dastardly act. Just as they reached the second arcade they heard another discordant hymn rise amid the shuffling din.

There were no street-walkers in Paddy's Market, Ned could see. He had caught his foot clumsily on the dress of one above the town-hall, a dashing demi-mondaine with rouged cheeks and unnaturally bright eyes and a huge velvet-covered hat of the Gainsborough shape and had been covered with confusion when she turned sharply round on him with a 'Now, clumsy, I'm not a door-mat.' Then he had noticed that the sad sisterhood were out in force where the bright gas-jets of the better-class shops illuminated the pavement, swaggering it mostly where the kerbs were lined with young fellows, fairly-well dressed as a rule, who talked of cricket and race horses and boating and made audible remarks concerning the women, grave and gay, who passed by in the throng. Nearing the poorer end of George–street, they seemed to disappear, both sisterhood and kerb loungers, until near the Haymarket itself they found the larrikin element gathered strongly under the flaring lights of hotel-bars and music hall entrances. But in Paddy's Market itself there were not even larrikins. Ned did not even notice anybody drunk.

He had seen drinking and drunkenness enough that day. Wherever there was poverty he had seen viciousness flourishing. Wherever there was despair there was a drowning of sorrow in drink. They had passed scores of public houses, that afternoon, through the doors of which workmen were thronging. Coming along George street, they had heard from more than one bar-room the howling of a drunken chorus. Men had staggered by them, and women too, frowsy and besotted. But there was none of this in Paddy's Market. It was a serious place, these long dingy arcades, to which people came to buy cheaply and carefully, people to whom every penny was of value and who had none to throw away, just then at least, either on a brain-turning carouse or on a painted courtesan. The people here were sad and sober and sorrowful. It seemed to Ned that here was collected, as in the centre of a great vortex, all the pained and tired and ill-fed and wretched faces that he had been seeing all day. The accumulation of misery pressed on him till it sickened him at the heart. It felt as though something clutched at his throat, as though by some mechanical means his skull was being tightened on his brain. His thoughts were interrupted by an exclamation from Nellie.

'There's a friend of mine,' she explained, making her way through the crowd to a brown-bearded man who was seated on the edge of an empty stall, apparently guarding a large empty basket in which were some white cloths. The man's features were fine and his forehead massive, his face indicating a frail constitution and strong intellectuality. He wore an apron rolled up round his waist. He seemed very poor.

'How d'ye do, Miss Lawton?' said he getting off the stall and shaking hands warmly. 'It's quite an age since I saw you. You're looking as well as ever.' Ned saw that his thin face beamed as he spoke and that his dark brown eyes, though somewhat hectic, wore singularly beautiful.

'I'm well, thanks,' said Nellie, beaming in return. 'And how are you? You seem browner than you did. What have you been doing to yourself?'

'Me! I've been up the country a piece trying my hand at farming. Jones is taking up a selection, you know, and I've been helping him a little now times aren't very brisk. I'm keeping fairly well, very fairly, I'm glad to say.'

'This is Mr. Hawkins, Mr. Sim,' introduced Nellie; the men shook hands.

'Come inside out of the rush,' invited Sim, making room for them in the entrance-way of the stall. 'We haven't got any armchairs, but it's not so bad up on the table here if you're tired.'

'I'm not tired,' said Nellie, leaning against the doorway. Ned sat up on the stall by her side; his feet were sore, unused to the hard paved city streets.

'I suppose Mr. Hawkins is one of us,' said Sim, perching himself up again.

'I don't know what you call "one of us",' answered Nellie, with a smile. 'He's a beginner. Some day he may get as far as you and Jones and the rest of the dynamiters.'

Sim laughed genially. 'Do you know, I really believe that Jones would use dynamite if he got an opportunity,' he commented. 'I'm not joking. I'm positively convinced of it.'

'Has he got it as bad as that?' asked Nellie. Ned began to feel interested. He also noticed that Sim used book-words.

'Has he got it as bad as that! "Bad" isn't any name for it. He's the stubbornest man I ever met, and he's full of the most furious hatred against the capitalists. He has it as a personal feeling. Then the life he's got is sufficient to drive a man mad.'

'Selecting is pretty hard,' agreed Nellie, sadly.

'Nellie and I know a little about that, Mr. Sim,' said Ned.

'Well, Jones' selection is a hard one,' went on Sim, good-humouredly. 'I prefer to sell trotters, when I sell out like this, to attempting it. The soil is all stones, and there is not a drop of water when the least drought comes on. Poor Jones toils like a team of horses and hardly gets sufficient to keep him alive. I never saw a man work as he does. For a man who thinks and has ideas to be buried like that in the bush is terrible. He has no one to converse with. He goes mooning about sometimes and muttering to himself enough to frighten one into a fit.'

'Does he still do any printing?' asked Nellie, archly.

'Oh, the printing,' answered Sim, laughing again. 'He initiated me into the art of wood-engraving. You see, Mr. Hawkins'—turning to Ned—'Jones hasn't got any type, and of course he can't afford to buy it, but he's got hold of a little second-hand toy printing press. To print from he takes a piece, of wood, cut across the grain and rubbed smooth with sand, and cuts out of it the most revolutionary and blood-curdling leaflets, letter by letter. If you only have patience it's quite easy after a few weeks' practice.'

'Does he print them?' asked Ned

'Print them! I should say he did. Every old scrap of paper he can collect or got sent him he prints his leaflets on and gets them distributed all over the country. Many a night I've sat up assisting with the pottering little press. Talk about Nihilism! Jones vows that there is only one way to cure things and that is to destroy the rule of Force.'

'He's along while starting,' remarked Nellie with a slight sneer. 'Those people who talk so much never do anything.'

'Oh, Jones isn't like that,' answered Sim, with cheerful confidence. 'He'll do anything that he thinks is worth while. But I suppose I'm horrifying you, Mr. Hawkins? Miss Lawton here knows what we are and is accustomed to our talk.'

'It'll take considerable to horrify me,' replied Ned, standing down as Nellie straightened herself out for a move-on. 'You can blow the whole world to pieces for all I care. There's not much worth watching in it as far as I can see.'

'You're pretty well an anarchist,' said the brown-bearded trotter-seller, his kindly intellectual face lighted up. 'It'll come some day, that's one satisfaction. Do you think that many here will regret it?' He waved his hand to include the crowd that moved to and fro before them, its voices covered with the din of its dragging feet.

'That'll do, Sim!' said Nellie. 'Don't stuff Ned's head with those absurd anarchistical night-mares of yours. We're going; we've got somewhere to go. Good-bye! Tell Jones you saw me when you write, and remember me to him, will you? I like him—he's so good-hearted, though he does rave.'

'He's as good-hearted a man as there is in New South Wales,' corroborated Sim, shaking hands. 'I'm expecting to meet a friend—here or I'd stroll along. Good-bye! Glad to have met you, Mr. Hawkins.'

He re-mounted the stall again as they moved off. In another minute he was lost to their sight as they were swallowed up once more in the living tide that ebbed and flowed through Paddy's Market.

After that Ned did not notice much, so absorbed was he. He vaguely knew that they drifted along another arcade and then crossed a street to an open cobble-paved space where there were shooting-tunnels and merry-go-rounds and try-your-weights and see-how-much-you-lifts. He looked dazedly at wizen-faced lads who gathered round ice-cream stalls, and at hungry folks who ate stewed peas. Everything seemed grimy and frayed and sordid; the flaring torches smelt of oil; those who shot, or ate, or rode, by spending a penny, were the envied of standers-by. Amid all this drumming and hawking and flaring of lights were swarms of boys and growing girls, precocious and vicious and foul-tongued.

Ten o'clock struck. 'For God's sake, let us get out of this, Nellie!' cried Ned, as the ringing bell-notes roused him.

'Have you had enough of Sydney?' she asked, leading the way out.

'I've had enough of every place,' he answered hotly. She did not say any more.

As they stood in George-street, waiting for their 'bus, a highheeled, tightly-corsetted, gaily-hatted larrikiness flounced out of the side door of a hotel near by. A couple of larrikin acquaintances were standing there, shrivelled young men in high-heeled pointed-toed shoes, belled trousers, gaudy neckties and round soft hats tipped over the left ear.

'Hello, you blokes!' cried the larrikiness, slapping one on the shoulder. 'Isn't this a blank of a time you're having?'

It was her ideal of pleasure, hers and theirs, to parade the street or stand in it, to gape or be gaped at.

CHAPTER V
WERE THEY CONSPIRATORS?

NEITHER Ned nor Nellie spoke as they journeyed down George street in the rumbling 'bus. 'I've got tickets,' was all she said as they entered the ferry shed at the Circular Quay. They climbed to the upper deck of the ferry boat in silence. He got up when she did and went ashore by her side without a word. He did not notice the glittering lights that encircled the murky night. He did not even know if it were wet or fine, or whether the moon shone or not. He was in a daze. The horrors of living stunned him. The miseries of poor Humanity choked him. The foul air of these noisome streets sickened him. The wretched faces he had seen haunted him. The oaths of the gutter children and the wailing of the blind beggar-girl seemed to mingle in a shriek that shook his very soul.

If he could have persuaded himself that the bush had none of this, it would have been different. But he could not. The stench of the stifling shearing-sheds and of the crowded sleeping huts where men are packed in rows like trucked sheep came to him with the sickening smell of the slums. On the faces of men in the bush he had seen again and again that hopeless look as of goaded oxen straining through a mud-hole, that utter degradation, that humble plea for charity. He had known them in Western Queensland often in spite of all that was said of the free, brave bush. It was not new to him, this dark side of life; that was the worst of it. It had been all along and he had known that it had been, but never before had he understood the significance of it, never before had he realised how utterly civilisation has failed. And this was what crushed him—the hopelessness of it all, the black despair that seemed to fill the universe, the brutal weariness of living, the ceaseless round of sorrow and sin and shame and unspeakable misery.

Often in the bush it had come to him, lying sleepless at night under the star-lit sky, all alone excepting for the tinkling of his horse-bell: 'What is to be the end for me? What is there to look forward to?' And his heart had sunk within him at the prospect. For what was in front? What could be? Shearing and waiting for shearing—that was his life. Working over the sweating sheep under the hot iron shed in the sweltering summer time; growing sick and losing weight and bickering with the squatter till the few working months wore over; then an occasional job, but mostly enforced idling till the season came round again; looking for work from shed to shed; struggling against conditions; agitating; organising; and in the future years, aged too soon, wifeless and childless, racked with rheumatism, shaken with fevers, to lie down to die on the open plain perchance or crawl, feebled and humbled, to the State-charity of Dunwich. He used to shut his eyes to force such thoughts from him, fearing lest he go mad, as were those travelling swagmen he met sometimes, who muttered always to themselves and made frantic gestures as they journeyed, solitary, through the monotonous wilderness. He had flung himself into unionism because there was nothing else that promised help or hope and because he hated the squatters, who took, as he looked at it, contemptible advantage of the bushmen. And he had felt that with unionism men grew better and heartier, gambling less and debating more, drinking less and planning what the union would do when it grew strong enough. He had worked for the union before it came, had been one of those who preached it from shed to shed and argued for it by smouldering camp fires before turning in. And he had seen the union feeling spread until the whole Western country throbbed with it and until the union itself started into life at the last attempt of the squatter to force down wages and was extending itself now as fast as even he could wish to see it. 'We only want what is fair,' he had told Nellie; 'we're not going in for anything wild. So long as we get a pound a hundred and rations at a fair figure we're satisfied.' And Nellie had shown him things which had struck him dumb and broken through the veneer of satisfaction that of late had covered over his old doubts and fears.

'What is to be the end for me?' he used to think, then force himself not to think in terror. Now, he himself seemed so insignificant, the union he loved so seemed so insignificant, he was only conscious for the time being of the agony of the world at large, which dulled him with the reflex of its pain. Oh, these puny foul-tongued children! Oh, these haggard weary women! Oh, these hopeless imbruted men! Oh, these young girls steeped in viciousness, these awful streets, this hateful life, this hell of Sydney. And beyond it—hell, still hell. Ah, he knew it now, unconsciously, as in a swoon one hears voices. The sorrow of it all! The hatefulness of it all! The weariness of it all! Why do we live? Wherefore? For what end, what aim? The selector, the digger, the bushman, as the townman, what has life for them? It is in Australia as all over the world. Wrong triumphs. Life is a mockery. God is not. At least, so it came gradually to Ned as he walked silently by Nellie's side.

They had turned down a tree-screened side road, descending again towards the harbour. Nellie stopped short at an iron gate, set in a hedge of some kind. A tree spanned the gateway with its branches, making the gloomy night still darker. The click of the latch roused her companion.

'Do you think it's any good living?' he asked her. She did not answer for a moment or two, pausing in the gateway. A break in the western sky showed a grey cloud faintly tinged with silver.

She looked fixedly up at it and Ned, his eyes becoming accustomed to the gloom, thought he saw her face working convulsively. But before he could speak again, she turned round sharply and answered, without a tremor in her voice:

'I suppose that's a question everybody must answer for themselves.'

'Well, do you?'

'For myself, yes.'

'For others, too?'

'For most others, no.' The intense bitterness of her tone stamped her words into his brain.

'Then why for you any more than anybody else?'

'I'll tell you after. We must go in. Be careful! You'd better give me your hand!'

She led the way along a short paved path, down three or four stone steps, then turned sharply along a small narrow verandah. At the end of the verandah was a door. Nellie felt in the darkness for the bell-button and gave two sharp rings.

'Where are you taking me, Nellie?' he asked. 'This is too swell a place for me. It looks as though everybody was gone to bed.'

In truth he was beginning to think of secret societies and mysterious midnight meetings. Only Nellie had not mentioned anything of the kind and he felt ashamed of acknowledging his suspicions by enquiring, in case it should turn out to be otherwise. Besides, what did it matter? There was no secret society which he was not ready to join if Nellie was in it, for Nellie knew more about such things than he did. It was exactly the place for meetings, he thought, looking round. Nobody would have dreamt that it was only half an hour ago that they two had left Paddy's Market. Here was the scent of damp earth and green trees and heavily perfumed flowers; the rustling of leaves; the fresh breath of the salt ocean. In the darkness, he could see only a semi-circling mass of foliage under the sombre sky, no other houses nor sign of such. He could not even hear the rumbling of the Sydney streets nor the hoarse whispering of the crowded city; not even a single footfall on the road they had come down. For the faint lap-lap-lapping of water filled the pauses, when the puffy breeze failed to play on its leafy pipes. Here a Mazzini might hide himself and here the malcontents of Sydney might gather in safety to plot and plan for the overthrow of a hateful and hated 'law and order.' So he thought.

'Oh, they're not gone to bed,' replied Nellie, confidently. 'They live at the back. It overlooks the harbour that side. And you'll soon see they're not as swell as they look. They're splendid people. Don't be afraid to say just what you think.'

'I'm not afraid of that, if you're not.'

'Ah, there's someone.'

An inside door opened and closed again, then they heard a heavy footstep coming, which paused for a moment, whereat a flood of colour streamed through a stained glass fanlight over the door.

'That's Mr. Stratton,' announced Nellie.

Next moment the door at which they stood was opened by a bearded man, wearing loose grey coat and slippers.

'Hello, Nellie!' exclaimed this possible conspirator, opening the door wide. 'Connie said it was your ring. Come straight in, both of you. Good evening, sir. Nellie's friends are our friends and we've heard so much of Ned Hawkins that we seem to have known you a long while.' He held out his hand and shook Ned's warmly, giving a strong, clinging, friendly grip, not waiting for any introduction. 'Of course, this is Mr. Hawkins, Nellie?' he enquired, seriously, turning to that young woman, whose hands he took in both of his while looking quizzingly from Ned to her and back to Ned again.

'Yes, of course,' she answered, laughing. Ned laughed. The possible conspirator laughed as he answered, dropping her hands and turning to shut the door: 'Well, it mightn't have been. By the way, Nellie, you must have sent an astral warning that you were coming along. We were just talking about you.'

*   *   *

They had been discussing Nellie in the Stratton circle, as our best friends will when we are so fortunate as to interest them.

In the pretty sitting-room that overlooked the rippling water, Mrs. Stratton perched on the music stool, was giving, amid many interjections, an animated account of the opera: a dark-haired, grey-eyed, full-lipped woman of thirty or so, with decidedly large nose and broad rounded forehead, somewhat under the medium height apparently but pleasingly plump as her evening dress disclosed. She talked rapidly, in a sweet expressive voice that had a strange charm. Her audience consisted of an ugly little man, with greyish hair, who stood at a bookcase in the corner and made his remarks over his shoulder; a gloomy young man, who sat in a reclining chair, with his arm hanging listlessly by his side; and a tall dark-moustached handsome man, broadly built, who sat on the edge of a table smoking a wooden pipe, and who, from his observations, had evidently accompanied her home from the theatre after the second act. There was also her husband, who leant over her, his back turned to the others, unhooking her fur-edged opera cloak, a tall fair brown bearded man, evidently the elder by some years, whose blue eyes were half hidden beneath a strongly projected forehead. He fumbled with the hooks of the cloak, passing his hands beneath it, smiling slyly at her the while. She, flushing like a girl at the touch, talked away while pressing her knee responsively against his. It was a little love scene being enacted of which the others were all unconscious unless for a general impression that this long-married couple were as foolishly in love as ever and indulged still in all the mild raptures of lovers.

'Ever so much obliged,' she said, pausing in her talk and looking at him at last, as he drew the cloak from her shoulders.

'You should be,' he responded, straightening himself out. 'It's quite a labour unhooking one of you fine ladies.'

'Don't call me names, Harry, or I'll get somebody else to take it off next time. I'm afraid it's love's labour lost. It's quite chilly, and I think I'll wrap it round me.'

'Well, if you will go about half undressed,' he commented, putting the cloak round her again.

'Half undressed! You are silly. The worst of this room is there's no fire in it. I think one needs a fire even in summer time, when it's damp, to take the chill off. Besides, as Nellie says, a blazing fire is the most beautiful picture you can put in a room.'

'Isn't Nellie coming to-night?' asked the man who smoked the wooden pipe.

'Why, of course, Ford. Haven't I told you she said on Thursday that she would come and bring the wild untamed bushman with her? Nellie always keeps her word.'

'She's a wonderful girl,' remarked Ford.

'Wonderful? Why wonderful is no name for it,' declared Stratton, lighting a cigar at one of the piano candles. 'She is extraordinary.'

'I tell Nellie, sometimes, that I shall get jealous of her, Harry gets quite excited over her virtues, and thinks she has no faults, while poor I am continually offending the consistencies.'

'Who is Nellie?' enquired the ugly little man, turning round suddenly from the book case which he had been industriously ransacking.

'I like Geisner,' observed Mrs. Stratton, pointing at the little man. 'He sees everything, he hears everything, he makes himself at home, and when he wants to know anything he asks a straightforward question. I think you've met her, though, Geisner.'

'Perhaps. What is her other name?'

'Lawton—Nellie Lawton. She came here once or twice when you were here before, I think, and for the last year or so she's been our—our—what do you call it, Harry? You know—the thing that South Sea Islanders think is the soul of a chief.'

'You're ahead of me, Connie. But it doesn't matter; go on.'

'There's nothing to go on about. You ought to recollect her, Geisner. I'm sure you met her here.'

'I think I do. Wasn't she a tall, between-colours girl, quite young, with a sad face and queer stern mouth—a trifle cruel, the mouth, if I recollect. She used to sit across there by the piano, in a plain black dress, and no colour at all except one of your roses.'

'Good gracious! What a memory! Have you got us all ticketed away like that?'

'It's habit,' pleaded Geisner. 'She didn't say anything, and only that she had a strong face, I shouldn't have noticed her. Has she developed?'

'Something extraordinary,' struck in Stratton, puffing great clouds of smoke. 'She speaks French, she reads music, she writes uncommonly good English, and in some incomprehensible way she has formed her own ideas of Art. Not bad for a dress-making girl who lives in a Sydney back street and sometimes works sixteen hours a day, is it?'

'Well, no. Only you must recollect, Stratton, that if she's been in your place pretty often, most of the people she meets here must have given her a wrinkle or two.'

'You're always in opposition, Geisner,' declared Mrs. Stratton. 'I never heard you agree with anybody else's statement yet. Nellie is wonderful. You can't shake our faith in that. There is but one Womanity and Nellie is its prophet.'

'It's all right about her getting wrinkles here, Geisner,' contributed Ford, 'for of course she has. It was what made her, Mrs. Stratton getting hold of her. But at the same time she is extraordinary. When she's been stirred up I've beard her tackle the best of the men who come here and down them. On their own ground too. I don't see how on earth she has managed to do it in the time. She's only twenty now.'

'I'll tell you, if you'll light the little gas stove for me, Ford, and put the kettle on,' said Mrs. Stratton, drawing her cloak more tightly round her shoulders. 'I know some of you men don't believe it, but it is the truth nevertheless that Feeling is higher than Reason. Isn't it chilly? You see, after all, you can only reason as to why you feel. Well, Nellie feels. She is an artist. She has got a soul.'

'What do you call an artist?' queried Geisner, partly for the sake of the argument, partly to see the little woman flare up.

'An artist is one who feels—that's all. Some people can fashion an image in wood or stone, or clay, or paint, or ink, and then they imagine that they are the only artists, when in reality three-quarters of them aren't artists at all but the most miserable mimics and imitators—highly trained monkeys, you know. Nellie is an artist. She can understand dumb animals and hear music in the wind and the waves, and all sorts of things. And to her the world is one living thing, and she can enjoy its joys and worry over its sorrows, and she understands more than most why people act as they do because she feels enough to put herself in their place. She is such an artist that she not only feels herself but impels those she meets to feel. Besides, she has a freshness that is rare nowadays. I'm very fond of Nellie.'

'Evidently,' said Geisner; 'I've got quite interested. Is she dressmaking still?'

'Yes; I wanted her to come and live with us but she wouldn't. Then Harry got her a better situation in one of the government departments. You know how those things are fixed. But she wouldn't have it. You see she is trying to get the girls into unions.'

'Then she is in the movement?' asked Geisner, looking up quickly.

Mrs. Stratton lifted her eye-brows. 'In the movement! Why, haven't you understood? My dear Geisner, here we've been talking for fifteen minutes and—there's Nellie's ring. Harry, go and open the door while I pour the coffee.'

The opera cloak dropped from her bare shoulders as she rose from the stool. She had fine shoulders, and altogether was of fashionable appearance, excepting that there was about her the impalpable, but none the less pronounced, air of the woman who associates with men as a comrade. As she crossed the room to the verandah she stopped beside the gloomy young man, who had said nothing. He looked up at her affectionately.

'You are wrong to worry,' she said, softly. 'Besides, it makes you bad company. You haven't spoken to a soul since we came in. For a punishment come and cut the lemon.'

They went out on to the verandah together, her hand resting on his arm. There, on a broad shelf, a kettle of water was already boiling over a gas stove.

'What are you thinking of,' she chattered. 'We shall have some more of your ferocious poetry, I suppose. I notice that about you, Arty. Whenever you get into your blue fits you always pour out blood and thunder verses. The bluer you are the more volcanic you get. When you have it really bad you simply breathe dynamite, barricades, brimstone, everything that is emphatic. What is it this time?'

He laughed. 'Why won't you let a man stay blue when he feels like it?'

She did not seem to think an answer necessary, either to his question or her own. 'Have you a match?' she went on. 'Ah! There is one thing in which a man is superior to woman. He can generally get a light without running all over the house. That is so useful of him. It's his one good point. I can't imagine how any woman can tolerate a man who doesn't smoke. I suppose one get's used to it, though.'

He laughed again, turning up the gas-jet he had lighted, which flickered in the puffs of wind that came off the water below. 'I could tell you a good story about that.'

'That is what I like, a good story. Gas is a nuisance. I wish we had electric lights. Sydney only wants two things to be perfect, never to rain and moonlight all the time. Why I declare! If there aren't Hero and Leander! Well, of all the spooniest, unsociable, selfish people, you two are the worst. You haven't even had the kindness to let us know you were in all the time, and you actually see Arty and me toiling away at the coffee without offering to help. I've given you up long ago, Josie, but I did expect better things of you, George.'

While she had been speaking, pouring the boiling water into the coffee-pot meanwhile, Arty cutting lemons into slices, the two lovers discovered by the flickering gaslight got out of a hammock slung across the end of the verandah and came forward.

'You seemed to be getting along so well we didn't like to disturb you, Mrs. Stratton,' explained George, shaking hands. He was bronzed and bright-eyed, not handsome but strong and kindly-looking; he had a kindly voice, too; he wore a white flannel boating costume under a dark cloth coat. Josie, also wore a sailor dress of dark blue with loose white collar and vest; a scarlet wrap covered her short curly hair; her skin was milkwhite and her features small and irregular. Josie and Connie could never be mistaken for anything but sisters, in spite of the eleven years between them. Only Josie was pretty and plastic and passionless, and Connie was not pretty nor plastic nor passionless. They were the contrast one sees so often in children kin-born of the summer and autumn of life.

'Don't tell me!' said Mrs. Stratton. 'I know all about that.'

'Connie knows,' said Josie, putting her arms over her sister's shoulders—the younger was the taller—and drawing her face back. 'Do you know, Arty, I daren't go into a room in a house I know without knocking. The lady has been married twelve years and when her husband is away he writes to her every day, and though they have quite big children they send them to bed and sit for hours in the same chair, billing and cooing. I've known them—'

'I wonder who they can be,' interrupted Mrs. Stratton, twisting herself free, her face as red as Josie's shawl. 'There's Nellie's voice. They'll be wondering what we're doing here. Do come along!' And seizing a tray of cups and saucers, on which she had placed the coffeepot and the saucer of sliced lemon, she beat a dignified retreat amid uproarious laughter.

*   *   *

Ned found himself in a narrow hall that ran along the side of the house at right angles to the verandah and the road. The floor was covered with oil-cloth; the walls were hung with curios, South Sea spears and masks, Japanese armour, boomerangs, nullahs, a multitude of quaint workings in wood and grass and beads. Against the wall facing the door was an umbrella stand and hat rack of polished wood, with a mirror in the centre. There were two pannelled doors to the left; a doorless stairway, leading downwards, and a large window to the right; at the end of the passage a glazed door, with coloured panes. A gas jet burned in a frosted globe and seeing him look at this Stratton explained the contrivance for turning the light down to a mere dot which gave no gleam but could be turned up again in a second.

'My wife is enthusiastic about household invention,' he concluded, smiling. 'She thinks it assists in righting women's wrongs. Eh, Nellie? The freed and victorious female will put her foot on abject man some day? Eh?'

Nellie laughed again. She held the handle of the nearest door in one hand. Mr. Stratton had turned to take Ned's hat, apologising for neglecting to think of that before. Ned saw the girl's other hand move quickly up to where the gas bracket met the wall and then the light went out altogether. 'That's for poking fun,' he heard her say. The door slammed, a key turned in it and he heard her laughing on the other side.

'Larrikin!' shouted Stratton, boisterously. 'Come out here and see what we'll do to you. She's always up to her tricks,' he added, striking a match and turning the gas on again. 'She is a fine girl. We are as fond of her as though she were one of the family. She is one of the family, for that matter.'

Ned hardly believed his ears or his eyes, either. He had not seen Nellie like this before. She had been grave and rather stern. Only at the gate he had thought he detected in her voice a bitterness which answered well to his own bitter heartache; he had thought he saw on her face the convulsive suppression of intense emotion. Certainly this very day she had shown him the horrors of Sydney and taught him, as if by magic, the misery of living. Now, she laughed lightly and played a trick with the quickness of a thoughtless school girl. Besides, how did it happen that she was so at home in this house of well-to-do people, and so familiar with this man of a cultured class? Ned did not express his thoughts in such phrases of course, but that was the effect of them. He had laughed, but he was still sad and sick at heart and somehow these pleasantries jarred on him. It looked as if there were some secret understanding certainly, some bond that he could not distinguish, between the girl of the people and this courteous gentleman. Nellie had told him simply that the Strattons were 'interested in the Labour movement' and were very nice, but Stratton spoke of her as 'one of the family' and she turned out his gas and locked one of his own doors in his face. If it was a secret society, well and good, no matter how desperate its plan. But why did they laugh and joke and play tricks? He was not in the humour. For the time his soul abhorred what seemed to him frippery. He sought intuitively to find relief in action and he began impatiently to look for it here.

'Hurry, Nellie!' cried Stratton. 'Coffee's nearly ready.'

'You won't touch me?' answered her merry voice.

'No, we'll forgive you this once, but look out for the next time.'

She opened the door forthwith and stepped out quickly. Ned caught a glimpse of a large bedroom through the doorway. She had taken off her hat and gloves and smoothed the hair that lay on her neck in a heavy plait. At the collar of the plain black dress that fell to her feet over the curving lines of her supple figure she had placed a red rose, half blown. She was tall and straight and graceful, more than beautiful in her strong fresh womanhood, as much at home in such a house as this as in the wretched room where he had watched her sewing slop-clothes that morning. His aching heart went out towards her in a burst of unspoken feeling which he did not know at the time to be Love.

'Mrs. Stratton always puts a flower for me. She loves roses.' So she said to Ned, seeing him looking astonishedly at her. Then she slipped one hand inside the arm that Stratton bent towards her, and took hold of Ned's arm with the other. Stratton turned down the gas. Linked thus together the three went cautiously down the dim passage hall-way, towards the glass door through one side of which coloured light came.

'Anybody particular here?' asked Nellie.

'That's a nice question,' retorted Stratton. 'Geisner is here, if you call him "anybody particular".'

'Geisner! Is he back again?' exclaimed the girl. Ned felt her hand clutch him nervously. A sudden repulsion to this Geisner shot through him. He pulled his arm from her grasp.

They had reached the end of the passage, however, and she did not notice. Stratton turned the handle and opened the door, held back the half-drawn curtain that hung on the further side and they passed in. 'Here we are,' he cried. 'Geisner says he recollects you, Nellie.'

Ned could have described the room to the details if he had been struck blind that minute. It was a double room, long and low and not very broad, running the whole width of the house, for there were windows on two sides and French lights on another. The glazed door opened in the corner of the windowless side. Opposite were the French lights, the further one swung ajar and showing a lighted verandah beyond from which came a flutter of voices. Beyond still were dim points of light that he took at first for stars. Folding doors, now swung right back, divided the long linoleum-floored room into two apartments, a studio and a sitting-room. The studio in which they stood was littered with things strange to him; an easel, bearing a half-finished drawing; a black-polished cabinet; a table-desk against the window, on it slips of paper thrown carelessly about, the ink-well open, a file full of letters, a handful of cigarettes, a tray of tobacco ash, a bespattered palette, pens, coloured crayons, a medley of things; a revolving office chair with a worn crimson footrug before it; a many-shelved glass case against the blank wall, crammed to overflowing with shells and coral and strange grasses, with specimens of ore, with Chinese carvings, with curious lacquer-work; a large brass-bound portfolio stand; on the painted walls plaster-casts of hands and arms and feet, boxing gloves, fencing foils, a glaring tiger's head, a group of photographs; in the corner, a suit of antique armour stood sentinel over a heap of dumb-bells and Indian clubs.

In the sitting room beyond the folded doors, a soft coloured rug carpet lay loosely on the floor. There were easy chairs there and a red lounge that promised softness; a square cloth-covered table; a whatnot in the corner; fancy shelves; a pretty walnut-wood piano, gilt lined, the cover thrown back, laden with music; on the music-stool a woman's cloak was lying, on the piano a woman's cap. A great book-case reached from ceiling to floor, filled with books, its shelves fringed with some scalloped red stuff. Everywhere were nick-nacks in china, in glass, in terra-cotta, in carved woods, in ivory; photo frames; medallions. On the walls, bright with striped hangings, were some dainty pictures. Half concealed by the hangings was another door. Lying about on the table, here and there on low shelves, were more books. The ground-glass globes of the gaslights were covered with crimson shades. There was a subdued blaze of vivid colouring, of rich toned hues, of beautiful things loved and cherished, over all. Sitting on the edge of the table was the moustached man who smoked the wooden pipe. And turning round from the book-case, an open book in his hand, was the ugly little man. Ned felt that this was Geisner.

The ugly little man put down his book, and came forward holding out his hand. He smiled as he came. Ned was angered to see that when he smiled his face became wonderfully pleasant.

'Yes; I think we know one another, Miss Lawton,' he said, meeting them on the uncarpeted floor.

'I am so glad you are here to-night,' she replied, greeting him warmly, almost effusively. 'I recollect you so well. And Ned will know you, too— Mr. Geisner, Mr. Hawkins.' Ned felt his reluctantly extended hand enclosed in a strong friendly clasp.

'Hawkins is the Queenslander we were expecting,' said Stratton cheerfully. 'You will excuse my familiarity, won't you?' he added, laying his hand on Ned's shoulder. 'We don't "Mister" our friends much here. I think it sounds cold and distant; don't you?'

'We don't "Mister" much where I come from,' answered Ned. He felt at home already. The atmosphere of kindness in this place stole over him and prevented him thinking that it was too 'swell' for him.

'I don't know Queensland much—,' Geisner was beginning, when the farther verandah door was swung wide and the dark-haired little woman swept in, tray in hand, the train of her dress trailing behind her.

'I heard you, Nellie dear,' she cried. 'That unfeeling Josie was saying the cruellest things to me. I feel as red as red.' Putting the tray down on the table she hurried to them, threw her plump bare arms round Nellie's neck and kissed her warmly on both cheeks. Then she drew back quickly and raised her finger threateningly. 'Worrying again, Nellie, I can tell. My word! What with you and what with Arty I'm made thoroughly wretched. You mayn't think so to look at me, Mr. Hawkins,' she rattled on, holding out her hand to Ned; 'but it is so. You see I know you. I heard Nellie introducing you. That husband of mine must leave all conventionalism to his guests, it seems. You're incorrigible, Harry.'

There was a welcome in her every word and look. She put him on a friendly footing at once.

'You have enough conventionalism to-night for us both, my fine lady,' twitted Stratton, pinching her arm.

'Stop that! Stop, this minute! Nellie, hit him for me. Mr. Hawkins, this is Bohemia. You do as you like. You say what you like. You are welcome to-night for Nellie's sake. You will be welcome always because I like your looks. I do, Harry, so there. And I'm going to call you Ned because Nellie always does. Oh! I forgot—Mr. Hawkins, Mr. Ford. Mr. Ford thinks he can cartoon. I don't know what you think you can do. And now, everybody, come to coffee.'

The others came in from the verandah, still laughing, whereat Mrs. Stratton flushed red again and denounced Josie and George for hiding away, then introduced them and Arty to Ned. There was a babel of conversation for awhile, Josie and George talking of their boating, Connie and Ford of the opera, Stratton and Arty of a picture they had seen that evening. Geisner sat by Ned and Nellie, the three chatting of the beauty of Sydney harbour, the little man waxing indignant at the vandalism which the naval authorities were perpetrating on Garden Island. Mrs. Stratton, all the time, attended energetically to her coffee-pot: Finally she served them all, in small green-patterned china cups, with strong black coffee guiltless of milk, in each cup a slice of lemon floating, in each saucer a biscuit.

'I hope you like your coffee, Ned,' she exclaimed, a moment after. 'I forgot to ask you. I'm always forgetting to ask newcomers. You see all the "regulars" like it this way.'

'I've never tasted it this way before,' answered Ned. 'I suppose liking it's a habit, like smoking. I think I'll try it.'

She nodded, being engaged in slowly sipping her own. Geisner looked at Ned keenly. There was silence for a little while, broken only by the clatter of cups and an occasional observation. From outside came the ceaseless lap-lap-lapping of the waves, as if rain water was gurgling down from the roof.

CHAPTER VI

'WE HAVE SEEN THE DRY BONES BECOME MEN'

NED'S thoughts were in tumult, as he sat balancing his spoon on his cup after forcing himself to swallow the, to him, unpleasant drink that the others seemed to relish so. There were no conspirators here, that was certain. Nellie he could understand being one, even with the red rose at her neck, but not this friendly chattering woman whose bare arms and shoulders shimmered in the tinted light and from whose silk dress a subtle perfume stole all over the room; and most certainly not this pretty, mild-looking girl in sailor-costume who appeared from the previous conversation to have passed the evening swinging in a hammock with her sweetheart. And the men! Why, they got excited over music and enraptured over the 'tone' of somebody's painting, while Geisner had actually gone back to the book-case, coffee cup in hand, and stood there nibbling a biscuit and earnestly studying the titles of books. It was pleasant, of course, too pleasant. It seemed a sin to enjoy life like this on the very edge of the horrible pit in which the poor wore festering like worms in an iron pot. Was it for this that Nellie had brought him here? To idle away an evening among well-meaning people who were 'interested in the Labour movement' and in some strange way, some whim probably, had taken to this working girl who in her plain black dress queened them all. He looked round the room and hated it. To his sickened soul its beauty blasphemed the lot of the toilers, insulted the wretchedness, the foulness, the hideousness, that he had seen this very day, that he had known and struggled against, all unconsciously, throughout his wayward life. And Geisner, Geisner at whom Nellie was looking fondly, Geisner who he supposed had written a book or a bit of poetry or could play the flute, and who raved about the spoiling of a bit of an island when the happiness of millions upon millions was being spoiled—well, he would just like to tell Geisner what he thought of him in emphatic bush lingo. Nellie, herself, seemed peacefully happy. Yet Mrs. Stratton had accused her of 'worrying.' When Ned thought of this he felt as he did when fording a strange creek, running a banker. He did not know what was underneath.

'Try a cigar, Hawkins?' asked Stratton, pushing a box towards him.

'Thank you, but I don't smoke.'

'Don't you really! Do you know I thought all bushmen were great smokers.'

'Some are and some aren't,' said Ned. 'We're not all built to one pattern any more than folks in town.'

'That's right, Ned,' put in Connie, suddenly recollecting that she was chilly. 'Will you hand me my cloak, please? You see,' she went on as he brought it, 'Harry imagines every bushman as just six feet high, proportionally broad, with bristling black beard streaked with grey, longish hair, bushy eyebrows, bloodshot eyes, moleskins, jean shirt, leathern belt, a black pipe, a swag—you call it "swag", don't you?—over his shoulders, and a whisky bottle in his hand whenever he is "blowing in his cheque", which is what Nellie says you call "going on the spree". Complimentary, isn't it?'

'Connie's libelling both me and my typical bushman,' said Stratton, lighting his cigar, having passed the box around. Ned was laughing against his will. Connie had mimicked her husband's imaginary bushman in a kindly humorous way that was very droll.

The musical debate had started up again behind them. Ford and George argued for the traditional rendering of music. Nellie and Arty battled for the musical zeit-geist, the national sense that sees through mere notation to the spirit that breathes behind. They waxed warm and threw authorities and quotations about, hardly waiting for each other to finish what they wished to say. Connie turned round to the disputants and threw herself impetuously into the quarrel, strengthening with her wit and trained criticism the cause of the zeit-geist. Stratton, to Ned's surprise, putting his arms over her shoulders, opposed her arguments and controverted her assertions with unsparing keenness. Josie leaned back on the lounge and smiled across at Ned. The smile said plainly: 'It really doesn't matter, does it?' Ned, fuming inwardly, thought it certainly did not. What a waste of words when the world outside needed deeds! This verbiage was as empty as the tobacco smoke which began to hang about the room in bluish clouds.

Suddenly Mrs. Stratton stood up. 'Geisner!' she cried. 'I'm ashamed of you. You hear us getting overwhelmed by these English heresies, and you don't come to the rescue. We have talked ourselves dry and you haven't said a word. Who says wine?'

Geisner slowly put down his book and went to the piano. 'This is the only argument worth the name,' he said. He ran his fingers over the keys, struck two or three chords apparently at hap-hazard, then sat down to play. A volume of sound rose, of clashing notes in fierce, swinging movement, a thrilling clamour of soul-stirring melody, at once short and sharp and long-drawn, at once soft as a mother's lullaby and savage as a hungry tiger's roar. It was the song of the world, the Marseillaise, the song that rises in every land when the oppressed rise against the oppressor, the song that breathes of wrongs to be revenged and of liberty to be won, of flying foes in front and a free people marching, and of blood shed like water for the idea that makes all nations kin. The hand of a master struck the keys and brought the notes out, clear and rhythmic, full strong notes that made the blood boil and the senses swim.

As the glorious melody rose and fell, sinking to a murmur, swelling out in heroic strains that rang like trumpet pealings, a great lump rose in Ned's throat and a mist of unquenchable tears filled his eyes. Roget de Lisle, dead and dust for generations, rose from the silent grave and spoke to him, spoke as heart speaks to heart, spoke and called and lived and breathed and was there, spoke of tortured lives and enslaved millions and of the fetid streets of great towns and of the slower anguish of the plundered country side, spoke of an Old Order based on the robbery of those who labour and on their weakness and on their ignorant sloth, spoke of virtue trampled down and little children weeping and Humanity bleeding at every pore and womanhood shamed and motherhood made a curse, spoke of all he hated and all he loved, pilloried the Wrong in front of him and bade him—to arms, to arms. 'To arms!' with the patriot army whose trampling was the background of the music. 'To arms!' with those whose desperate hands feared nothing and at whose coming thrones melted and kingdoms vanished and tyranny fled. To arms! To certain victory! To crash forward like a flood and sweep before the armed people all those who had worked it wrong!

Down Ned's cheeks the great tears rolled. He did not heed them. Why did not some one beat this mighty music through the Sydney slums, through those hateful back streets, through those long endless rows of mortgaged cottages and crowded apartment-houses? Why was it not carried out to the great West, hymned from shed to shed, told of in the huts and by the waterholes, given to the diggers in the great claims, to the drovers travelling stock, borne wherever a man was to be found who had a wrong to right and a long account to square? Ah! How they would all leap to it! How they would swell its victorious chanting and gather in their thousands and their hundred thousands to march on, march on, tramping time to its majestic notes! If he could only take it to them! If he could only make them feel as he felt! If he could only give to them in their poverty and misery all this wondrous music sounding here in this luxurious room! He could not; he could not. This Geisner could and would not, and he who would could not. The tears rained down his cheeks because of his utter impotence.

The music stopped. With a start he came to himself, ashamed of his weakness, and hastily blew his nose, fussing pretentiously with his handkerchief. But only one had noticed him—Geisner, who seemed to see and hear everything. Connie was sobbing quietly with her arms round

Harry's neck, holding his head closely to her as he bent over her chair; all the while her foot beat time. Arty had suddenly grown moody again and sat with bent head, his cigar gone out in his listless hand. Ford had got up and was perched again on a corner of the table, smoking critically, apparently wholly engaged in watching the smoke wreaths he blew. George and Josie had taken each other's hands and sat breathlessly side by side on the lounge. Nellie lay back in her chair, her face flushed, a twisted handkerchief stretched over her eyes by both hands.

'I think that's the official version,' observed Geisner, running his fingers softly over the keys again.

'It's above disputation, whatever it is,' remarked Ford.

'Why should it be, if all true music isn't? And why should not this be the best rendering?'

He struck the grand melody again and it sounded softened, spiritualised, purified. Its fierce clamour, its triumphant crashing, were gone. It told of defeat and overthrow, of martyrs walking painfully to death, of prison cells and dungeons that never see the sun, of life-work unrewarded, of those who give their lives to Liberty and die before its shackled limbs are struck free. But it told, too, of an ideal held more sacred than life, rising ever from defeat, filling men's hearts and brains and driving them still to raise again the flag of Freedom against hopeless odds. It was a death march rolling out, the death march of sad-souled patriots going sorrowfully to seal their faith with all their earthly hopes and human loves and to meet, calm and pale, all that Fate has in store. They said to Liberty: 'In death we salute thee.' Without seeing her or knowing her, while the world around still slept in ignorance of her, they gave all up for her and in darkness died. Only they knew that there was no other way, that unless each man of himself dared to raise the chant and march forward alone, if need be, Liberty could never be.

'Well,' said Geisner, coming unconcernedly into the circle where they sat in dead silence. 'Don't you think the last rendering is the best, and isn't it the best simply because it expresses the composer's idea in the particular phase that we feel most at this present time?'

'Gracious! Don't start the argument again!' entreated Connie, vivacious again, though her eyes were red. 'You'll never convert Ford or George or Harry here. They'll always have some explanation. Puritanism crushed the artistic sense out of the English, and they are only getting it back slowly by a judicious crossing with other peoples who weren't Puritanised into Philistinism. England has no national music. She has no national painting. She has no national sculpture. She has to borrow and adapt everything from the Continent. I nearly said she has no art at all.'

'Here, I say,' protested Ford. 'Aren't you coming it a little too strong? You've got the floor, Geisner. I've heard you stand up for English Art. Stand up now, won't you?'

'Does it need standing up for?' asked Geisner. 'Why, Connie doesn't forget that Puritanism with all its faults was in its day a religious movement, that is an emotional fervour, a veritable poem. That the Puritan cut love-locks off, wore drab, smashed painted windows and suppressed instrumental music in churches, is no proof of their being utterly inartistic. Their art-sense would simply find vent and expression in other directions if it existed strongly enough. And what do we find? This, that the Puritan period produced two of the masterpieces of English Art—Milton's 'Paradise Lost' and Bunyan's 'Pilgrim's Progress.' As an absolute master of English, of sentences rolling magnificently in great waves of melodious sound, trenchant in every syllable, not to be equalled even by Shakespeare himself, Milton stands out like a giant. As for Bunyan, the Englishman who has never read 'Pilgrim's Progress' does not know his mother tongue.'

'Oh! Of course, we all admit English letters,' interjected Connie.

'Do we?' answered Geisner, warming with his theme. 'I'm not so sure of that; else, why should English people themselves put forward claims to excellencies which their nation has not got, and why should others dub them inartistic because of certain things lacking in the national arts? As far as music goes what has France got if you take away the Marseillaise? It is Germany, the kin of the English, which has the modern music. France has painting, England has literature and poetry—in that she leads the whole world.'

'Still, to-day! How about Russia? How about France even—Flaubert, Zola, Daudet, Ohnet, a dozen more?'

'Still! Ay, still and ever! Will these men live as the English writers live, think you? Look back a thousand years and see English growing, see how it comes to be the king of languages, destined, if civilisation lasts, to be the one language of the civilised world. There, in the Viking age, the English sweep the seas, great burly brutes, as Taine shows them to us, gorging on half-raw meat, swilling huge draughts of ale, lounging naked by the sedgy brooks under the mist-softened sun that cannot brown their fair pink bodies, until hunger drives them forth to foray; drinking and fighting and feasting and shouting and loving as Odin loved Frega. And the most honoured of all was the singer who sang in heroic verse of their battling and their love-making and their hunting. English was conceived then, and it was worthy conceiving.'

'Other nations have literature,' maintained Connie.

'What other living nations?' demanded Geisner. 'Look at English! An endless list, such as surely before the world never saw. You cannot even name them all. Spenser and Chaucer living still. Shakespeare, whoever he was, immortal for all time, dimming like a noontide sun a galaxy of stars that to other nations would be suns indeed! Take Marlow, Beaumont and Fletcher, a dozen playwrights! The Bible, an imperishable monument of the people's English! Milton, Bunyan and Baxter, Wycherly and his fellows! Pope, Ben Johnson, Swift, Goldsmith, Junius, Burke, Sheridan! Scott and Byron, De Quincey, Shelley, Lamb, Chatterton! Moors and Burns wrote in English too! Look at Wordsworth, Dickens, George Eliot, Swinburne, Tennyson, the Brontés! There are gems upon gems in the second class writers, books that in other countries would make the writer immortal. Over the sea, in America, Poe, Whittier, Bret Harte, Longfellow, Emerson, Whitman. Here in Australia, the seed springing up!

Even in South Africa, that Olive Schreiner writing like one inspired. By heavens! There are moments when I feel it must be a proud thing to be an Englishman.'

'Bravo, Geisner! You actually make me for the minute,' cried Ford.

'You should be! Has any other people anything to compare? There is not one other whose great writers could not almost be counted on the fingers of one hand. Spain has Cervantes and he is always being thrown at us. Germany has Goethe, Heine, Schiller. France so seldom sees literary genius that a man like Victor Hugo sends her into hysterics of self-admiration. But I'm afraid I'm lecturing.'

'It's all right, Geisner,' remarked Connie. 'It's not only what you say but how you say it. But what are you driving at?'

'Just this! Nations seldom do all things with equal vigour and fervour and opportunity, so one excels another and is itself excelled. England excels in the simplest and strongest form of expression, literature. She is defective in other forms and borrows from us. But so we others borrow from her. Puritanism did not crush English art. English art, in the national way of expressing the national feeling, kept steadily on.'

'Thanks! I think I'll sit down,' he added, as Stratton handed him a tumbler half-filled with wine and a water-bottle. He filled the tumbler from the bottle, put them on the table, took cigarettes in a case from his pocket and lighted one at a gas jet behind him.

'Do you take water with your wine?' asked Stratton of Ned.

'I don't take wine at all, thank you,' said Ned.

'What!' exclaimed Connie, sitting up. 'You don't smoke and you don't drink wine. Why, you are a regular Arab. But you must have something. Arty! Rouse up and light the little stove again! You'll have some tea, Ned. Oh! It's no trouble. Arty will make it for me and it will do him good. What do you think of this oration of Geisner's?'

'I suppose it's all right,' said Ned. 'But I can't see what good it does myself.'

'How's that?'

'Well, it's no use saying one thing and meaning another. This talk of "art" seems to me selfish while the world to most people is a hell that it's pain to live in. I am sorry if I say what you don't like.'

'Never mind that,' said Connie, as cheerfully as ever. 'You've been worrying, too. Have it out, so that we can all jump on you at once! I warn you, you won't have an ally.'

'I suppose not,' answered Ned, hotly. 'You are all very kind and mean well, but do you know how people live, how they exist, what life outside is?'

Geisner had sat down in a low chair near by, his cigarette between his lips, his glass of wine and water on a shelf at his elbow. The others looked on in amazement at the sudden turn of the conversation. Connie smiled and nodded. Ned stared fiercely round at Geisner, who nodded also.

'Then listen to me,' said Ned, bitterly. 'Is it by playing music in fine parlours that good is to be done? Is it by drinking wine, by smoking, by laughing, by talking of pictures and books and music, by going to theatres, by living in clover while the world starves? Why do you not play that music in the back streets or to our fellows?' he asked, turning to Geisner again. 'Are you afraid? Ah, if I could only play it!'

'Ned!' cried Nellie, sharply. But he went on, talking at Geisner:

'What do you do for the people outside? For the miserable, the wretched, those, weary of life? I suppose you are all "interested in the Labour movement". Well, what does all this do for it? What do you do for it? Would you give up anything, one puff of smoke, one drink of wine—'

'Stop, Ned! For shame's sake! How dare you speak to him like that?' Nellie interrupted, jumping up and coming between the two men. Ned leaned eagerly forward, his hands on his knees, his eyes flaming, his face quivering, his teeth showing. Geisner leaned back quietly, alternately sipping his wine and water and taking a whiff from his cigarette.

'Never mind,' said Geisner. 'Sit down, Nellie. It doesn't matter.' Nellie sat down but she looked to Mrs. Stratton anxiously. The two women exchanged glances. Mrs. Stratton came quickly across to Geisner.

'It does matter,' she said to him, laying her hands on his head and shoulder and facing Ned thus. 'Not to you, of course, but to Ned there. He does not understand, and I don't think you understand everything either. It takes a woman to understand it all, Ned,' and she laughed at the angry man. 'Why do you say such things to Geisner? He does not deserve them.'

Ned did not answer.

'I'm not defending the rest of us, only Geisner. If you only knew all he has done you would think of him as we do.'

'Connie!' exclaimed Geisner, flushing. 'Don't.'

'Oh! I shall. If men will keep their lights under bushel baskets they must expect to get the covers knocked off sometimes. Ned! This man is a martyr. He has suffered so for the people, and he has borne it so bravely.'

There was a hush in the room. Ned could see Connie's full underlip pouted tremulously and her eyes swimming, her hands moved caressingly to and fro. His face relaxed its passion. The tears came again into his eyes, also. Geisner smoked his cigarette, the most unmoved of any.

'If you had only known him years ago,' went on Connie, her voice trembling. 'He used to take me on his knee when I was a little girl, and keep me there for hours while great men talked great things and he was greatest of them all. He was young then and rich and handsome and fiery, and with a brain—oh, such a brain!—that put within his reach what other men care for most. And he gave it all up, everything—even Love,' she added, softly. 'When he played the Marseillaise just now, I thought of it. One day he came to our house and played it so, and outside the people in the streets were marching by singing it, and—and—' she set her teeth on a great sob. 'My father never came back nor my brother, and Harry there came one night and took Josie and me away. We had no mother. And when we saw this man again he was what he is now. It was worse than death, ten thousand times worse. Oh! Geisner, Geisner!' The head her hand rested on had sunk down. What were the little man's thoughts? What were they?

'But his heart is still the same, Ned,' she cried, triumphantly, her sweet voice ringing clear again. 'Ah, yes! His heart is still the same, as brave and true and pure and strong. Oh, purer, better! If it came again, Ned, he would do it. Sometimes, I think, he doubts himself but I know. He would do it all again and suffer it all—that worse than death he suffered. For, you see, he only lives to serve the Cause, in a different way to the old way but still to serve it. And I serve the Cause also as best I can, even if I wear—' she shrugged her shoulders. 'And Harry serves it still as loyally as when, a beardless lad, he risked his life to care for a slaughtered comrade's orphan children. And Ford, too, and Nellie here, and Arty and Josie and George. But Geisner serves it best of all if it be best to give most. He has given most all his life and he gives most still. And we love him for it. And that love, perhaps, is sweeter to him than all he might have been.'

She knelt by his side as she ceased speaking, and put her arms round his neck as he crouched there. 'Geisner!' Nellie who was nearest heard her whisper in her childhood's tongue. 'Geisner! We have seen the dry bones become men. We have poured our blood and our brain into them and if only for a moment they have lived, they have lived. Ah, comrade, do you recollect how you breathed soul into them when they shrank back that day? They moved, Geisner. They moved. We felt them move. They will move again, some day, dear heart. They will move again.' Then, choking with sobs, she laid her head on his knees. He put his arms tenderly round her and they saw that this immovable little man was weeping like a child. One by one the others went softly out to the verandah. Only Ned remained. He had buried his face in his hands and sat, overwhelmed with shame, wishing that the floor would open and swallow him. From outside came the ceaseless lap-lap-lapping of water, imperceptibly eating away the granite rock, caring not for time, blindly working, destroying the old and building up the new.

The touch of a hand roused Ned. He looked up. Mrs. Stratton had gone through the door concealed by the hangings. Geisner stood before him, calmly lighting another cigarette with a match. There was no trace of emotion on his face. He turned to drop the match into an ash tray, then held out both hands, on his face the kindly smile that transfigured him. Ned grasped them eagerly, wringing them in a grip that would have made most men wince. They stood thus silently for a minute or two, looking at one another, the young, hot-tempered bushman, the grey-haired, cool-tempered leader of men; between them sprang up, as they stood, the bond of that friendship which death itself only strengthens. The magnetism of the elder, his marvellous personality, the strength and majesty of the mighty soul that dwelt in his insignificant body, stole into Ned's heart and conquered it. And the spirit of the younger, his fierce indignation, his angry sorrow, his disregard for self, his truth, his strong manhood, appealed to the weary man as an echoing of his own passionate youth. Then they loosened hands and without a word Geisner commenced to walk slowly backwards and forwards, his hands behind him, his head bent down.

Ned watched him, studying him feature by feature. Yes, he had been handsome. He was ugly only because of great wrinkles that scored his cheeks and disfigured the fleshless face and discoloured skin. His eyebrows and eyelashes were very thin, too. His hair looked dried up and was strongly greyed; it had once been almost black. His lips were thin, his mouth shapeless, only because he had closed them in his fight against pain and anguish and despair and they had set thus by the habit of long years. His nose was still fine and straight, the nostrils swelling wide. His forehead was rugged and broad under its wrinkles. His chin was square. His frame still gave one the impression of tireless powers of endurance. His blue eyes still gleamed unsubdued in their dark, overhanging caverns. Yes! He had lived, this man. He had lived and suffered and kept his manhood still. To be like him! To follow him into the Valley of the Shadow! To live only for the Cause and by his side to save the world alive! Ned thought thus, as Connie came back, her face bathed and beaming again, her theatre dress replaced by a soft red dressing gown, belted loosely at the waist and trimmed with an abundance of coffee coloured lace. Her first words were a conundrum to Ned:

'Geisner! Haven't you dropped that unpleasant trick of yours after all these years? Two long steps and a short step! Turn! Two long steps and a short stop! Turn! Now, just to please me, do three long steps.'

He smiled. 'Connie, you are becoming quite a termagant.'

She looked at Ned questioningly: 'Well?'

'Oh, Ned and I are beginning to understand one another,' said Geisner.

'Of course,' she replied. 'All good men and women are friends if they get to the bottom of each other. Let us go on the verandah with the rest. Do you know I feel quite warm now. I do believe it was only that ridiculous dress which made me feel so cold. Give me your arm, Ned. Bring me along a chair, Geisner.'

CHAPTER VII

A MEDLEY OF CONVERSATION

NED dreaded that rejoining the others on the verandah, but he need not have. They had forced the conversation at first, but gradually it became natural. It had turned on the proper sphere of woman, and went on without being interrupted by the new-comers. Nobody took any notice of them. The girls were seated. Stratton lay smoking in the hammock. The other men perched smoking on the railing. The gaslight had been turned down and in the gloom the cigar ends gleamed with each respiration. In spite of the damp it was very cosy. From the open door behind a ray of light fell upon the darkness-covered water below. Beyond were circling the lights of Sydney. Dotting the black night here and there were the signal lamps of anchored ships.

'We want perfect equality for woman with man,' asserted Ford, in a conclusive tone of voice.

'We want woman in her proper sphere,' maintained Stratton, from the hammock.

'What do you call "her proper sphere"?' asked Nellie.

'This: That she should fulfil the functions assigned to her by Nature. That she should rule the home and rear children. That she should be a wife and a mother. That she should be gentle as men are rough, and, to pirate the Americanism, as she rocked the cradle should rock the world.'

'How about equality?' demanded Ford.

'Equality! What do you mean by equality? Is it equality to scramble with men in the search for knowledge, narrow hipped and flat-chested? Is it equality to grow coarse and rough and unsexed in the struggle for existence? Ah! Let our women once become brutalised, masculinised, and there will be no hope for anything but a Chinese existence.'

'Who wants to brutalise them?' asked Ford.

'What would your women be like?' asked Nellie.

'Look out for Madame there, Stratton!' said George.

'What would my women be like? Full-lipped and broad-hearted, fit to love and be loved! Full-breasted and broad-hipped fit to have children! Full-brained and broad-browed, fit to teach them! My women should be the embodiment of the nation, and none of them should work except for those they loved and of their own free will.'

'Sort of queen bees!' remarked Nellie. 'Why have them work at all?'

'Why? Is it "work" for a mother to nurse her little one, to wash it, to dress it, to feed it, to watch it at night, to nurse it when it sickens, to teach it as it grows? And if she does that does she not do all that we have a right to ask of her? Need we ask her to earn her own living and bear children as well? Shall we make her a toy and a slave, or harden her to battle with men? I wouldn't. My women should be such that their children would hold them sacred and esteem all women for their sakes. I don't want the shrieking sisterhood, hard-voiced and ugly and unlovable, perpetuated. And they will not be perpetuated. They can't make us marry them. Their breed must die out.'

'In other words,' observed Nellie; 'you would leave the present relationship of woman to Society unchanged, except that you would serve her out free rations.'

'No! She should be absolutely mistress of her own body, and sole legal guardian of her own children.'

'Which means that you would institute free divorce, and make the family matriarchal instead of patriarchal; replace one lopsided system by another.'

'Give it him, Nellie,' put in Connie. 'I haven't heard those notions of his for years. I thought he had recanted long ago.'

'Well, yes! But you needn't be so previous [sic] in calling it lop-sided,' said Stratton.

'It is lop-sided, to my mind!' replied Nellie. 'What women really want is to be left to find their own sphere, for whenever a man starts to find it for them he always manages to find something else. No man understands woman thoroughly. How can he when she doesn't even understand herself? Yet you propose to crush us all down to a certain pattern, without consulting us. That's not democratic. Why not consult us first I should like to know?'

'Probably because they wouldn't agree to it if you led the opposition, Nellie. We are all only democratic when we think Demos is going our way.' This from Ford.

Arty slipped quietly off the railing and went into the sitting-room. Connie leaned back and watched him through the open door. 'He's started to write,' she announced. 'He's been terribly down lately so it'll be pretty strong, poor fellow.' She laughed good-naturedly; the others laughed with her. 'Go on, Nellie dear. It's very interesting, and I didn't mean to interrupt.'

'Oh! He won't answer me,' declared Nellie, in a disgusted tone.

'I should think not,' retorted Stratton. 'I know your womanly habit of tying the best case into a tangled knot with a few Socratic questions. I leave the truth to prove itself.'

'Just so! But you won't leave the truth about woman to prove itself. You want us to be good mothers, first and last. Why not let us be women, true women, first, and whatever it is fitting for us to be afterwards?'

'I want you to be true women.'

'What is a true woman? A true woman to me is just what a true man is— one who is free to obey the instincts of her nature. Only give us freedom, opportunity, and we shall be at last all that we should be.'

'Is it not freedom to be secure against want, to be free to—'

'To be mothers.'

'Yes; to be mothers—the great function of women. To cradle the future. To mould the nation that is to be.'

'That is so like a man. To be machines, you mean—well cared for, certainly, but machines just the same. Don't you know that we have been machines too long? Can't you see that it is because we have been degraded into machines that Society is what it is?'

'How?' questioned Stratton.

'He knows it well, Nellie,' cried Connie, clapping her hands.

'Because you can't raise free men from slave women. We want to be free, only to be free, to be let alone a little, to be treated as human beings with souls, just as men do. We have hands to work with, and brains to think with, and hearts to feel with. Why not join hands with us in theory as you do in fact? Do you tell us now that you won't have our help in the movement? Will you refuse us the fruit of victory when the fight is won? If I thought you would, I for one would cease to care whether the Cause won or not.'

'I, too, Nellie. We'd all go on strike,' cried Connie.

'What is it to you whether women are good mothers or not? What objections can you have to our rivalling men in the friendly rivalry that would be under fair conditions? Are our virtues, our woman instincts, so weak and frail that you can't trust us to go straight if the whole of life is freely open to us? Why, when I think of what woman's life is now, what it has been for so long, I wonder how it is that we have any virtues left.' She spoke with intense feeling.

'What are we now,' she went on, 'in most cases? Slaves, bought and sold for a home, for a position, for a ribbon, for a piece of bread. With all their degradation men are not degraded as we are. To be womanly is to be shamed and insulted every day. To love is to suffer. To be a mother is to drink the dregs of human misery. To be heartless, to be cold, to be vicious and a hypocrite, to smother all one's higher self, to be sold, to sell one's self, to pander to evil passions, to be the slave of the slave, that is the way to survive most easily for a woman. And see what we are in spite of everything! Geisner said he would sometimes be proud if he were an Englishman. Sometimes I'm foolish enough to be proud I'm a woman.

'Why should we be mothers, unless it pleases us to be mothers? Why should we not feel that life is ours as men may feel it, that we help hold up the world and owe nothing to others except that common debt of fraternity which they owe also to us? Don't you think that Love would come then as it could in no other way? Don't you think that women, who even now are good mothers generally, would be good mothers to children whose coming was unstained with tears? And would they be worse mothers if their brains were keen and their bodies strong and their hearts brave with the healthy work and intelligent life that everybody should have, men and women alike?'

'You seem to have an objection to mothers somehow, Nellie,' observed Geisner.

'Oh, I have! It seems to me such a sin, such a shameful sin, to give life for the world that we have. I can understand it being a woman's highest joy to be a mother. I have seen poor miserable women looking down at their puny nursing babies with such unutterable bliss on their faces that I've nearly cried for pure joy and sympathy. But in my heart all the time I felt that this was weakness and folly; that what was bliss to the mother, stupefying her for a while to the hollowness and emptiness of her existence, was the beginning of a probable life of misery to the child that could end only with death. And I have vowed to myself that never should child of mine have cause to reproach me for selfishness that takes a guise which might well deceive those who have nothing but the animal instincts to give them joy in living.'

'You will never have children?' asked Geisner.

'I will never marry,' she answered. 'There is little you can teach a girl who has worked in Sydney, and I know there are ideas growing all about which to me seem shameful and unwomanly, excepting that they spare the little ones. For me, I shall never marry. I will give my life to the movement, but I will give no other lives the pain of living.'

'You will meet him some day, Nellie,' said Connie.

'Then I will be strong if it breaks my heart.' Ned often thought of this in after days. Just then he hardly realised how the girl's words affected him. He was so breathlessly interested. Never had he heard people talk like this before. He began to dimly understand how it touched the Labour movement.

'You will miss the best part of life, my dear,' said Connie. 'I say it even after what you have seen of that husband of mine.'

'You are wrong, Nellie,' said Geisner, slowly. 'Above us all is a higher Law, forcing us on. To give up what is most precious for the sake of the world is good. To give up that which our instincts lead us to for fear of the world cannot but be bad. For my part, I hold that no door should be closed to woman, either by force of law or by force of conventionalism. But if she claims entrance to the Future, it seems to me that she should not close Life's gate against herself.'

'I would close Life's gate altogether if I could,' cried Nellie, passionately. 'I would blot Life out. I would—oh, what would I not do? The things I see around me day after day almost drive me mad.'

There was silence for a moment, broken then by Connie's soft laugh. 'Nellie, my dear child,' she observed, 'you seem quite in earnest. I hope you won't start with us.'

'Don't mind her, Nellie,' said Josie, softly, speaking for the first time. 'Connie laughs because if she didn't she would cry.'

'I know that,' said Nellie. 'I don't mind her. Is there one of us who does not feel what a curse living is?'

Geisner's firm voice answered: 'And is there one of us who does not know what a blessing living might be? Nellie, my girl, you are sad and sorrowful, as we all are at times, and do not feel yet God in all working itself out in unseen ways.'

'God!' she answered, scornfully. 'There is no God. How can there be?'

'I do not know. It is as one feels. I do not mean that petty god of creeds and religions, the feeble image that coarse hands have made from vague glimpses caught by those who were indeed inspired. I mean the total force, the imperishable breath, of the universe. And of that breath, my child, you and I and all things are part.'

Stratton took his cigar from his mouth and quoted:

> I am the breath of the lute, I am the mind of man,
> Gold's glitter, the light of the diamond and the sea-pearl's lustre wan.
>
> I am both good and evil, the deed and the deed's intent—

'Yes,' said Geisner; 'that and more. Brahma and more than Brahma. What Prince Buddha thought out too. What Jesus the Carpenter dimly recognised. Not only Force, but Purpose, or what for lack of better terms we call Purpose, in it all.'

'And that Purpose; what is it?' Ned was surprised to hear his own voice uttering his thought.

'Who shall say? There are moments, a few moments, when one seems to feel what it is, moments when one stands face to face with the universal Life and realises wordlessly what it means.' Geisner spoke with grave solemnity. The others, hardly breathing, understood how this man had thought these things out.

'When one is in anguish and sorrow unendurable. When one has seen one's soul stripped naked and laid bare, with all its black abysses and unnatural sins; the brutishness that is in each man's heart known and understood—the cowardice, the treachery, the villainy, the lust. When one knows oneself in others, and sinks into a mist of despair, hopeless and heart-wrung, then come the temptations, as the prophets call them, the miserable ambitions dressed as angels of light, the religions which have become more drugged pain-lullers, the desire to suppress thought altogether, to end life, to stupefy one's soul with bodily pain, with mental activity. And if,' he added slowly, 'if one's pain is for others more than for oneself, if in one's heart Humanity has lodged itself, then it may be that one shall feel and know. And from that time you never doubt God. You may doubt yourself but never that all things work together for good.'

'I do not see it,' cried Nellie.

'Hush!' said Connie. 'Go on, Geisner.'

'To me,' the little man went on, as if talking rather to himself than to the others. 'To me the Purpose of Life is self-consciousness, the total Purpose I mean. God seeking to know God. Eternal Force one immeasurable Thought. Humanity the developing consciousness of the little fragment of the universe within our ken. Art, the expression of that consciousness, the outward manifestation of the effort to solve the problem of Life. Genius, the power of expressing in some way or other what many thought but could not articulate. I do not mean to be dogmatic. Words fail us to define our meaning when we speak of these things. Any quibbler can twist the meaning of words, while only those who think the thought can understand. That is why one does not speak much of them. Perhaps we should speak of them more.'

'It is a barren faith to me,' said Nellie.

'Then I do not express it well,' said Geisner. 'But is it more barren-sounding than utter Negation? Besides, where do we differ really? All of us who think at all agree more or less. We use different terms, pursue different lines of thought, that is all. It is only the dullard, who mistakes the symbol for the idea, the letter for the spirit, the metaphor for the thought within, who is a bigot. The true thinker is an artist, the true artist is a thinker, for Art is the expression of thought in thing. The highest thought, as Connie rightly told us before you came, is Emotion.'

'I recollect the Venus in the Louvre,' interjected Harry. 'When I saw it first it seemed to me most beautiful, perfect, the loveliest thing that ever sculptor put chisel to. But as I saw it more I forgot that it was beautiful or perfect. It grew on me till it lived. I went day after day to see it, and when I was glad it laughed at me, and when I was downhearted it was sad with me, and when I was angry it scowled, and when I dreamed of Love it had a kiss on its lips. Every mood of mine it changed with; every thought of mine it knew. Was not that Art, Nellie?'

'The artist in you,' she answered.

'No. More than that. The artist in the sculptor, breathing into the stone a perfect sympathy with the heart of men. His genius grasped this, that beauty, perfect beauty, is the typifying not of one passion, one phase of human nature, but of the aggregation of all the moods which sway the human mind. There is a great thought in that. It is "the healthy mind in the healthy body", as the sculptor feels it. And "the healthy mind in the healthy body" is one of the great thoughts of the past. It is a thought which is the priceless gift of Greek philosophy to the world. I hold it higher than that of the Sphinx, which Ford admires so.'

'What does the Sphinx mean?' asked Ned.

'Much the same, differently expressed,' answered Ford. 'That Life with us is an intellectual head based on a brutish body, fecund and powerful; that Human Nature crouches on the ground and reads the stars; that man has a body and a mind, and that both must be cared for.'

'They had a strange way of caring for both, your Egyptians,' remarked Nellie. 'The people were all slaves and the rulers were all priests.'

At this criticism, so naïve and pithy and so like Nellie, there was a general laugh.

'At least the priests were wise and the slaves were cared for,' retorted Ford, nothing abashed. 'I recollect when I was a little fellow in England. My people were farm labourers, west of England labourers. We lived in a little stone cottage that had little diamond-paned windows. The kitchen floor was below the ground, and on wet days my mother used to make a little dam of rags at the door to keep the trickling water back. We lived on bread and potatoes and broad beans, and not too much of that. We got a little pig for half-a-crown, and killed it when it was grown to pay the rent. Don't think such things are only done in Ireland! We herded together like pigs ourselves. The women of the place often worked in the fields. The girls, too, sometimes. You know what that means where the people are like beasts, the spirit worn out of them. The cottages were built two together, and our neighbour's daughter, a girl of eighteen or so, had two children. It was not thought anything. The little things played at home with our neighbour's own small children, and their grandmother called them hard names when they bothered her.

'My father was a bent-shouldered hopeless man, when I recollect him. He got six shillings a week then, with a jug of cider every day. When he stopped from the wet, and there was no work in the barns, his wages were stopped. So he worked in the wet very often, for it generally rains in England, you know. The wet came through our roof. Gives the natives such pretty pink skins, eh, Geisner?' and he laughed shortly. 'My father got rheumatism, and used to keep us awake groaning at nights. He had been a good-looking young fellow, my old granny used to say. I never saw him good-looking. In the winter we always had poor relief. We should have starved if we hadn't. My father got up at four and came home after dark. My mother used to go weeding and gleaning. I went to scare crows when I was five years old. All the same, we were a family of paupers. Proud to be an Englishman, Geisner! Be an English pauper, and then try!'

'You'll never get to the priests, Ford, if you start an argument,' interposed Mrs. Stratton.

'I'll get to them all right. Our cottage was down a narrow, muddy lane. On one side of the lane was a row of miserable stone hovels, just like ours. On the other was a great stone wall that seemed to me, then, to be about a hundred feet high. I suppose it was about twenty feet. You could just see the tops of trees the other side. Some had branches lopped short to prevent them coming over the wall. At the corner of the highway our lane ran to was a great iron gate, all about it towering trees, directly inside a mound of shrub-covered rockery that prevented anybody getting a peep further. The carriage drive took a turn round this rockery and disappeared. Once, when the gate was open and nobody about, I got a peep by sneaking round this rockery like a little thief. There was a beautiful lawn and clumps of flowers, and a summer house and a conservatory, and a big grey-fronted mansion. I thought heaven must be something like that. It made me radical.'

'How do you mean?' asked Mrs. Stratton.

'Well, it knocked respect for constituted authority out of me. I didn't know enough to understand the wrong of one lazy idler having this splendid place while the people he lived on kennelled in hovels. But it struck me as so villainously selfish to build that wall, to prevent us outside from even looking at the beautiful lawn and flowers. I was only a little chap but I recollect wondering if it would hurt the place to let me look, and when I couldn't see that it would I began to hate the wall like poison. There we were, poor, ragged, hungry wretches, without anything beautiful in our lives, so miserable and hopeless that I didn't even know it wasn't the right thing to be a pauper, and that animal ran up a great wall in our faces so that we couldn't see the grass—curse him!' Ford had gradually worked himself into a white rage.

'He didn't know any better,' said Geisner. 'Was he the priest?'

'Yes, the rector, getting £900 a year and this great house, and paying a skinny curate £60 for doing the work. A fat impostor, who drove about in a carriage, and came to tell the girl next door as she lay a-bed that she would go to hell for her sin and burn there for ever. I hated his wall and him too. Out in the fields I used to draw him on bits of slate. In the winter when there weren't any crows or any weeding I went to school. You see, unless you sent your children to the church school a little, and went to church regularly, you didn't get any beef or blanket at Christmas. I tell you English charity is a sweet thing. Well, I used to draw the parson at school, a fat, pompous, double chinned, pot-bellied animal, with thin side-whiskers, and a tall silk hat, and a big handful of a nose. I drew nothing else. I studied the question as it were and I got so that I could draw the brute in a hundred different ways. You can imagine they weren't complimentary, and one day the parson came to the school, and we stood up in class with slates to do sums, and on the back of my slate was one of the very strongest of my first attempts at cartooning. It was a hot one.' And at the remembrance Ford laughed so contagiously that they all joined. 'The parson happened to see it. By gum! It was worth everything to see him.'

'What did he do?'

'What didn't he do? He delivered a lecture, how I was a worthy relative of an uncle of mine who'd been shipped out this way years before for snaring a rabbit, and so on. I got nearly skinned alive, and the Christmas beef and blanket wore stopped from our folks. And there another joke comes in. An older brother of mine, fourteen years old, I was about twelve, took to going to the Ranters' meetings instead of to church. My mother and father used to tie him up on Saturday nights and march him to church on Sunday like a young criminal going to gaol. They were afraid of losing the beef and blanket, you see. He sometimes ran out of church when they nodded or weren't looking, and the curate was always worrying them about him. It was the deadliest of all sins, you know, to go to the Ranters. Well, when the beef and blanket were stopped, without any chance of forgiveness, we all went to the Ranters.'

'I've often wondered where you got your power from, Ford,' remarked Connie. 'I see now.'

'Yes, that great wall made me hate the great wall that bars the people from all beautiful things; that fat hypocrite made me hate all frauds. I can never forget the way we all swallowed those things as sacred. When I get going with a pencil I feel towards whatever it is just as I felt to the parson, and I try to make everybody feel the same. Yet would you believe it, I don't care much for cartooning. I want to paint.'

'Why don't you?' asked Nellie.

'Well, there's money you know. Then it was sheer luck that made me a cartoonist and I can't expect the same run of luck always.'

'Don't believe him, Nellie,' said Connie. 'He feels that he has a chance now to give all frauds such a hammering that he hesitates to give it up. You've paid the parson, Ford, full measure, pressed down and running over!'

'Not enough!' answered Ford. 'Not enough! Not till the wall is down flat all the world over! Do you think Egypt would have lasted 20,000 years if her priests had been like my parson, and her slaves like my people?'

'I'd forgotten all about Egypt,' said Nellie. 'But I suppose her rulers had sense enough to give men enough to eat and enough to drink, high wages and constant employment, as M'Ilwraith used to say. Yes; it was wiser than the rulers of to-day are. You can rob for a long while if you only rob moderately. But the end comes some time to all wrong. It's coming faster with us, but it came in Egypt, too.'

'Here is Arty, finished!' interrupted Connie, who every little while had looked through the door at the young man. She jumped up. 'Come along in and see what it is this time.'

They all went in, jostling and joking one another. Arty was standing up in the middle of the room looking at some much blotted slips of paper. He appeared to be very well satisfied, and broke into a broad smile as he looked up at them all. Geisner and Ned found themselves side by side near the piano, over the keys of which Geisner softly ran his fingers with loving touch. 'You are in luck to-night,' he remarked to Ned. 'You know Arty's signature, of course. He writes as ——,' mentioning a well-known name.

'Of course I know. Is that him?' answered Ned, astonished. 'Verses which bore that signature were as familiar to thousands of western bushmen as their own names. Who is Ford?' he added.

'Ford! Oh, Ford signs himself ——.' Geisner mentioned another signature.

'Is he the one who draws in the *Srutineer*?' demanded Ned more astonished than ever.

'Yes; you know his work?'

'Know his work! Had not every man in Australia laughed with his pitiless cartoons at the dignified magnates of Society and the utter rottenness of the powers that be?'

'And what is Mr. Stratton?'

'A designer for a livelihood. An artist for love of Art. His wife is connected with the press. You wouldn't know her signature, but some of her work is very fine. George there is a journalist.'

'But I thought the newspapers were against unions.'

'Naturally they are. They are simply business enterprises, conducted in the ordinary commercial way for a profit, and therefore opposed to everything which threatens to interfere with profit-making. But the men and women who work on the press are very different. They are really wage-workers to begin with. Besides, they are often intelligent enough to sympathise thoroughly with the Labour movement in spite of the surroundings which tend to separate them from it. Certainly, the most popular exponents of Socialism are nearly all press writers.'

'We are only just beginning to hear about these things in the bush,' said Ned. 'What is Socialism?'

'That's a big question,' answered Geisner. 'Socialism is—'

He was interrupted. 'Silence, everybody!' cried Mrs. Stratton. 'Listen to Arty's latest!'

CHAPTER VIII

THE POET AND THE PRESSMAN

'SILENCE, everybody!' commanded Mrs. Stratton. 'Listen to Arty's latest!'

She had gone up to him as they all came in. 'Is it good?' she asked, looking over his arm. For answer he held the slips down to her and changed them as she read rapidly, only pausing occasionally to ask him what a more than usually obscured word was. There was hardly a line as originally written. Some words had been altered three and four times. Whole lines had been struck out and fresh lines inserted. In some verses nothing was left of the original but the measure and the rhymes.

'No wonder you were worrying if you had all this on your mind,' she remarked, as he finished, smiling at him. 'Let me read it to them.'

He nodded. So when the buzz of conversation had stopped she read his verses to the others, holding his arm in the middle of the room, her sweet voice conveying their spirit as well as their words. And Arty stood by her, jubilant, listening proudly and happily to the rhythm of his new-born lines, for all the world like a young mother showing her new-born babe.

THE VISION OF LABOUR.*

There's a sound of lamentation 'mid the murmuring nocturne noises,
And an undertone of sadness, as from myriad human voices,

---

* Kindly written by Mr. F.J. Broomfield for insertion here.

And the harmony of heaven and the music of the spheres,
And the ceaseless throb of Nature, and the flux and flow of years,
Are rudely punctuated with the drip of human tears
     As Time rolls on!

Yet high above the beat of surf, and Ocean's deep resounding,
And high above the tempest roar of wind on wave rebounding,
There's a burst of choral chanting, as of victors in a fight,
And a battle hymn of triumph wakes the echoes of the night,
And the shouts of heroes mingle with the shriekings of affright—
     As Time rolls on!

There's a gleam amid the darkness, and there's sight amid the blindness,
And the glow of hope is kindled by the breath of human kindness,
And a phosphorescent glimmer gilds the spaces of the gloom,
Like the sea-lights in the midnight, or the ghost-lights of the tomb,
Or the livid lamps of madness in the charnel-house of doom—
     As Time rolls on!

And amidst the weary wand'rers on the mountain crags belated
There's a hush of expectation, and the sobbings are abated,
For a word of hope is spoken by a prophet versed in pain,
Who tells of rugged pathways down to fields of golden grain,
Where the sun is ever shining, and the skies their blessings rain
     As Time rolls on!

Where the leafy chimes of gladness in the tree-tops aye are ringing,
Answering to the joyous chorus which the birds are ever singing;

Where the seas of yellow plenty toss with music in the wind;

Where the purple vines are laden, and the groves with fruit are lined;

Where all grief is but a mem'ry, and all pain is left behind—

>   As Time rolls on!

But it lies beyond a desert 'cross which hosts of Death are marching,

And a hot sirocco wanders under skies all red and parching,

Lined with skeletons of armies through the centuries fierce and acre

Bones of heroes and of sages marking Time's lapse year by year,

Unmoistened by the night-dews 'mid the solitudes of fear

>   As Time rolls on!

'Well done, Arty'! cried Ford. 'I'd like to do a few "thumbnails" for that.'
'Let me see it, please! Why don't you say "rushes" for "wanders" in the last verse, Arty?' asked George, reaching out his hand for the slips.

'Go away!' exclaimed Mrs. Stratton, holding them out of reach. 'Can't you wait two minutes before you begin your sub-editing tricks? Josie, keep him in order!'

'He's a disgrace,' replied Josie. 'Don't pay any heed to him, Arty! They'll cut up your verses soon enough, and they're just lovely.'

The others laughed, all talking at once, commending, criticising, comparing. Arty laughed and joked and quizzed, the liveliest of them all. Ned stared at him in astonishment. He seemed like somebody else. He discussed his own verses with a strange absence of egotism. Evidently he was used to standing fire.

'The metaphor in that third verse seems to me rather forced,' said Stratton finally. 'And I think George is right. "Rushes" does sound better than "wanders". I like that "rudely punctuated" line, but I think I'd go right through it again if it was mine.'

'I think I will, too,' answered Arty. 'There are half-a-dozen alterations I want to make now. I'll touch it up to-morrow. It'll keep till then.'

'That sort of stuff would keep for years if it wasn't for the *Scrutineer*,' said Stratton. 'Very few papers care to publish it nowadays.'

'The *Scrutineer* is getting just like all the rest of them,' commented George. 'It's being run for money, only they make their pile as yet by playing to the gallery while the other papers play to the stalls and dress circle.'

'It has done splendid work for the movement, just the same,' said Ford. 'Admit it's a business concern and that everybody growls at it, it's the only paper that dares knock things.'

'It's a pity there isn't a good straight daily here,' said Geisner. 'That's the want all over the world. It seems impossible to get them, though.'

'Why is it?' demanded Nellie. 'It's the working people who buy the evening papers at least. Why shouldn't they buy straight papers sooner than these sheets of lies that are published?'

'I've seen it tried,' answered Geisner, 'but I never saw it done. The *London Star* is going as crooked as the others I'm told.'

'I don't see why the unions shouldn't start dailies,' insisted Nellie. 'I suppose it costs a great deal but they could find the money if they tried hard.'

'They haven't been able to run weeklies yet,' said George, authoritatively. 'And they never will until they get a system, much less run dailies.'

'Why?' asked Ned. 'You see,' he continued, 'our fellows are always talking of getting a paper. They get so wild sometimes when they read what the papers say about the unions and know what lies most of it is that I've seen them tear the papers up and dance a war-dance on the pieces.'

'It's along story to explain properly,' said George. 'Roughly it amounts to this that papers live on advertisements as well as on circulation and that advertisers are sharp business men who generally put the boycott on papers that talk straight. Then the cable matter, the telegraph matter, the news matter, is all procured by syndicates and companies and mutual arrangement between papers which cover the big cities between them and run on much the same lines, the solid capitalistic lines, you know. Then newspaper stock, when it pays, is valuable enough to make the holder a capitalist; when it doesn't pay he's still more under the thumb of the advertisers. The whole complex organisation of the press is against the movement and only those who're in it know how complex it is.'

'Then there'll never be a Labour press, you think?'

'There will be a Labour press, I think,' said George, turning Josie's hair round his fingers. 'When the unions get a sound system it'll come.'

'What do you mean by your sound system, George?' asked Geisner.

'Just this! That the unions themselves will publish their own papers, own their own plant, elect their own editors, paying for it all by levies or subscriptions. Then they can snap their fingers at advertisers and as every union man will get the union paper there'll be a circulation established at once. They can begin with monthlies and come down to weeklies. When they have learnt thoroughly the system, and when every colony has its weekly or weeklies, then they'll have a chance for dailies, not before.'

'How would you get your daily?' enquired Geisner.

'Expand the weeklies into dailies simultaneously in every Australian capital,' said George, waxing enthusiastic. 'That would be a syndicate at once to co-operate on cablegrams and exchange intercolonial telegrams. Start with good machinery, get a subsidy of 6d. a month for a year and 3d. a month afterwards, if necessary, from the unions for every member, and then bring out a small-sized, neat, first-rate daily for a ha'penny, three-pence a week, and knock the penny evenings off their feet.'

'A grand idea!' said Geisner, his eyes sparkling. 'It sounds practical. It would revolutionise politics.'

'Who'd own the papers, though, after the unions had subsidised them?' asked Ned, a little suspiciously.

'Why, the unions, of course,' said George. 'Who else? The unions would find the machinery and subsidise the papers on to their feet, for you couldn't very well get every man to take a daily. And the unions would elect trustees to hold them and manage them and an editor to edit each one and would be able to dismiss editors or trustees either if it wasn't being run straight. There'd be no profits because every penny made would go to make the papers better, there being no advertising income or very little. And every day, all over the continent, there would be printing hundreds of thousands of copies, each one advancing and defending the Labour movement.'

'It's a grand idea,' said Geisner again, 'but who'd man the papers, George. Could Labour papers afford to pay managers and editors what the big dailies do?'

'I don't know much about managers, but an editor who wouldn't give up a lot to push the Cause can't think much of it. Why, we're nothing but literary prostitutes,' said George, energetically. 'We just write now what we're told, selling our brains as women on the streets do their bodies, and some of us don't like it, some of the best too, as you know well, Geisner. My idea would be to pay a living salary, the same all round, to every man on the literary staff. That would be fair enough as an all round wage if it was low pay for editing and leader writing and fancy work. Many a good man would jump at it, to be free to write as he felt, and as for the rest of the staff by paying such a wage we'd get the tip-top pick of the ordinary men who do the pick-up work that generally isn't considered important but in my opinion is one of the main points of a newspaper.'

'Would you take what you call a "living salary" on such a paper?' asked Connie.

'I'd take half if Josie—' He looked at her with tender confidence. The love-light was in her answering eyes. She nodded, proud of him.

'And they'd all publish my poetry?' asked Arty.

'Would they? They'd jump at it.'

'Then when they come along, I'll write for a year for nothing.'

'How about me?' asked Ford, 'Where do I come in?'

'And me?' asked Connie.

'You can all come in,' laughed George. 'Geisner shall do the political and get his editor ten years for sedition. Stratton will supply the mild fatherly sociological leaders. Mrs. Stratton shall prove that there can't be any true Art so long as we don't put the police on to everything that is ugly and repulsive. Nellie, here, shall blossom out as the Joan of Arc of women's rights, with a pen for a sword. And Arty we'll keep chained upon the premises and feed him with peppercorns when we want something particularly hot. Ford can retire to painting and pour his whole supply of bile out in one cartoon a week that we'll publish as a Saturday's supplement. Hawkins shall be our own correspondent who'll give the gentle squatter completely away in weekly instalments. And Josie and I'll slash the stuffing out of your 'copy' if you go writing three columns when there's only room for one. We'll boil down on our papers. Every line will be essence of extract. Don't you see how it's done already?'

'We see it,' said Nellie, stifling a yawn. 'The next thing is to get the unions to see it.'

'That's so,' retorted George, 'so I'll give you my idea to do what you can with.'

'We must go,' said Nellie, getting up from her chair. 'It must be after one and I'm tired.'

'It's ten minutes to two,' said Ford, having pulled out his watch.

'Why don't you stay all night, Nellie,' asked Connie. 'We can put Ned up, if he doesn't mind a shake-down. Then we can make a night of it. Geisner is off again on Monday or Tuesday.'

'Tuesday,' said Geisner, who had gone to the book-shelf again.

'Then I'll come Monday evening,' said Nellie, for his tone was an invitation. 'I feel like a walk, and I don't feel like talking much.'

'All right,' said Connie, not pressing, with true tact. 'Will you come on Monday too, Ned?' she asked, moving to the door under the hangings with Nellie. Josie slipped quickly out on to the verandah with George.

'I must be off on Monday,' replied Ned, regretfully. 'There's a shed starts the next week, and I said I'd be up there to see that it shore union. I'm very sorry, but I really can't wait.'

'I'm so sorry, too. But it can't be helped. Some other time, Ned.' And nodding to him Connie went out with Nellie.

'So we shan't see you again,' said Stratton, lighting a cigar at the gas. Ford had resumed his puffing at his black pipe and his seat on the table.

'Not soon at any rate,' answered Ned. I shall be in Western Queensland this time next week.'

'The men are organising fast up that way, aren't they?' asked Stratton.

'They had to,' said Ned. 'What with the Chinese and the squatters doing as they liked and hating the sight of a white man, we'd all have been cleared out if we hadn't organised.'

'Coloured labour has been the curse of Queensland all through,' remarked Ford.

'I think it has made Queensland as progressive as it is, too,' remarked Geisner. 'It was a common danger for all the working classes, and from what I hear has given them unity of feeling earlier than that has been acquired in the south.'

'Some of the old-fashioned union ideas that they have in Sydney want knocking badly,' remarked Arty, smoking cheerfully.

'They'll be knocked safely enough if they want knocking,' said Geisner. 'There are failings in all organisation methods everywhere as well as in Sydney. New Unionism is only the Old Unionism reformed up to date. It'll need reforming itself as soon as it has done its work.'

'Is the New Unionism really making its way in England, Geisner?' asked Stratton.

'I think so. A very intelligent man is working with two or three others to organise the London dock laborers on the new lines. He told me he was confident of success but didn't seem to realise all it meant. If those men can be organised and held together for a rise in wages it'll be the greatest strike that the world has seen yet. It will make New Unionism.'

'Do you think it possible?' asked Ford. 'I know a little about the London dockers. They are the drift of the English labour world. When a man is hopeless he goes to look for work at the docks.'

'There is a chance if the move is made big enough to attract attention and if everything is prepared beforehand. If money can be found to keep a hundred thousand penniless men out while public opinion is forming they can win, I think. Even British public opinion can't yet defend fourpence an hour for casual work.'

'Men will never think much until they are organised in some form or other,' said Stratton. 'Such a big move in London would boom the organisation of unskilled men everywhere.'

'More plots!' cried Connie, coming back, followed by Nellie, waterproofed and hatted.

'It's raining,' she went on, to Ned, 'so I'll give you Harry's umbrella and let Ford take his waterproof. You'll have a damp row, Nellie. I suppose you know you've got to go across in George's boat, Ned.'

Ned didn't know, but just then George's 'Ahoy!' sounded from outside.

'We mustn't keep him waiting in the wet,' exclaimed Nellie. She shook hands with them all, kissing Mrs. Stratton affectionately. Ned felt as he shook hands all round that he was leaving old friends.

'Come again,' said Stratton, warmly. 'We shall always be glad to see you.'

'Indeed we shall,' urged Connie. 'Don't wait to come with Nellie. Come and see us any time you're in Sydney. Day or night, come and see if we're in and wait here if we're not.'

Geisner and Stratton put on their hats and went with them down the verandah steps to the little stone quay below. Josie was standing there, in the drizzle, wrapped in a cloak and holding a lantern. In a rowing skiff, alongside, was George; another lantern was set on one of the seats.

'Are you busy to-morrow afternoon?' asked Geisner of Ned, as Nellie was being handed in, after having kissed Josie.

'Not particularly,' answered Ned.

'Then you might meet me in front of the picture gallery between one and two, and we can have a quiet chat.'

'All aboard!' shouted George.

'I'll be there,' answered Ned, shaking hands again with Geisner and Stratton and with Josie, noticing that that young lady had a very warm clinging hand.

'Good-bye! Good-bye! Good-bye!' From the three on shore.

'Good-bye! Good-bye! Good-bye!' From the three in the boat as George shoved off.

'Good-bye!' cried Connie's clear voice from the verandah. 'Put up the umbrella, Ned!'

Ned obediently put up the umbrella she had lent him, overcoming his objections by pointing out that it would keep Nellie's hat from being spoiled. Then George's oars began to dip into the water, and they turned their backs to the pleasant home and faced out into the wind and wet.

The last sound that came to them was a long melodious cry that Josie sent across the water to George, a loving 'Good-bye!' that plainly meant 'Come back!'

CHAPTER IX
'THIS IS SOCIALISM!'

THE working of George's oars and the rippling of water on the bow were all that broke the silence as the skiff moved across the harbour. Suddenly Ned lost sight of the swinging lantern that Josie had held at the little landing stairs and without it could not distinguish the house they had left. Here and there behind them were lights of various kinds and sizes, shining blurred through the faint drizzle. He saw similar lights in front and on either hand. Yet the darkness was so deep now that but for the lantern on the fore thwarts he could not have seen George at all.

There were no sounds but those of their rowing.

Nellie sat erect, half hidden in the umbrella Ned held over her. George pulled a long sweeping stroke, bringing it up with a jerk that made the rowlocks sound sharply. When he bent back they could feel the light boat lift under them. He looked round now and then, steering himself by some means inscrutable to the others, who without him would have been lost on this watery waste.

All at once George stopped rowing. 'Listen!' he exclaimed.

There was a swishing sound as of some great body rushing swiftly through the water near them. It ceased suddenly; then as suddenly sounded again.

'Sharks about,' remarked George, in a matter-of-fact tone, rowing again with the same long sweeping stroke as before.

Nellie did not stir. She was used to such incidents, evidently. But Ned had never before been so close to the sea-tigers and felt a creepy sensation. He would much rather, he thought, be thirty-five miles from water with a lame horse than in the company of sharks on a dark wet night in the middle of Sydney harbour.

'Are they dangerous?' he asked, with an attempt at being indifferent.

'I suppose so,' answered George, in a casual way. 'If one of them happened to strike the boat it might be unpleasant. But they're terrible cowards.'

'Are there many?'

'In the harbour? Oh, yes, it swarms with them. You see that light,' and George pointed to the left, where one of the lights had detached itself from the rest and shone close at hand. 'That's on a little island and in the convict days hard cases were put on it—I think it was on that island or one like it—and the sharks saw that none of them swam ashore.' 'They seem to have used those convicts pretty rough,' remarked Ned. 'Rough's no name,' said George after a few minutes. 'It was as vile and unholy a thing, that System, as anything they have in Russia. A friend of mine has been working the thing up for years, and is going to start writing it up soon. You must read it when it comes out. It'll make you hate everything that has a brass button on. I tell you, this precious Law of ours has something to answer for. It was awful, horrible, and it's not all gone yet, as I know.'

He rowed on for a space in silence.

'There's one story I think of, sometimes, rowing across here, and hearing the sharks splash. At one place they used to feed the dead convicts to the sharks so as to keep them swarming about, and once they flung one in before he was dead.'

Nellie gave a stifled exclamation. Ned was too horror-struck to answer; above the clicking of the oars in the rowlocks he fancied he could hear the swish of the savage sharks rushing through the water at their living prey. He was not sorry when George again rested on his oars to say:

'Will you land at the point this time, Nellie?'

'Yes, I think so.'

'Well, here you are! We've had a pretty fastish pull over, considering.'

Two or three more strokes brought them to a flight of low stone steps. By the light of the lantern Ned and Nellie were disembarked.

'I won't keep you talking in the rain, Nellie,' said George. 'I'm sorry you are going away so soon, Hawkins. We could have given you some boating if you had time. You might come out to-morrow afternoon—that's this afternoon—if you haven't anything better to do.'

'I'm very much obliged, but I was going to meet Mr. Geisner.'

'That settles it then. Anybody would sooner have a yarn with Geisner. We'll fix some boating when you're down again. You'll come again. Won't he, Nellie? Good-bye and a pleasant trip! Good-bye, Nellie.' And having shaken hands by dint of much arm stretching, George pushed his boat away from the steps and pulled away.

Nellie stood for a minute watching the lantern till it turned the point, heading eastward. Then straightening the waterproof over her dress she took Ned's arm and they walked off.

'He's a nice sort of chap,' remarked Ned, referring to George.

'Yes, he's a great oarsman. He rows over to see Josie. Mrs. Stratton calls them Hero and Leander.'

'Why? Who were they?'

'Oh! Leander was Hero's sweetheart and used to swim across the water to her so that nobody should see him.'

'They're to be married, I suppose?'

'Yes, next month.'

'Those Strattons are immense—what's that noise, Nellie?' he interrupted himself. A strange groaning from close at hand had startled him.

'Somebody asleep, I suppose,' she answered, more accustomed to the Sydney parks. But she stopped while, under the umbrella, he struck a match with a bushman's craft.

By the light of the match they saw a great hollow in the rocks that bordered on one side the gravelled footway. The rocks leaned out and took in part of the path, which widened underneath. Sheltered thus from the rain and wind a number of men were sleeping, outcast, some in blankets, some lying on the bare ground. The sound they had beard was a medley of deep breathing and snoring. It was but a glimpse they caught as the match flared up for a minute. It went out and they could see nothing, only the faint outline of path and rock. They could hear still the moaning sound that had attracted them.

They walked on without speaking for a time.

'How did you know the Strattons?' resumed Ned.

'At the picture gallery one Sunday. She was writing some article defending their being opened on the "Sawbath" and I had gone in. I like pictures—some pictures, you know. We got talking and she showed me things in the pictures I'd never dreamed of before. We stayed there till closing time and she asked me to come to see her.

'She's immense!'

'I'm so glad you like her. Everybody does.'

'Has she any children?'

'Four. Such pretty children. She and her husband are so fond of each other. I can't imagine people being happier.'

'I suppose they're pretty well off, Nellie?'

'No, I don't think they're what you'd call well off. They're comfortable, you know. She has to put on a sort of style, she's told me, to take the edge off her ideas. If you wear low-necked dress you can talk the wildest things, she says, and I think it's so. That's business with her. She has to mix with low-necked people a little. It's her work.'

'Does she have to work?'

'No. I suppose not. But I think she prefers to. She never writes what she doesn't think, which is pleasanter than most writers find it. Then I should think she'd feel more independent, however much she cares for her husband. And then she has a little girl who's wonderfully clever at colours, so she's saving up to send her to Paris when she's old enough. They think she'll become a great painter—the little girl, I mean.'

'What does that Josie do?'

'She's a music-teacher.'

'They're all clever, aren't they?'

'Yes. But, of course, they've all had a chance. Ford is the most remarkable. He never got any education to speak of until he was over twenty. The Strattons have been born as they live now. They've had some hard times, I think, from what they say now and then, but they've always been what's called "cultured". Everybody ought to be as they are.'

'I think so, too, Nellie, but can everybody be as well off as they are?'

'They're not well off, I told you, Ned. If they spend £5 a week it's as much as they do. Of course that sounds a lot, but since if things were divided fairly everybody who works ought to get far more, it's not extravagant riches. Wine and water doesn't cost more than beer, and the things they've got were picked up bit by bit. It's what they've got and the way it's put that looks so nice. There's nothing but what's pretty, and she is always adding something or other. She idolises Art and worships everything that's beautiful.'

'Do you think it's really that sort of thing that makes people better?' said Ned.

'How can it help making them better if their hearts are good? When what is ugly and miserable in life jars on one at every turn because one loves so what is harmonious and beautiful, there seems to me to be only one of two things to be done, either to shut your eyes to others and become a selfish egotist or to try with all your strength to bring a beautiful life to others. I'm speaking, of course, particularly of people like the Strattons. But I think that hatred of what is repulsive is a big influence with all of us.'

'You mean of dirty streets, stuffy houses and sloppy clothes?'

'Oh! More than that. Of ugly lives, of ugly thoughts, of others, and ourselves perhaps, just existing like working bullocks when we might be so happy, of living being generally such a hateful thing when it might be so sweet!'

'I suppose the Strattons are happy?'

'Not as happy as everybody might be if the world was right. They understand music and pictures and colouring and books. He reads science a lot and paints—funny mixture, isn't it?—and she teaches the children a great deal. They go boating together. They both work at what they like and are clever enough to be fairly sure of plenty to do. They have friends who take an interest in the things that interest them and their children are little angels. They aren't short of money for anything they need because they really live simply and so have plenty to spend. And, then, they are such kind people. She has a way with her that makes you feel better no matter how miserable you've been. That's happiness, I think, as far as it goes. But she feels much as I do about children. She is so afraid that they will not be happy and blames herself for being selfish because other people's children never have any happiness and would do anything to alter things so that it would be different. Still, of course, they have a happy life as far as the life itself goes. I think, the way they live, they must both feel as if they were each better and knew more and cared for each other more the older they get.'

'It must be very pleasant,' said Ned, after a pause. They had reached the higher ground and were passing under branches from which the rain-drops, collected, fell in great splashes on the umbrella.

'Yes,' said Nellie, after another pause.

'Do they go to church?' Ned began again.

'I never heard them say they did.'

'They're not religious then?'

'What do you call religious?'

'They don't believe anything, do they?'

'I think they believe a very great deal. Far more than most people who pretend to believe and don't,' answered Nellie. There was a longer pause. Then:

'What do they believe?'

'In Socialism.'

'Socialism! Look here, Nellie! What is Socialism?'

They had passed the fig-tree avenue, turning off it by a cross path, where a stone fountain loomed up gigantic in the gloom and where they could hear a rushing torrent splashing. They were in the region of gas-lamps again. Nellie walked along with a swiftness that taxed Ned to keep abreast of her. She seemed to him to take pleasure in the wet night. In spite of their long walking of the day before and the lateness of the hour she had still the same springy step and upright carriage. As they passed under the lamps he saw her face, damp with the rain, but flushed with exercise, her eyes gleaming, her mouth open a little. He would have liked to have taken her hand as she steadied the umbrella, walking arm in arm with him, but he did not dare. She was not that sort of girl.

He had felt a proud sense of proprietorship in her at the Strattons'. It had pleased him to see how they all liked her, but pleased him most of all that she could talk as an equal with these people, to him so brilliant and clever. The faint thought of her which had been unconsciously with him for years began to take shape. How pleasant it would be to be like the Strattons, to live with Nellie always, and have friends to come and see them on a Saturday night! How a man would work for a home like that, so full of music, so full of song, so full of beauty, so full of the thoughts which make men like unto gods and of the love which makes gods like unto men! Why should not this be for him as well as for others when, as Nellie said, it really cost only what rich people thought poverty, and far less than the workingman's share if things were fairly divided? And why should it not be for his mates as well as for himself? And why, most of all, why not for the wretched dwellers in the slums of Sydney, the weary women, the puny children, the imbruted men? For the first time in his life, he coveted such things with a righteous covetousness, without hating those who had them, recognising without words that to have and to appreciate such a life was to desire ceaselessly to bring it within the reach of every human being. He could not see how this was all to come about. He would have followed blindly anybody who played the Marseillaise as Geisner did. He was ready to echo any ringing thought that appealed to him as good and noble. But he did not know. He could see that in the idea called by Mrs. Stratton 'the Cause' there was an understood meaning which fitted his aspirations and his desires. He had gathered, his narrow bigotry washed from him, that between each and all of those whom he had just left there was a bond of union, a common thought, an accepted way. He had met them strangers, and had left them warm friends. The cartoonist, white with rage at the memory of the high rectory wall that shut the beautiful from the English poor; the gloomy poet whose verses rang still in his ears and would live in his heart for ever; the gray-eyed woman who idolised Art, as Nellie said, and fanned still the fire in which her nearest kin had perished; the pressman, with his dream of a free press that would not serve the money power; the painter to whom the chiselled stone spoke; the pretty girl who had been cradled amid barricades; the quiet musician for whom the bitterness of death was past, born leader of men, commissioned by that which stamped him what he was; the dressmaking girl, passionately pleading the cause of Woman; even himself, drinking in this new life as the ground sucks up the rain after a drought; between them all there was a bond—'the Cause.' What was this Cause? To break down all walls, to overthrow all wrong, to destroy the ugliness of human life, to free thought, to elevate Art, to purify Love, to lift mankind higher, to give equality to women, to—to—he did not see exactly where he himself came in—all this was the Cause. Yet he did not quite understand it, just the same. Nor did he know how it was all to come about. But he intended to find out. So he asked Nellie what the Strattons believed, feeling instinctively that there must be belief in something.

'What do they believe?' he had asked.

'In Socialism,' Nellie had answered.

'Socialism! Look here, Nellie! What is Socialism?' he had exclaimed.

They neared a lamp, shining mistily in the drizzle. Close at hand was a seat, facing the grass. In the dim light was what looked like a bundle of rags thrown over the seat and trailing to the ground. Nellie stopped. It was a woman, sleeping.

There, under a leafy tree, whose flat branches shielded her somewhat from the rain, slept the outcast. She had dozed off into slumber, sitting there alone. She was not lying, only sitting there, her arm flung over the back of the seat, her head fallen on her shoulder, her face upturned to the pitying night. It was the face of a street-walker, bloated and purplish, the poor pretence of colour gone, the haggard lines showing, all the awful life of her stamped upon it; yet in the lamplight, upturned in its helplessness, sealed with the sleep that had come at last to her, sore-footed, as softly as it might have come to a little baby falling asleep amid its play, there enhaloed it the incarnation of triumphant suffering. On the swollen cheeks of the homeless woman the night had shed its tears of rain. There amid the wind and wet, in the darkness, alone and weary, shame-worn and sin-sodden, scorned by the Pharisee, despised by the vicious, the harlot slept and forgot. Calm as death itself was the face of her. Softly and gently she breathed, as does the heavy-eyed bride whose head the groom's arm pillows. Nature, our Mother Nature, had taken her child for a moment to her breast and the outcast rested there awhile, all sorrows forgotten, all desires stilled, all wrongs and sins and shame obscured and blotted out. She envied none. Equal was she with all. Great indeed is Sleep, which teaches us day by day that none is greater in God's sight than another, that as we all came equal and naked from the unknown so naked and equal we shall all pass on to the Unknown again, that this life is but as a phantasy in which it is well to so play one's part that nightly one falls asleep without fear and meets at last the great sleep without regret!

But, oh, the suffering that had earned for this forsaken sister the sweet sleep she slept! Oh, the ceaseless offering of this sin-stained body, the contumelious jeers she met, the vain search through streets and avenues this wild night, for the blind lust that would give her shelter and food! Oh, the efforts to beg, the saints who would not wait to listen to such a one, the sinners who were as penniless! Oh, the shivering fits that walk, walk, walk, when the midnight hours brought silence and solitude, the stamps that racked her poor limbs when she laid down, exhausted, in dripping garments, on the hard park seats, the aching feet that refused at last the ceaseless tramping in their soaked and broken shoes! Oh, the thoughts of her, the memories, the dreams of what had been and what might be, as she heard the long hours toll themselves away! Oh, the bitter tears she may have shed, and the bitter words she may have uttered, and the bitter hate that may have overflowed in her against that vague something we call Society! And, oh, the sweet sleep that fell upon her at last, unexpected—as the end of our waiting shall come, when we weary most— falling upon her as the dew falls, closing her weary eye-lids, giving her peace and rest and strength to meet another to-day!

Ned stopped when Nellie did, of course. Neither spoke. A sense of great shame crept upon him, he hardly knew why. He could not look at Nellie. He wished she would move on and leave him there. The silent pathos of that sleeping face cried to him. Lowest of the low, filthy, diseased probably, her face as though the womanliness had been stamped from her by a brutal heel of iron, she yet was a woman. This outcast and Nellie were of one sex; they all three were of one Humanity.

A few hours before and he would have passed her by with a glance of contemptuous pity. But now, he seemed to have another sense awakened in him, the sense that feels, that sympathises in the heart with the hearts of others. It was as though he himself slept there. It was as though he understood this poor sister, whom the merciful called erring, and the merciless wicked, but of whom the just could only say: she is what we in her place must have become. She was an atom of the world of suffering by which his heart was being wrung. She was one upon whom the Wrong fell crushingly, and she was helpless to resist it. He was strong, and he had given no thought to those who suffered as this poor outcast suffered. He had lived his own narrow life, and shared the sin, and assisted Wrong by withholding his full strength from the side of Right. And upon him was the responsibility for this woman. He, individually, had kicked her into the streets, and dragged her footsore through the parks, and cast her there to bear testimony against him to every passer-by; he, because he had not fought, whole-souled, with those who seek to shatter the something which, without quite understanding, he knew had kicked and dragged and outcasted this woman sleeping here. Ned always took his lessons personally. It was perhaps, a touch in him of the morbidity that seizes so often the wandering Arabs of the western plains.

Suddenly Nellie let go the umbrella, leaving it in his hand. She bent forward, stooped down. The strong young face, proud and sad, so pure in its maiden strength, glowing with passionate emotion, was laid softly against that bruised and battered figurehead of shipwrecked womanhood; Nellie had kissed the sleeping harlot on the cheek.

Then, standing erect, she turned to Ned, her lips parted, her face quivering, her eyes flashing, her hand resting gently on the unconscious woman.

'You want to know what Socialism is,' she said, in a low, trembling voice. 'This is Socialism.' And bending down again she kissed the poor outcast harlot a second time. The woman never stirred. Seizing Ned's arm Nellie drew him away, breaking into a pace that made him respect her prowess as a walker ever after.

Until they reached home neither spoke. Nellie looked sterner than ever. Ned was in a whirl of mental excitement. Perhaps if he had been less natural himself the girl's passionate declaration of fellowship with all who are wronged and oppressed—for so he interpreted it by the light of his own thoughts—might have struck him as a little bit stagey. Being natural, he took it for what it was, an outburst of genuine feeling. But if Nellie had really designed it she could not have influenced him more deeply. Their instincts, much akin, had reached the same idea by different ways. Her spontaneous expression of feeling had fitted in her mind to the Cause which possessed her as a religious idea, and had capped in him the human yearnings which were leading him to the same goal. And so, what with his overflowing sympathy for the sleeping outcast, and his swelling love for Nellie, and the chaotic excitement roused in him by all he had seen and heard during the preceding hours, that kiss burnt itself into his imagination and became to him all his life through as a sacred symbol. From that moment his life was forecast—a woman tempted him and he ate.

For that kiss Ned gave himself into the hands of a fanaticism, eating of the fruit of the Tree of Knowledge, striving to become as a god knowing good from evil. For that kiss he became one of those who have the Desire which they know can never be satiated in them. For that kiss he surrendered himself wholly to the faith of her whose face was sad and stern-mouthed, content ever after if with his whole life he could fill one of the ruts that delay the coming of Liberty's triumphal car. To that turning-point in his life, other events led up, certainly, events which of themselves would likely have forced him to stretch out his hand and pluck and eat. It is always that way with life changes. Nothing depends altogether upon one isolated act. But looking back in after years, when the lesser influences had cleared away in the magic glass of Time, Ned could ever see, clear and distinct as though it were but a minute since, the stern red lips of that pale, proud, passionate face pressed in trembling sisterliness to the harlot's purple cheek.

As she put the key in the door Nellie turned to Ned, speaking for the first time:

'You'd better ask Geisner about Socialism when you see him to-morrow—I mean this afternoon.'

Ned nodded without speaking. Silently he let her get his candle, and followed her up the stairs to the room concerning which the card was displayed in the window below. She turned down the bedclothes, then held out her hand.

'Good-night or good-morning, whichever it is!' she said, smiling at him. 'You can sleep as long as you like Sunday morning, you know. If you want anything knock the wall there.'

'Good-night, Nellie!' he answered, slowly, holding her fingers in his. Then, before she could stop him, he lifted her hand to his lips. She did not snatch it away but looked him straight in the eyes, without speaking; then went out, shutting the door softly behind her. She understood him partly; not altogether, then.

Left alone in the scantily-furnished room, Ned undressed, blew out the candle and went to bed. But until he fell asleep, and in his dreams afterwards, he still saw Nellie bending down over a purpled, sin-stained face, and heard her sweet voice whisper tremblingly:

'This is Socialism!'

CHAPTER X
WHERE THE EVIL REALLY LIES

GEISNER was betimes at his appointment in the Domain. It was still the dinner hour, and though it was Sunday there were few to be seen on the grass or along the paths. So Ned saw him afar off, pacing up and down before the Art Gallery like a sentinel, an ordinary looking man to a casual passer-by, one whom you might pass a hundred times on the street and not notice particularly, even though he was ugly. Perhaps because of it.

Neither of them cared to stroll about, they found. Accordingly they settled down at a shady patch on a grassy slope, the ground already dried from the night's rain by the fierce summer sunshine of the morning. Stretched out there, Geisner proceeded to roll a cigarette and Ned to chew a blade of grass.

Below them a family were picnicking quietly. Dinner was over; pieces of paper littered the ground by an open basket. The father lay on his side smoking, the mother was giving a nursing baby its dinner, one little child lay asleep under a tree and two or three wore were playing near at hand.

'That reminds me of Paris,' remarked Geisner, watching them.

'I suppose you are French?'

'No. I've been in France considerably.'

'It's a beautiful country, isn't it?'

'All countries are beautiful in their way. Sydney Harbour is the most beautiful spot I know. I hardly know where I was born. In Germany I think.'

'Things are pretty bad in those old countries, aren't they?'

'Things are pretty bad everywhere, aren't they?'

'Yes,' answered Ned, meditatively. 'They seem to be. They're bad enough here and this is called the workingman's paradise. But a good many seem glad enough to get here from other countries. It must be pretty bad where they come from.'

'So it is. It is what it is here, only more so. It is what things will be in a very few years here if you let them go on. As a matter of fact the old countries ought to be more prosperous than the new ones, but our social system has become so ill-balanced that in the countries where there are most people at work those people are more wretched than where there are comparatively few working.'

'How do you mean?'

'Well, this way. The wealth production of thickly settled countries is proportionately greater than that of thinly settled countries. Of course, there would be a limit somewhere, but so far no country we know of has reached it.'

'You don't mean that a man working in England or France earns more than a man working in Australia?' demanded Ned, sitting up. 'I thought it was the other way.'

'I don't mean he gets more but I certainly mean that he produces more. The appliances are so much better, and the sub-division of labour, that is each man doing one thing until he becomes an expert at it, is carried so much further by very virtue of the thicker population.'

'That's to say they have things fixed so that they crush more to the ton of work.'

'About that. Taking the people all round, and throwing in kings and queens and aristocrats and the parsons that Ford loves so, every average Englishman produced yesterday more wealth—more boots, more tools, more cloth, more anything of value—than every average Australian. And every average Belgian produced yesterday, or any day, more wealth than every average Englishman. These are facts you can see in any collection of statistics. The conservative political economists don't deny them; they only try to explain them away.'

'But how does it come? Men produce more there than we do here and earn less. How's that?'

'Simply because they're robbed more.'

'Look here, Mr. Geisner!' said Ned, gathering his knees into his arms. 'That's what I want to know. I know we're robbed. Any fool can see that those who work the least or don't work at all get pretty much everything, but I don't quite see how they get it. We're only just beginning to think of these things in the bush, and we don't know much yet. We only know there's something wrong, but we don't know what to do except to get a union and keep up wages.'

'That's the first step, to get a union,' said Geisner. 'But unless unionists understand what it's all about they'll only be able to keep up wages for a little while. You see, Ned, this is the difficulty: a man can't work when he likes.'

'A man can't work when he likes!'

'No; not the average man and it's the average man who has to be considered always. Let's take a case—yourself. You want to live. Accordingly, you must work, that is you must produce what you need to live upon from the earth by your labour or you must produce something which other working men need and these other men will give you in exchange for it something they have produced which you need. Now, let's imagine you wanting to live and desiring to start to-morrow morning to work for your living. What would you do?'

'I suppose I'd ask somebody.'

'Ask what?'

'Well, I'd have to ask somebody or other if there was any work.'

'What work?'

'Well, if they had a job they wanted me to do, that I could do, you know.'

'I don't "You know" anything. I want you to explain. Now what would you say?'

'Oh! I'd kind of go down to the hut likely and see the boys if 'twas any use staying about and then, perhaps, or it might be before I went to the hut, that would be all according, I'd see the boss and sound him.'

'How sound him?'

'Well, that would be all according, too. If I was pretty flush and didn't care a stiver whether I got a job or not I'd waltz right up to him just as I might to you to ask the time, and if he came any of his law-de-dah squatter funny business on me I'd give him the straight wire, I promise you. But it stands to reason—don't it?—that if I've been out of graft for months and haven't got any money and my horses are played out and there's no chance of another job, well, I'm going to humour him a bit more than I'd like to, ain't I?'

Geisner laughed 'You see it all right, Ned. Suppose the first man you sounded said no?'

'I'd try another.'

'And if the other said no?'

'Well, I'd have to keep on trying.'

'And you'd get more inclined to humour the boss every time you had to try again.'

'Naturally. That's how they get at us. No man's a crawler who's sure of a job.'

'Then you might take lower wages, and work longer hours, after you'd been out of work till you'd got thoroughly disheartened than you would now.'

'I wouldn't. Not while there was—I might have to, though I say I'd starve or steal first. There are lots who do, I suppose.'

'Lots who wouldn't dream of doing it if there was plenty of work to be had?'

'Of course. Who'd work for less than another man if he needn't, easily? There isn't one man in a thousand who'd do another fellow out of a job for pure meanness. The chaps who do the mischief are those who're so afraid the boss'll sack them, and that another boss won't take them on, that they'd almost lick his boots if they thought it would please him.'

'Now we're coming to it. It is work being hard to get that lowers wages and increases hours, and makes a workman, or workwoman either, put up with what nobody would dream of putting up with if they could help it?'

'Of course that's it.'

'Now! Is the day's work done by a poorly-paid man less than that done by a highly-paid one?'

'No,' answered Ned. 'I've seen it more,' he added.

'How's that?'

'Well, when a man's anxious to keep a job and afraid he won't get another he'll often nearly break his back bullocking at it. When he feels independent he'll do the fair thing, and sling the job up if the boss tries to bullock him. It's the same thing all along the line, it seems to me. When you can get work easily you get higher wages, shorter hours, some civility, and only do the fair thing. When you can't, wages come down, hours spin out, the boss puts on side, and you've got to work like a nigger.'

'Then, roughly speaking, the amount of work you do hasn't got very much to do with the pay you get for it?'

'I suppose not. It's not likely a man ever gets more than his work is worth. The boss would soon knock him off and let the work slide. I suppose a man is only put on to a job when its worth more than the boss has to pay for getting it done. And I reckon the less a man can be got to do it for the better it is for the fellow who gets the job done.'

'That's it. Suppose you can't get work no matter how often you ask, what do you do?'

'Keep on looking. Live on rations that the squatters serve out to keep men travelling the country so they can get them if they want them or on mutton you manage to pick up or else your mates give you a bit of a lift. You must live. It's beg or steal or else starve.'

'I think men and women are beginning to starve in Australia. Many are quite starving in the old countries and have been starving longer. That's why the workers are somewhat worse off there than here. The gold rushes gave things a lift here and raised the condition of the workers wonderfully. But the same causes that have been working in the old countries have been working here and are fast beating things down again.'

'A gold rush!' exclaimed Ned. 'That's the thing to make wages rise, particularly if it's a poor man's digging.'

'What's that?'

'Don't you know? An alluvial field is where you can dig out gold with a pick and shovel and wash it out with a pannikin. You don't want any machines, and everybody digs for himself, or mates with other fellows, and if you want a man to do a job you've got to pay him as much as he could dig for himself in the time.'

'I see. "Poor man's digging", you call it, eh? You don't think much of a reefing field?'

'Of course not,' answered Ned, smiling at this apparent ignorance. 'Reefing fields employ men, and give a market, and a few strike it, but the average man, as you call him, hasn't got a chance. It takes so much capital for sinking and pumping and crushing, and things of that sort, that companies have to be formed outside, and the miners mostly work just for wages. And when a reefing field gets old it's as bad as a coal-field or a factory town. You're just working for other people, and the bigger the dividends the more anxious they seem to be to knock wages.'

'Then this is what it all amounts to. If you aren't working for yourself you're working for somebody else who pays as little as he can for as much as he can get, and rubs the dirt in, often, into the bargain.'

'A man may not earn wages working for himself,' answered Ned.

'You mean he may not produce for himself as much value as men around him receive in wages for working for somebody else. Of course! You might starve working on Mount Morgan or Broken Hill with a pick and pannikin, though on an alluvial your pick and pannikin would be all you needed. That's the kernel of the industrial question. Industry has passed out of the alluvial stage into the reefing. We must have machinery to work with or we may all starve in the midst of mountains of gold.'

'I don't quite see how you mean.'

'Just this. If every man could take his pick on his shoulders and work for himself with reasonable prospect of what he regarded as a sufficient return he wouldn't ask anybody else for work.'

'Not often, anyway.'

'But if he cannot so work for himself he must go round looking for the man who has a shaft or a pump or a stamping mill and must bargain for the owner of machinery to take the product of his labour for a certain price which of course isn't it's full value at all but the price at which, owing to his necessities, he is compelled to sell his labour.

'Things are getting so in all branches of industry, in squatting, in manufacturing, in trading, in ship-owning, in everything, that it takes more and more capital for a man to start for himself. This is a necessary result of increasing mechanical powers and of the economy of big businesses as compared to small ones. For example, if there is a great advantage in machine clipping, as a friend of mine who understands such things tells me there is, all wool will some day be clipped that way. Then, the market being full of superior machine-clipped wool, hand-clipped would have little sale and only at lower price. The result would be that all wool-growers must have machines as part of their capital, an additional expense, making it still harder for a man with a small capital to start wool-growing.

'All this means,' continued Geisner, 'that more and more go round asking for work as what we call civilisation progresses, that is as population increases and the industrial life becomes more complicated. I don't mean in Australia only. I'm speaking generally. They can only work when another man thinks he can make a profit out of them, and there are so many eager to be made a profit on that the owner of the machine has it pretty well his own way. This system operates for the extension of its own worst feature, the degradation of the working masses. You see, such a vast amount of industrial work can be held over that employers, sometimes unconsciously, sometimes deliberately, hold work over until times are what they call "more suitable", that is when they can make bigger profits by paying less in wages. This has a tendency to constantly keep wages down, besides affording a stock argument against unionist agitations for high wages. But, in any case, the fits of industrial briskness and idleness which occur in all countries are enough to account for the continual tendency of wages to a bare living amount for those working, as many of those not working stand hungrily by to jump into their places if they get rebellious or attempt to prevent wages going down.'

'That's just how it is,' said Ned. 'But we're going to get all men into unions, and then we'll keep wages up.'

'Yes; there is no doubt that unions help to keep wages up. But, you see, so long as industrial operations can be contracted, and men thrown out of work, practically at the pleasure of those who employ, complete unionism is almost impracticable if employers once begin to act in concert. Besides, the unemployed are a menace to unionism always. Workmen can never realise that too strongly.'

'What are we to do then if we can't get what we want by unionism?'

'How can you get what you want by unionism? The evil is in having to ask another man for work at all—in not being able to work for yourself. Unionism, so far, only says that if this other man does employ you he shall not take advantage of your necessity by paying you less than the wage which you and your fellow workmen have agreed to hold out for. You must destroy the system which makes it necessary for you to work for the profit of another man, and keeps you idle when he can't get a profit out of you. The whole wage system must be utterly done away with.' And Geisner rolled another cigarette as though it was the simplest idea in the world.

'How? What will you do instead?'

'How! By having men understand what it is, and how there can be no true happiness and no true manliness until they overthrow it! By preaching socialistic ideas wherever men will listen, and forcing them upon them where they do not want to listen! By appealing to all that is highest in men and to all that is lowest—to their humanity and to their selfishness! By the help of the education which is becoming general, by the help of art and of science, and even of this vile press that is the incarnation of all the villainies of the present system! By living for the Cause, and by being ready to die for it! By having only one idea: to destroy the Old Order and to bring in the New!' Geisner spoke quietly, but in his voice was a ring that made Ned's blood tingle in his veins.

'What do you call the Old Order?' asked Ned, lying back and looking up at the sky through the leaves.

'Everything that is inhuman, everything that is brutal, everything which relies upon the taking advantage of a fellow-man, which leads to the degradation of a woman or to the unhappiness of a child. Everything which is opposed to the idea of human brotherhood. That which produces scrofulous kings, and lying priests, and greasy millionaires, and powdered prostitutes, and ferret-faced thieves. That which makes the honest man a pauper and a beggar, and sets the clever swindler in parliament. That which makes you what you are at twenty-four, a man without a home, with hardly a future. That which tries to condemn those who protest to starvation, and will yet condemn them to prison here in Australia as readily as ever it did in Europe or Russia.

'You want to know what makes this,' he went on. 'Well, it is what we have been talking of, that you should have to ask another man for work so that you may live. It doesn't matter what part of the world you are in or under what form of government, it is the same everywhere. So long as you can't work without asking another man for permission you are exposed to all the ills that attend poverty and all the tyranny that attends inordinate power and luxury. When you grip that, you understand half the industrial problem.'

'And the other half, what's that?' asked Ned.

'This, that we've got over the alluvial days, if they ever did exist industrially, and are in the thick of reefing fields and syndicates. So much machinery is necessary now that no ordinary single man can own the machinery he needs to work with as he could in the old pick and pannikin days. This makes him the slave of those who do own it for he has to work to live. Men must all join together to own the machinery they must have to work with, so that they may use it to produce what they need as they need it and will not have to starve unless some private owner of machinery can make a profit out of their labour. They must pull together as mates and work for what is best for all, not each man be trying only for himself and caring little whether others live or die. We must own all machinery co-operatively and work it co-operatively.'

'How about the land? Oughtn't that to be owned by the people too?'

'Why, of course. The land is a part of the machinery of production. Henry George separates it but in reality it is simply *one* of the means by which we live, nowadays, for no man but an absolute savage can support himself on the bare land. In the free land days which Henry George quotes, the free old German days when we were all barbarians and didn't know what a thief was, not only was the land held in common but the cattle also. Without its cattle a German tribe would have starved on the richest pastureland in Europe, and without our machinery we would starve were the land nationalised to-morrow. At least I think so. George's is a scheme by which it is proposed to make employers compete so fiercely among one another that the workman will have it all his own way. It works this way. You tax the landowner until it doesn't pay him to have unused land. He must either throw it up or get it used somehow and the demand for labour thus created is to lift wages and put the actual workers in what George evidently considers a satisfactory position. That's George's Single Tax scheme.'

132

'You don't agree with it?' asked Ned.

'I am a Socialist. Between all Socialists and all who favour competition in industry, as the Single Tax scheme does, there is a great gulf fixed. Economically, I consider it fallacious, for the very simple reason that capitalism continues competition, not to selling at cost price but to monopoly, and I have never met an intelligent Single Taxer, and I have met many, who could logically deny the possibility of the Single Tax breaking down in an extension of this very monopoly power. Roughly, machinery is necessary to work land most profitably, profitably enough even to get a living off it. Suppose machine holders, that is capitalists, extend their organisation a little and "pool" their interests as land users, that is refuse to compete against one another for the use of land! Nellie was telling me that at one land sale on the Darling Downs in Queensland the selectors about arranged matters among themselves beforehand. The land sold, owing to its situation, was only valuable to those having other land near and so was all knocked down at the upset price though worth four times as much. It seems to me that in just the same way the capitalists, who alone can really use land remember, for the farmer, the squatter, the shopkeeper, the manufacturer, the merchant, are nowadays really only managers for banks and mortgage companies, will soon arrange a way of fixing the values of land to suit themselves. But apart from that, I object to the Single Tax idea from the social point of view. It is competitive. It means that we are still to go on buying in the cheapest market and selling in the dearest. It is tinged with that hideous Free Trade spirit of England, by which cotton kings became millionaires while cotton spinners were treated far worse than any chattel slaves. There are other things to be considered besides cheapness, though unfortunately, with things as they are we seem compelled to consider cheapness first.'

They lay for some time without speaking.

CHAPTER XI
'IT ONLY NEEDS ENOUGH FAITH'

'YOU think land and stock and machinery should be nationalised, then?' asked Ned, turning things over in his mind.

'I think land and machinery, the entire means and processes of the production and exchange of wealth, including stock, should be held in common by those who need them and worked co-operatively for the benefit of all. That is the socialistic idea of industry. The State Socialists seek to make the State the co-operative medium, the State to be the company and all citizens to be equal shareholders as it were. State Socialism is necessarily compulsory on all. The other great socialistic idea, that of Anarchical Communism, bases itself upon voluntaryism and opposes all organised Force, whether of governments or otherwise.'

'Then Anarchists aren't wicked men?'

'The Anarchist ideal is the highest and noblest of all human ideals. I cannot conceive of a good man who does not recognise that when he once understands it. The Anarchical Communists simply seek that men should live in peace and concord, of their own better nature, without being forced, doing harm to none, and being harmed by none. Of course the blind revolt against oppressive and unjust laws and tyrannical governments has become associated with Anarchy, but those who abuse it simply don't know what they do. Anarchical Communism, that is men working as mates and sharing with one another of their own free will, is the highest conceivable form of Socialism in industry.'

'Are you an Anarchist?'

'No. I recognise their ideal, understand that it is the only natural condition for a community of general intelligence and fair moral health, and look to the time when it will be instituted. I freely admit it is the only form of Socialism possible among true Socialists. But the world is full of mentally and morally and socially diseased people who, I believe, must go through the school of State Socialism before, as a great mass, they are true Socialists and fit for voluntary Socialism. Unionism is the drill for Socialism and Socialism is the drill for Anarchy and Anarchy is that free ground whereon true Socialists and true Individualists meet as friends and mates, all enmity between them absorbed by the development of an all-dominant Humanity.'

'Mates! Do you know that's a word I like?' said Ned. 'It makes you feel good, just the sound of it. I know a fellow, a shearer, who was witness for a man in a law case once, and the lawyer asked him if he wasn't mates with the chap he was giving evidence for.

'No,' says Bill, 'we ain't mates.'

'But you've worked together?' says the lawyer. 'Oh, yes!' says Bill.

'And travelled together?'

'Oh, yes!'

'And camped together?'

'Oh, yes!'

'Then if you're not mates what is mates?' says the lawyer in a bit of a tear.

'Well, mister,' says Bill, 'mates is them wot's got one pus. If I go to a shed with Jack an' we're mates an' I earn forty quid and Jack gets sick an' only earns ten or five or mebbe nothin' at all we puts the whole lot in one pus, or if it's t'other way about an' Jack earns the forty it don't matter. There's one pus no matter how much each of us earns an' it b'longs just the same to both of us alike. If Jack's got the pus and I want half-a-crown, I says to Jack, says I, "Jack, gimme the pus." An' if Jack wants ten quid or twenty or the whole lot he just says to me, "Bill," says he "gimme the pus." I don't ask wot he's goin' to take and I don't care. He can take it all if he wants it, 'cos it stands to reason, don't it, mister?' says Bill to the lawyer, 'that a man wouldn't be so dirt mean as to play a low-down trick on his own mate. So you see, mister, him an' me warn't mates 'cos we had two pusses an' mates is them wot's got one pus.'

Geisner laughed with Ned over the bush definition of 'mates'.

'Bill was about right,' he said, 'and Socialism would make men mates to the extent of all sharing up with one another. Each man might have a purse but he'd put no more into it than his mate who was sick and weak.'

'We'd all work together and share together, I take it,' said Ned. 'But suppose a man wouldn't work fairly and didn't want to share?'

'I'd let him and all like him go out into the bush to see how they could get on alone. They'd soon get tired. Men must co-operate to live civilised.'

'Then Socialism is co-operation?' remarked Ned.

'Co-operation as against competition is the main industrial idea of Socialism. But there are two Socialisms. There is a socialism with a little "s" which is simply an attempt to stave off the true Socialism. This small, narrow socialism means only the state regulation of the distribution of wealth. It has as its advocates politicians who seek to modify the robbery of the workers, to ameliorate the horrors of the competitive system, only in order to prevent the upheaval which such men recognise to be inevitable if things keep on unchanged.'

'But true Socialism? I asked Nellie last night what Socialism was, but she didn't say just what.'

'What did she say?'

'Well! We were coming through the Domain last night, this morning I mean. It was this morning, too. And on a seat in the rain, near a lamp, was a poor devil of a woman, a regular hardtimer, you know, sleeping with her head hung over the back of the seat like a fowl's. I'd just been asking Nellie what Socialism was when we came to the poor wretch and she stopped there. I felt a bit mean, you know, somehow, but all at once Nellie bent her head and kissed this street-walking woman on the cheek, softly, so she didn't wake her. 'That's Socialism,' says Nellie, and we didn't speak any more till we got to her place, and then she told me to ask you what Socialism was.' Ned had shifted his position again and was sitting now on his heels. He had pulled out his knife and was digging a little hole among the grass roots.

Geisner, who hardly moved except to roll cigarettes and light them, lay watching him. 'I think she's made you a Socialist,' he answered, smiling.

'I suppose so,' answered Ned, gravely. 'If Socialism means that no matter what you are or what you've been we're all mates, and that Nellie's going to join hands with the street-walker, and that you're going to join hands with me, and that all of us are going to be kind to one another and have a good time like we did at Mrs. Stratton's last night, well, I'm a Socialist and there's heaps up in the bush will be Socialists too.'

'You know what being a Socialist means, Ned?' asked Geisner, looking into the young man's eyes.

'I've got a notion,' said Ned, looking straight back.

'There are socialists and Socialists, just as there is socialism and Socialism. The ones babble of what they do not feel because it's becoming the thing to babble. The others have a religion and that religion is Socialism.'

'How does one know a religion?'

'When one is ready to sacrifice everything for it. When one only desires that the Cause may triumph. When one has no care for self and does not fear anything that man can do and has a faith which nothing can shake, not even one's own weakness!'

There was a pause. 'I'll try to be a Socialist of the right sort,' said Ned.

'You are young and hopeful and will think again and again that the day of redemption is dawning, and will see the night roll up again. You will see great movements set in and struggle to the front and go down when most was expected of them. You will see in the morning the crowd repent of its enthusiasm of the night before. You will find cowards where you expected heroes and see the best condemned to the suffering and penury that weaken the bravest. Your heart will ache and your stomach will hunger and your body will be bent and your head gray and then you may think that the world is not moving and that you have wasted your life and that none are grateful for it.'

'I will try not,' said Ned.

'You will see unionism grow, the New Unionism, which is simply the socialistic form of unionism. You will see, as I said before, penal laws invoked against unionism here in Australia, under the old pretence of "law and order". You will see the labour movement diverted into political action and strikes fought and lost and won at the polling booths.'

'Will it not come then?'

'How can it come then? Socialism is not a thing which can be glued like a piece of veneering over this rotten social system of ours. It can only come by the utter sweeping away of competition, and that can only come by the development of the socialistic idea in men's hearts.'

'Do you mean that unions and political action and agitations don't do any good?'

'Of course they do good. A union may make an employer rob his men of a few shillings weekly less. An act of Parliament may prevent wage-slaves from being worked sixteen hours a day. An act of Parliament, granted that Parliament represented the dominant thought of the people, could even enforce a change of the entire social system. But before action must come the dominant thought. Unions and Parliaments are really valuable as spreading the socialistic idea. Every unionist is somewhat socialist so far as he has agreed not to compete any longer against his fellows. Every act of Parliament is additional proof that the system is wrong and must go before permanent good can come. And year after year the number of men and women who hold Socialism as a religion is growing. And when they are enough you will see this Old Order melt away like a dream and the New Order replace it. That which appears so impregnable will pass away in a moment. So!' He blew a cloud of smoke and watched it disappear circling upwards.

'Listen!' he went on. 'It only needs enough Faith. This accursed Competitivism of ours has no friends but those who fear personal loss by a change of system. Not one. It has hirelings, Praetorian guards, Varangians, but not a devoted people. Its crimes are so great that he is a self-condemned villain who knowing them dreams of justifying them. There is not one man who would mourn it for itself if it fell to-morrow. A dozen times this century it has been on the verge of destruction, and what has saved it every time is simply that those who assailed it had not a supreme ideal common among them as to how they should re-build. It is exactly the same with political action as with revolutionary movements. It will fail till men have faith.'

'How can they get it?' asked Ned, for Geisner had ceased speaking and mused with a far-off expression on his face.

'If we ourselves have it, sooner or later we shall give it to others. Hearts that this world has wounded are longing for the ideal we bring; artist-souls that suffering has purified and edged are working for the Cause in every land; weak though we are we have a love for the Beautiful in us, a sense that revolts against the unloveliness of life as we have it, a conception of what might be if things were only right. In every class the ground is being turned by the ploughshare of Discontent; everywhere we can sow the seed broadcast with both hands. And if only one seed in a thousand springs up and boars, it is worth it.'

'But how can one do it best?'

'By doing always the work that comes to one's hand. Just now, you can go back to your union and knowing what the real end is, can work for organisation as you never did before. You can help throw men together, tie the bushmen to the coastmen, break down narrow distinctions of calling and make them all understand that all who work are brothers whether they work by hand or brain. That is the New Unionism and it is a step forward. It is drill, organisation, drill, and we, need it. Men must learn to move together, to discuss and to decide together. You can teach them what political action will do when they know enough. And all the time you can drive and hammer into them the socialistic ideas. Tell them always, without mincing matters, that they are robbed as they would probably rob others if they had a chance, and that there never can be happiness until men live like mates and pay nothing to any man for leave to work. Tell them what life might be if men would only love one another and teach them to hate the system and not individual men in it. Some day you will find other work opening out. Always do that which comes to your hand.'

'You think things will last a long time?' asked Ned, reverting to one of Geisner's previous remarks.

'Who can tell? While Belshazzar feasted the Medes were inside the gate. Civilisation is destroying itself. The socialistic idea is the only thing that can save it. I look upon the future as a mere race between the spread of Socialism as a religion and the spread of that unconditional Discontent which will take revenge for all its wrongs by destroying civilisation utterly, and with it much, probably most, that we have won so slowly and painfully, of Art and Science.'

'That would be a pity,' said Ned. He would have spoken differently had he not gone with Nellie last night, he thought while saying it.

'I think so. It means the whole work to be done over again. If Art and Science were based on the degradation of men I would say "away with them". But they are not. They elevate and ennoble men by bringing to them the fruition of elevated and noble minds. They are expressions of high thought and deep feeling; thought and feeling which can only do good, if it is good to become more human. The artist is simply one who has a little finer soul than others. Mrs. Stratton was saying last night before you came that Nellie is an artist because she has a soul. But it's only comparative. We've all got souls.'

'Mrs. Stratton is a splendid woman,' began Ned, after another pause.

'Very. Her father was a splendid man, too. He was a doctor, quite famed in his profession. The misery and degradation he saw among the poor made him a passionate Communist. Stratton's father was a Chartist, one of those who maintained that it was a bread-and-butter movement.'

For some few minutes neither spoke.

'One of the most splendid men I ever knew,' remarked Geisner, suddenly, 'was a workman who organised a sort of co-operative housekeeping club among a number of single fellows. They took a good-sized "fiat" and gradually extended it till they had the whole of the large house. Then this good fellow organised others until there were, I think, some thirty of them scattered about the city. They had cards which admitted any member of one house into any other of an evening, so that wherever a man was at night he could find friends and conversation and various games. I used to talk to him a great deal, helping him keep the books of an evening when he came home from his work. He had some great plans. Those places were hotbeds of Socialism,' he added.

'What became of him?'

Geisner shrugged his shoulders without answering.

'Isn't it a pity that we can't co-operate right through in the same way?' said Ned.

'It's the easiest way to bring Socialism about,' answered Geisner. 'Many have thought of it. Some have tried. But the great difficulty seems to be to get the right conditions. Absolute isolation while the new conditions are being established; colonists who are rough and ready and accustomed to such work and at the same time are thoroughly saturated with Socialism; men accustomed to discuss and argue and at the same time drilled to abide, when necessary, by a majority decision; these are very hard to get. Besides, the attempts have been on small scales, and though some have been fairly successful as far as they went, have not pointed the great lesson. One great success would give men more Faith than a whole century of talking and preaching. And it will come when men are ready for it, when the times are ripe.'

They were silent again.

'We would be free under Socialism?' asked Ned.

'What could stop us, even under State Socialism. The basis of all slavery and all slavish thought is necessarily the monopoly of the means of working, that is of living. If the State monopolises them, not the State

141

ruled by the propertied classes but the State ruled by the whole people, to work would become every man's right. Nineteen laws out of twenty could then be dropped, for they would become useless. We should be free as men have never been before, because the ideal of the State would be toleration and kindness.'

'Let's go and hear the speaking,' he added, jumping up. 'I've talked quite enough for once.'

'You couldn't talk too much for me,' answered Ned. 'You ought to come up to a shed and have a pitch with the chaps. They'd sit up all night listening. I've to meet Nellie between five and six at the top of the steps in the garden,' he added, a little bashfully. 'Have we time?'

'Plenty of time,' said Geisner, smiling. 'You won't miss her.'

CHAPTER XII
LOVE AND LUST

THE picnic party had moved on while they talked, but a multitude of sitters and walkers were now everywhere, particularly as they climbed the slope to the level. There the Sunday afternoon meetings were in full swing.

On platforms of varying construction, mostly humble, the champions of multitudinous creeds and opinions were holding forth to audiences which did not always greet their utterances approvingly. They stood for a while near a vigorous iconoclast, who from the top of a kitchen chair laid down the Law of the Universe as revealed by one Clifford, overwhelming with contumely a Solitary opponent in the crowd who was foolish enough to attempt to raise an argument on the subject of 'atoms'. Near at hand, a wild-eyed religionary was trying to persuade a limited and drifting audience that a special dispensation had enabled him to foretell exactly the date of the Second Coming of Christ. Then came the Single Tax platform, a camp-stool with a board on it, wherefrom a slender lad, dark-eyed and good-looking, held forth, with a flow of language and a power of expression that was remarkable, upon the effectiveness of a land tax as a remedy for all social ills.

Ned had never seen such a mass of men with such variegated shades of thought assembled together before. There was a well-dressed bald-headed individual laying down the axioms of that very Socialism of which Geisner and he had been talking. There was an ascetic looking man just delivering a popular hymn, which he sang with the assistance of a few gathered round, as the conclusion of open-air church. There was the

Anarchist he had seen at Paddy's Market, fervidly declaring that all government is wrong and that men are slaves and curs for enduring it and tyrants for taking part in it. There was the inevitable temperance orator, the rival touters for free trade and protection, and half-a-dozen others with an opinion to air. They harangued and shouted there amid the trees, on the grass, in the brilliant afternoon sunshine that already threw long shadows over the swaying, moving thousands.

It was a great crowd, a good many thousands altogether, men and women and children and lads. It was dressed in its Sunday best, in attire which fluctuated from bright tints of glaring newness to the dullness of well-brushed and obtrusive shabbiness. There were every-looking men you could think of and women and girls, young and old, pretty and plain and repulsive. But it was a working-people crowd. There was no room among it for the idlers. Probably it was not fashionable for them to be there.

And there was this about the crowd, which impressed Ned, everybody seemed dissatisfied, everybody was seeking for a new idea, for something fresh. There was no confidence in the Old, no content with what existed, no common faith in what was to come. There was on many a face the same misery that he had seen in Paddy's Market. There was no happiness, no face free from care, excepting where lovers passed arm-in-arm. There was the clash of ideas, the struggling of opinions, the blind leading the blind. He saw the socialistic orator contending with a dozen others. Who were the nostrum vendors? Which was the truth?

He turned round, agitated in thought, and his glance fell on Geisner, who was standing with bent head, his hands behind him, ugly, impassive. Geisner looked up quickly: 'So you are doubting already,' he remarked.

'I am not doubting,' answered Ned. 'I'm only thinking.'

'Well?'

'It is a good thought, that Socialism,' answered Ned slowly, as they walked on. 'There's nothing in it that doesn't seem fit for men to do. It's a part with Nellie kissing that woman in the wet. What tries to make us care for each other and prevent harm being done to one another can't be very far wrong and what tries to break down the state of affairs that is must be a little right. I don't care, either, whether it's right or wrong. It feels right in my heart somehow and I'll stand by it if I'm the only man left in the world to talk up for it.'

Geisner linked his arm in Ned's.

'Remember this when you are sorrowful,' he said. 'It is only through Pain that Good comes. It is only because the world suffers that Socialism is possible. It is only as we conquer our own weaknesses that we can serve the Cause.'

They strolled on till they came to the terraced steps of the Gardens. Before them stretched in all its wondrous glory the matchless panorama of grove and garden, hill-closed sea and villa'd shore, the blue sky and the declining sun tipping with gold and silver the dark masses of an inland cloud.

'What is Life that we should covet it?' said Geisner, halting there. 'What is Death that we should fear it so? What has the world to offer that we should swerve to the right hand or the left from the path our innermost soul approves? In the whole world, there is no lovelier spot than this, no purer joy than to stand here and look. Yet, it seems to me, Paradise like this would be bought dearly by one single thought unworthy of oneself.'

'We are here to-day,' he went on, musingly. 'To-morrow we are called dead. The next day men are here who never heard our names. The most famous will be forgotten even while Sydney Harbour seems unchanged. And Sydney Harbour is changing and passing, and the continent is changing and passing, and the world is changing and passing, and the whole universe is changing and passing.

'It is all change, universal change. Our religions, our civilisations, our ideas, our laws, change as do the nebulae and the shifting continents we build on. Yet through all changes a thread of continuity runs. It is all changing and no ending. Always Law and always, so far as we can see, what we call progression. A man is a fool who cares for his life. He is the true madman who wastes his years in vain and selfish ambition.

'Listen, Ned,' he pursued, turning round. 'There, ages ago, millions and millions of years ago, in the warm waters yonder, what we call Life on this earth began. Minute specks of Life appeared, born of the sunshine and the waters some say, coming in the fitness of Time from the All-Life others. And those specks of Life have changed and passed, and come and gone, unending, reproducing after their kind in modes and ways that changed and passed and still are as all things change and pass and are. And from them you and I and all the forms of Life that breathe to-day have ascended. We struggled up, obedient to the Law around us and we still struggle. That is the Past, or part of it. What is the Future, as yet no man knows. We do more than know—we feel and dream, and struggle on to our dreaming. And Life itself to the dreamer is as nothing only the struggling on.

'And this has raised us, Ned, this has made us men and opened to us the Future, that we learned slowly and sadly to care for each other. From the mother instinct in us all good comes. This is the highest good as yet, that all men should live their life and lay down their life when need is for their fellows. With all our blindness we can see that. With all our weakness we can strive to reach nearer that ideal. It is but Just that we should live so for others since happiness is only possible where others live so for us.'

He turned again and gazed intently across the sail-dotted harbour.

'There is one thing I would like to say.' He spoke without turning. 'Man without Woman is not complete. They two are but one being, complete and life-giving. Love when it comes is the keystone of this brief span of Life of ours. They who have loved have tasted truly of the best that Life can give to them. And this is the great wrong of civilisation to-day, that it takes Love from most and leaves in us only a feverish, degrading Lust. It is when we lust that Woman drags us down to the level of that Lust and blackens our souls with the blackness of hell. When we love Woman raises us to the level of Love and girds on us the armour that wards our own weakness from us.

'Love comes to few, I think. Society is all askew and, then, we have degraded women. So they are often well-nigh unfit for loving as men are often as unfit themselves. Physically unfit for motherhood, mentally unfit to cherish the monogamic idea that once was sacred with our people, sexually unfit to rouse true sex-passion—such women are being bred by the million in crowded cities and by degenerate country life. They match well with the slaves who 'move on' at the bidding of a policeman, or with the knaves who only see in Woman the toy of a feeble lust.

'There are two great reforms needed, Ned, two great reforms which must come if Humanity is to progress, and which must come, sooner or later, either to our race or to some other, because Humanity must progress. One reform is the Reorganisation of Industry. The other is the Recognition of Woman's Equality. These two are the practical steps by which we move up to the socialistic idea.

'If it ever comes to you to love and be loved by a true woman, Ned, let nothing stand between you and her. If you are weak and lose her you will have lost more than Life itself. If you are strong and win her you can never lose her again though the universe divided you and though Death itself came between you, and you will have lived indeed and found joy in living.'

'Should one give up the Cause for a woman?' asked Ned.

Geisner turned round at last and looked him full in the face.

'Lust only,' he answered, 'and there is no shame to which Woman cannot drag Man. Love and there is nothing possible but what is manly and true.'

As he spoke, along the terraced path below them came Nellie, advancing towards them with her free swinging walk and tall lissom figure, noticeable even at a distance among the Sunday promenaders.

'See?' said Geisner, smiling, laying his hand on Ned's arm. 'This is Paradise and there comes Eve.'

PART II

HE KNEW HIMSELF NAKED

In yesterday's reach and to-morrow's,
Out of sight though they lie of to-day,
There have been and there yet shall be sorrows
That smite not and bite not in play.

The life and the love thou despisest,
These hurt us indeed and in vain,
O wise among women, and, wisest,
Our Lady of Pain.
                                    —Swinburne

CHAPTER I

THE SLAUGHTER OF AN INNOCENT

MRS. Hobb's baby was dying.

'It had clung to its little life so long, in the close Sydney streets, in the stuffy, stifling rooms which were its home; it had battled so bravely; it was being vanquished at last.

'The flame of its life had flickered from its birth, had shrunk to a bluish wreathing many a time, had never once leapt upward in a strong red blaze. Again and again it had lain at its mother's breast, half-dead; again and again upon its baby face Death had laid the tips of its pinching fingers; again and again it had struggled moaning from the verge of the grave and beaten back the grim Destroyer by the patient filling of its tiny lungs. It wanted so to live, all unconsciously. The instinct to exist bore it up and with more than Spartan courage stood for it time and again in the well-nigh carried breach. Now, it was over, the battling, the struggling. Death loitered by the way but the fight was done.

'The poor little baby! Poor unknown soldier! Poor unaided heroic life that was spent at last! There were none to help it, not one. In all the world, in all the universe, there was none to give it the air it craved, the food it needed, the living that its baby-soul faded for not having. It had fought its fight alone. It lay dying now, unhelped and helpless, forsaken and betrayed.'

*   *   *

So thought Nellie, sitting there beside it, her head thrown back, over her eyes her hands clasped, down her cheeks the tears of passionate pity streaming.

*   *   *

'What had its mother done for it? The best she could, indeed, but what was that? The worst she could when she gave it life, when she bore it to choke and struggle and drown in the fetid stream that sweeps the children of the poor from infancy to age; the life she gave it only a flickering, half-lighted life; the blood she gave it thin with her own weariness and vitiate from its drunken sire; the form she gave it soft-boned and angle-headed, more like overgrown embryo than child of the boasted Australian land. Even the milk it drew from her unwieldy breasts was tainted with city smoke and impure food and unhealthy housing. Its playground was the cramped kitchen floor and the kerb and the gutter. Its food for a year had been the food that feeds alike the old and the young who are poor. All around conspired against it, yet for two years and more it had clung to its life and lived, as if defying Fate, as if the impulse that throbbed in it from the Past laughed at conditions and would have it grow to manhood in spite of all. In the strength of that impulse, do not millions grow so? But millions, like this little one, are crushed and overborne.

'It had no chance but the chance that the feeble spark in it gave it. It had no chance, even with that, to do more than just struggle through. None came to scatter wide the prison walls of the slum it lived in and give it air. None came to lift the burden of woe that pressed on all around it and open to it laughter and joy. None came to stay the robbery of the poor and to give to this brave little baby fresh milk and strengthening food. In darkness and despair it was born; in darkness and despair it lived; in darkness and despair it died. To it Death was more merciful than Life. Yet it was a crime crying for vengeance that we should have let it waste away and die so.'

*   *   *

So thought Nellie, weeping there beside it, all the woman in her aching and yearning for this poor sickly little one.

*　　　*　　　*

'It was murdered, murdered as surely as if a rope had been put round its neck and the gallows-trap opened under it; murdered as certainly as though, dying of thirst, it had been denied a sup of water by one who had to spare; murdered, of sure truth, as though in the dark one who knew had not warned it of a precipice in the path. It had asked so little and had been denied all; only a little air, only a little milk and fruit, only a glimpse of the grass and the trees, even these would have saved it. And oh! If also in its languid veins the love-life had bubbled and boiled, if in its bone and flesh a healthy parentage had commingled, if the blood its mother gave it had been hot and red and the milk she suckled it to white and sweet and clean from the fount of vigorous womanhood! What then? Then, surely it had been sleeping now with chubby limbs flung wide, its breathing so soft that you had to bend your ear to its red lips to hear it, had been lying wearied with dancing and mischief-making and shouting and toddling and falling, resting the night from a happy to-day till the dawn woke it betime for a happy to-morrow. All this it should have had as a birthright, with the years stretching in front of it, on through fiery youth, past earnest manhood, to a loved and loving old age. This is the due, the rightful due, of every child to whom life goes from us. And that child who is born to sorrow and sordid care, pot-bound from its mother's womb by encircling conditions that none single-handed can break, is wronged and sinned against by us all most foully. If it dies we murder it. If it lives to suffer we crucify it. If it steals we instigate, despite our canting hypocrisy. And if it murders we who hang it have beforehand hypnotised its will and armed its hand to slay.'

*　　　*　　　*

So Nellie thought, the tears drying on her cheeks, leaning forward to watch the twitching, purpled face of the hard-breathing child.

*   *   *

'Is there not a curse upon us and our people, upon our children and our children's children, for every little one we murder by our social sins? Can it be that Nemesis sleeps for us, he who never slept yet for any, he who never yet saw wrong go unavenged or heard the innocent blood cry unanswered from the ground?

'Can it be that he has closed his ears to the dragging footfalls of the harlot host and to the sobs of strong men hopeless and anguished because work is wanting and to the sighing of wearied women and to the death-rattle of slaughtered babes? Surely though God is not and Humanity is weak yet Nemesis is strong and sleepless and lingers not! Surely he will tear clown the slum and whelm the robbers in their iniquity and visit upon us all punishment for the crime which all alike have shared! Into the pit which we have left digged for the children of others shall not our own children fall? Is happiness safe for any while to any happiness is denied?

'It is a crime that a baby should live so and die so. It is a villainy and we all are villains who let it be. No matter how many are guilty, each one who lives with hands unbound is as guilty as any. It were better to die alone, fighting the whole world single-handed, refusing to share the sin or to tolerate it or to live while it was, than with halting speech to protest and with supple conscience to compromise. He is a coward who lets a baby die or a woman sink to shame or a fellow-man be humbled, alone and unassisted and unrighted. She is false to the divinity of womanhood who does not feel the tigress in her when a little one who might be her little one is tossed, stifled by unholy conditions, into its grave. But where are the men, now, who will strike a blow for the babies? Where are the women who will put their white teeth into the murderous hands of the Society that throttles the little ones and robs the weak and simple and cloaks itself with a 'law and order' which outrages the Supreme Law of that Humanity evolving in us?

154

'Surely we are all tainted and corrupted, even the best of us, by the scrofulous cowardice, the fearsome selfishness, of a decaying civilisation! Surely we are only fit to be less than human, to be slave to conditions that we ourselves might govern if we would, to be criminal accomplices in the sins of social castes, to be sad victims of inhuman laws or still sadder defenders of inhumanity! Oh, for the days when our race was young, when its women slew themselves rather than be shamed rid when its men, trampling a rotten empire down, feared neither God nor man and held each other brothers and hated, each one, the tyrant as the common foe of all! Better the days when from the forests and the steppes our forefathers burst, half-naked and free, communists and conquerors, a fierce avalanche of daring men and lusty women who beat and battered Rome down like Odin's hammer that they were! Alas, for the heathen virtues and the wild pagan fury for freedom and for the passion and purity that Frega taught to the daughters of the barbarian! And alas, for the sword that swung then, unscabbarded, by each man's side and for the knee that never bent to any and for the fearless eyes that watched unblenched while the gods lamed each other with their lightnings in the thunder-shaken storm! Gone forever seemed the days when the land was for all, and the cattle and the fruits of the field, and when, unruled by kings, untrammelled by priests, untyrannised by pretence of 'law,' our fathers drank in from Nature's breast the strength and vigour that gave it even to this little babe to fight its hopeless fight for life so bravely and so long. Odin was dead whose sons dared go to hell with their own people and Frega was no more whose magic filled with molten fire the veins of all true lovers and nerved with desperate courage the hand of her who guarded the purity of her body and the happiness of her child. The White Christ had come when wealth and riches and conquests had upheaped wrongs, upon the heads of the wrongers, the cross had triumphed over the hammer when the fierce freedom of the North had worn itself out in selfish foray; the shaven-pated priest had come to teach patience as God-given when a robber-caste grew up to whom it seemed wise to uproot the old ideas from the mind of the people whose spent courage it robbed. Alas, for the days when it was not righteous to submit to wrong nor wicked to strike tyranny to the ground, when one met it, no matter where! Alas, for the men of the Past and the women, their faith and their courage and their virtue and their gods, the hearts large to feel and the brains prompt to think and the arms strong to do, the bare feet that followed the plough and trod in the winepress of God and the brown hands that milked cows and tore kings from their thrones by their beard! They were gone and a feebler people spoke their tongue and bore their name, a people that bent its back to the rod and bared its head to the cunning and did not rise as one man when in its midst a baby was murdered while all around a helpless kinsfolk were being robbed and wronged.

'For the past, who would not choose it? Who would not, if they could, drop civilisation from them as one shakes off a horrid nightmare at the dawning of the day? Who would not be again a drover of cattle, a follower of the plough, a milker of cows, a spinner of wool-yarn by the fireside, to be, as well, strong and fierce and daring, slave to none and fearing none, ignorant alike of all the wisdom and all the woes of this hateful life that is?

'For only one moment of the past if the whole past could not be! Only to be free for a moment if the rest were impossible! Only to lose one's hair and bare one's feet and girdle again the single garment round one's waist and to be filled with the frenzy that may madden still as it maddened our mothers when the Roman legions conquered! Only to stand for a moment, free, on the barricade, outlawed and joyous, with Death, Freedom's impregnable citadel, opening its gates behind—and to pass through, the red flag uplifted in the sight of all men, with flaming slums and smoking wrongs for one's funereal pyre!'

*   *   *

So Nellie thought in her indignation and sorrow, changing the wet cloth on the baby's head, powerless to help it, uncomforted by creeds that moulder in the crimson-cushioned pews. She knew that she was unjust, carried away by her tumultuous emotions, knew also, in her heart, that there was something more to be desired than mere wild outbreaks of the despairing. Only she thought, as we all think, in phases, and as she would certainly have talked had opportunity offered while she was in the mood, and as she would most undoubtedly have written had she just then been writing. The more so as there was a wave of indignation and anger sweeping over Australia, sympathetic with the indignation and anger of the voteless workers in the Queensland bush. The companions of her childhood were to be Gatling-gunned because of the squatters, whose selfish greed and heartless indifference to all others had made them hateful to this selector's daughter. Because the bushmen would not take the squatters' wage and yield his liberty as a workman to the squatter's bidding and agree to this and to that without consultation or discussion, the scum of southern towns and the sifted blacklegs of southern 'estates' were to be drafted in hordes to Queensland to break down the unionism that alone protected the bushman and made him more of a man than he had been when the squatter could do as he would and did. From the first days she could remember she had heard how the squatters filched from the bushmen in their stores and herded the bushmen in vile huts and preferred every colour to white when there were workers wanted; and how the magistrates were all squatters or squatters' friends and how Government was for the squatters and for nobody else on the great Western plains; and she knew from Ned of the homeless, wandering life the bushmen led and how new thoughts were stirring among them and rousing them from their aimless, hopeless living. She knew more, too, knew what the bushman was: frank as a child, keeping no passing thought unspoken, as tender as a woman to those he cared for, responsive always to kindly, earnest words, boiling over with anger one moment and shouting with good humour the next, open-handed with sovereigns after months and years of lonely toiling or sharing his last plug of tobacco with a stranger met on the road. His faults she knew as well: his drunkenness often, his looseness of living, his excitability, all born of unnatural surroundings; but his virtues she knew as well, none better, and all her craving for the scent of the gums and to feel again the swaying saddle and to hear again the fathomless noon-day silence and to see again the stock rushing in jumbling haste for the water-hole, went out in a tempestuous sympathy for those who struggled for the union in the bush. And Ned! She hardly knew what she thought about Ned.

She was unjust in her thoughts, she knew, not altogether unjust but somewhat. There had been heroism in the passive struggle of six months before, when the seamen left the boats at the wharves for the sake of others and when the 'lumpers' threw their coats over their shoulders and stood by the seamen and when the miners came up from the mines so that no coal should go to help fight comrades they had never seen. Her heart had thrilled with joy to see so many grip hands and stand together, officers and stewards and gasmen and lightermen and engine-drivers and cooks and draymen, from Adelaide to far-off Cooktown, in every port, great and small, all round the eastern coast. As the strike dragged on she lived herself as she had lived in the starving hand-to-mouth days of her bitter poverty, to help find bread for the hungry families she knew. For Phillips and Macanany were on strike, while Hobbs, who had moved round the corner, had been sacked for refusing to work on the wharves; and many another in the narrow street and the other narrow streets about it were idling and hungering and waiting doggedly to see what might happen, with strike pay falling steadily till there was hardly any strike pay at all. And Nellie's heart, that had thrilled with joy when New Unionism uprose in its strength and drew the line hard and fast between the Labour that toiled and the Capitalism that reaped Labour's gains, ached with mingled pride and pain to see how hunger itself could not shake the stolid unionism about her. She saw, too, the seed that for years had been sown by unseen, unknown sowers springing up on every hand and heard at every street corner and from every unionist mouth that everything belonged of right to those who worked and that the idle rich were thieves and robbers. She smiled grimly to watch Mrs. Macanany and viragoes like her pouring oil on the flames and drumming the weak-kneed up and screaming against 'blacklegging' as a thing accurst. And when she understood that the fight was over, while apparently it was waxing thicker, she had waited to see what the end would be, longing for something she knew not what. She used to go down town, sometimes of an evening, to watch the military patrols, riding up and down with jingling bits and clanking carbines and sabres as if in a conquered city. She heard, in her workroom, the dull roar of the angry thousands through whose midst the insolent squatters drove in triumphal procession, as if inciting to lawlessness, with dragoon-guarded, police-protected drays of blackleg wool. Then the end came and the strike was over, leaving the misery it had caused and the bitter hatreds it had fostered and the stern lesson which all did not read as the daily papers would have had them. And now the same Organised Capitalism which had fought and beaten the maritime men and the miners, refusing to discuss or to confer or to arbitrate or to conciliate, but using its unjust possession of the means of living to starve into utter submission those whose labour made it rich, was at the same work in the Queensland bush, backing the squatters, dominating government, served by obsequious magistrates and a slavish military and aided by all who thought they had to gain by the degradation of their fellows or who had been ground so low that they would cut each other's throats for a crust or who, in their blind ignorance, misunderstood what it all meant. And there were wild reports afloat of resistance brooding in Queensland and of excited meetings in the bush and of troops being sent to disperse the bushmen's camps. Why did they endure these things, Nellie thought, watching and waiting, as impotent to aid them as she was to save the baby dying now beside her. Day by day she expected Ned.

She knew Ned was in the South, somewhere, though she had not seen him. He had come down on some business, in blissful ignorance of the nearness of the coming storm, but would be called back, she knew, now this new trouble had begun. And then he would be arrested, she was sure, because he was outspoken and fearless and would urge the men to stand out till the last, and would be sent to prison by legal trickery under this new law the papers said had been discovered; all so that the unions might break down and the squatters do as they liked. Which, perhaps, was why her thoughts for the time being were particularly tinged with pessimism.

If the vague something called 'law and order' was determined to be broken so that the bush could be dragooned for the squatter it seemed to her as well to make a substantial breakage while men were about it—and she did not believe they would.

She placed a cool damp cloth on the baby's head, wishing that its mother would come up, Mrs. Hobbs having been persuaded to go downstairs for some tea and a rest while Nellie watched by the sick child and having been entangled in household affairs the moment she appeared in the dingy kitchen where Mrs. Macanany, to the neglect of her own home, was 'seeing to things.' The hard breathing was becoming easier. Nellie brought the candle burning in a broken cup. The flushed face was growing paler and more natural. The twitching muscles were stilling. There was a change.

One unused to seeing Death approach would have thought the baby settling down at last to a refreshing, health-reviving sleep. Nellie had lived for years where the children die like rabbits, and knew.

'Mrs. Hobbs!' she called, softly but urgently, running to the stairs.

The poor woman came hastily to the foot. 'Quick, Mrs. Hobbs!' said Nellie, beckoning.

'Oh, Mrs. Macanany! The baby's dying!' cried poor Mrs. Hobbs, tripping on her dragging skirts in her frantic haste to get upstairs. Mrs. Macanany followed. The children set up a boohoo that brought Mr. Hobbs from the front doorstep where he had been sitting smoking. He rushed up the stairs also. When he reached the top he saw, by the light of the candle in Nellie's hand, a little form lying still and white; its mother crouched on the floor, wailing over it.

It was a small room, almost bare, the bedstead of blistered iron, the mattress thin, the bedding tattered and worn. A soapbox was the chair on which Nellie had been sitting; there was no other. Against the wall, above a rough shelf, was a piece of mirror-glass without a frame. The window in the sloping roof was uncurtained. On the poor bed, under the tattered sheet, was the dead baby. And on the floor, writhing, was its mother, Mrs.

Macanany trying to comfort her between the pauses of her own vehement neighbourly grief.

Nellie closed the dead baby's eyes, set the candle on the shelf and moved to the door where Mr. Hobbs stood bewildered and dumbfoundered, his pipe still in his hand. 'Speak to her!' she whispered to him. 'It's very hard for her.'

Mr. Hobbs looked hopelessly at his pipe. He did not recollect where to put it. Nellie, understanding, took it from his fingers and pushed him gently by the arm towards his wife. He knelt down by the weeping woman's side and put his hands on the head that was bent to the ground. 'Sue,' he said, huskily, not knowing what to say. 'Don't take on so! It's better for 'im.'

'It's not better,' she cried in answer, kneeling up and frantically throwing her arms across the bed. 'How can it be better? Oh, God! I wish I was dead. Oh, my God! Oh, my God! '

'Don't, Sue!' begged Mr. Hobbs, weeping in a clumsy way, as men usually do.

'It's not right,' cried the mother, rolling her head, half-crazed. 'It's not right, Jack. It's not right. It didn't ought to have died. It didn't ought to have died, Jack. It wouldn't if it had a chance, but it hadn't a chance. It didn't have a chance, Jack. It didn't have a chance.'

'Don't, Sue!' begged Mr. Hobbs again. 'You did what you could.'

'I didn't,' she moaned. 'I didn't. I didn't do what I could. There were lots of things I might have done that I didn't. I wasn't as kind as I might have been. I was cross to it and hasty. Oh, my God, my God! Why couldn't I have died instead? Why couldn't I? Why don't we all die? It's not right. It's not right. Oh, my God, my God!'

And she thought God, whatever that is, did not hear and would not answer, she not knowing that in her own pain and anguish were the seeds of progression and in her cries the whetting of the sickle wherewith all wrongs are cut down when they are ripe for the reaper. So she wept and lamented, bewailing her dead, rebellious and self-reproachful.

161

'Take the baby, dear?' quoth Mrs. Macanany, reappearing from a descent to the kitchen with a six months' infant squalling in her arms. 'Give it a drink now! It'll make you feel better.'

Poor Mrs. Hobbs clutched the baby-in-arms convulsively and sobbed over it, finding some comfort in the exertion. To Mrs. Macanany's muttered wrath Nellie intervened, however, with warnings of 'fits' as likely to follow the nursing of the child while its mother was so excited and feverish. Mr. Hobbs loyally seconded Nellie's amendment and with unexpected shrewdness urged the mother to control her grief for the dead for the sake of the living. Which succeeding, to some extent, they got the poor woman downstairs and comforted her with a cup of tea, Nellie undressing and soothing the crying children, who sobbed because of this vague happening which the eldest child of eleven explained as meaning that 'Teddy's going to be put in the deep hole.'

It was after ten when Nellie went. Mrs. Hobbs cried again as Nellie kissed her 'good-night.' Mr. Hobbs shook hands with genuine friendship. 'I don't know whatever we'd have done without you, Miss Lawton,' he said, bashfully, following her to the door.

'I don't know what they'll do without you, Mr. Hobbs,' retorted Nellie, whose quick tongue was noted in the neighbourhood.

He did not answer, only fumbled with the door-knob as she stood on the step in the brilliant moonlight.

'Give it up!' urged Nellie. 'It makes things worse and they're bad enough at the best. It's not right to your wife and the children.'

'I don't go on the spree often,' pleaded Mr. Hobbs.

'Not as often as some,' admitted Nellie, 'but if it's only once in a life-time it's too often. A man who has drink in him isn't a man. He makes himself lower than the beasts and we're low enough as it is without going lower ourselves. He hurts himself and he hurts his family and he hurts his mates. He's worse than a blackleg.'

'I don't see as it's so bad as that,' protested Mr. Hobbs.

'Yes, it is,' insisted Nellie, quickly. 'Every bit as bad. It's drink that makes most of the blacklegs, anyway. Most of them are men whose manhood has been drowned out of them with liquor and the weak men in the unions are the drunkards who have no heart when the whisky's out of them. Everybody knows that. And when men who aren't as bad feel down-hearted and despairing instead of bracing up and finding out what makes it they cheer up at a pub and imagine they're jolly good fellows when they're just cowards dodging their duty. They get so they can't take any pleasure except in going on the spree and if they only go on once in a month or two'—this was a hit at Hobbs—'they're the worse for it. Why, look here, Mr. Hobbs, if I hadn't been here you'd have gone to-night and brought home beer and comforted yourselves getting fuddled. That's so, you know, and it wouldn't be right. It's just that sort of thing'—she added softly—'that stops us seeing how it is the little ones die when they shouldn't. If everybody would knock off drinking for ten years, everybody, we'd have everything straightened out by then and nobody would ever want to go on the spree again.'

She stood with her back to the moonlight, fingering the post of the door. Mr. Hobbs fumbled still with the door-knob and looked every way but at her. She waited for an answer, but he did not speak.

'Come,' she continued, after a pause. 'Can't you give it up? I know it's a lot to do when one's used to it. But you'll feel better in the end and your wife will be better right away and the children, and it won't be blacklegging on those who're trying to make things better. No matter how poor he is if a man's sober he's a man, while if he drinks, no matter if he's got millions, he's a brute.'

'You never drink anything, Miss Lawton, do you?' asked Mr. Hobbs, swinging the door.

'I never touched it in my life,' said Nellie.

'Do you really think you're better for it?'

'I think it has kept me straight,' said Nellie, earnestly. 'I wouldn't touch a drop to save my life. Some people call us who don't drink fools just because a few humbugs make temperance a piece of cant. I think those who get drunk are fools or who drink when there's a prospect of themselves or those they drink with getting drunk. Drink makes a man an empty braggart or a contented fool. It makes him heartless not only to others but to himself.'

There was another pause.

'If you won't for the sake of your wife and your children and yourself and everybody, will you do it to please me?' asked Nellie, who knew that Mr. Hobbs regarded her as the one perfect woman in Australia and, woman-like, was prepared to take advantage thereof.

'You know, Miss Lawton, I'm not one of the fellows who swear off Monday mornings and get on the spree the next Saturday night. If I say I'll turn temperance I'll turn.' So quoth the sturdy Hobbs.

'I know that. If you were the other sort do you think I'd be bothering you?' retorted Nellie.

'Well, I'll do it,' said Mr. Hobbs. 'So help me—'

'Never mind that,' interrupted the girl. 'If a man's a man his word's his word, and if he's not all the swearing in the world won't make any difference. Let's shake on it!' She held out her hand.

Mr. Hobbs dropped the door-knob and covered her long, slender hand with his great, broad, horny-palmed one.

'Good night, Mr. Hobbs!' she said, the 'shake' being over. 'Get her to sleep and don't let her fret!'

'Good night, Miss Nellie!' he answered, using her name for the first time. He wanted to say something more but his voice got choked up and he shut the door in her face, so confused was he.

'Hello, Nellie!' said a voice that made her heart stand still, as she crossed the road, walking sadly homewards. At the same time two hands stretched out of the dense shadow into the lane of moonlight that shone down an alley way she was passing and that cut a dazzling swath in the blackness made still blacker by the surrounding brilliancy. 'I've been wondering if you ever would finish that pitch of yours.'

It was Ned.

CHAPTER II
ON THE ROAD TO QUEENSLAND

WHILE Nellie had been talking temperance to Mr. Hobbs, Ned had been watching her impatiently from the other side of the street. For an hour and more he had been prowling up and down, up and clown, between the Phillipses and the Hobbses, having learned from Mrs. Phillips, who looked wearier than ever, where the Hobbses lived now and why Nellie had gone there after hardly stopping to swallow her dinner. At seven he had acquired this information and returned soon after nine to find Nellie still at the house of sickness, now, alas, the house of death. So he had paced up and down, up and down, waiting for her. He had seen the Hobbs' door open at last and had watched impatiently, from the shadow opposite, the conversation on the door step. His heart gave a great leap as she stopped across the road full in the moonlight. He saw again the sad stern face that had lived as an ideal in his memory for two long eventful years. There was none like her in the whole world to him, not one.

The years had come to her in this stifling city, amid her struggling and wrestling of spirit, but the strong soul in her had borne her up through all, she had aged without wearying, grown older and sadder without withering from her intense womanhood. Broader of hip a little, as Ned could see with the keen eyes of love, not quite so slender in the waist, fuller in the uncorsetted bust, more sloping of shoulder as though the pillared neck had fleshed somewhat at the base; the face, too, had gathered form and force, in the freer curve of her will-full jaw, in the sterner compression of fuller lips that told their tale of latent passions strangely bordering on the cruel, in the sweeter blending of Celt and

Saxon shown in straight nose, strong cheek-bones and well-marked brows. She trod still with the swinging spring of the bill-people, erect and careless. Only the white gleam of her collar and a dash of colour in her hat broke the sombre hue that clothed her, as before, from head to foot.

Ned devoured her with his eyes as she came rapidly towards him, unconscious of his presence. She was full grown at last, in woman's virgin prime, her mind, her soul, her body, all full and strong with pure thoughts, natural instincts and human passions. Her very sadness gave her depths of feeling that never come to those who titter and fritter youth away. Her very ignoring of the love-instincts in her, absorbed as her thoughts were in other things, only gave those instincts the untrammelled freedom that alone gives vigorous growth. She was barbarian, as her thoughts had been beside the dying baby: the barbarian cultured, as Shakespeare was, the barbarian wronged, as was Spartacus, the barbarian hating and loving and yearning and throbbing, the creature of her instincts, a rebel against restrictions, her mind subject only to her own strong will. She was a woman of women, in Ned's eyes at least. One kiss from her would be more than all other women could give, be their self-abandonment what it might. To be her lover, her husband, a man might yield up his life with a laugh, might surrender all other happiness and be happy ever after. There was none like her in the whole world to Ned, not one—and he came to say good-bye to her, perhaps for ever.

In the black shadows thrown by the high-rising moon, the crossing alley-way cut a slice of brilliancy as if with a knife. From the shadow into the moonshine two hands stretched towards her as Ned's voice greeted her. She saw his tall form looming before her.

'Ned!' she cried, in answer, grasping both his hands and drawing him forward into the light. 'I was expecting you. I've been thinking of you every minute for the last week. How tired you look! You're not ill?'

'No! I'm all right,' he answered, laughing. 'It's those confounded trains. I can't sleep on them, and they always give me a headache. But you're looking well, Nellie. I can't make out how you do it in this stuffed-up town.'

'I'm all right,' She replied, noticing a red rose in his coat but saying nothing of it. 'Nothing seems to touch me. Did you come straight through?'

'Straight through. We rushed things all we could but I couldn't get away before. Besides, as long as I get Saturday's boat in Brisbane it'll be as soon as it's possible to get on. That gives me time to stay over to-night here. I didn't see you going down and I began to wonder if I'd see you going back. You can do a pitch, Nellie. When a fellow's waiting for you, too.'

Nellie laughed, then sobered down. 'The baby's dead,' she said, sadly. 'You recollect it was born when you were here before, the day we went to the Strattons.'

'I don't wonder,' he answered, looking round at the closed-in street, with its dull, hopeless, dreary rows of narrow houses and hard roadway between. 'But I suppose you're tired, Nellie. Let's go and get some oysters!'

'I don't care to, thanks. I feel like a good long walk,' she went on, taking his arm and turning him round to walk on with her. 'I'm thirsting for a breath of fresh air and to stretch myself. I'm a terrible one for walks, you know.'

'Not much riding here, Nellie;' walking on.

'That's why I walk so. I can go from here right down to Lady Macquarie's Chair in under half-an-hour. Over two miles! Not bad, eh, Ned?'

'That's a good enough record. Suppose we go down there now, Nellie, only none of your racing time for me. It's not too late for you?'

'Too late for me! My word! I'm still at the Phillipses and they don't bother. I wouldn't stay anywhere where I couldn't come and go as I liked. I'd like to go it you're not too tired.'

'It'll do me good,' said Ned, gleefully. So they set off, arm in arm. After they had walked a dozen yards he stopped suddenly.

'I've brought you a rose, Nellie,' he exclaimed, handing it to her. 'I'm so pleased to see you I forgot it.'

'I knew it was for me,' she said, fondly, pinning it at her throat. 'How ever did you recollect my colour?'

'Do you think I forget anything about you, Nellie?' he asked. She did not answer and they walked on silently.

'Where is Geisner?' he enquired, after a pause. 'I don't know. Why?'

'Oh, nothing. Only he'd advise us a little.'

After a pause: 'What do you think of things, Ned?'

'What do I think? We couldn't get any wires through that explained anything. There was nothing on but the ordinary strike business when I came down. I suppose some of the chaps have been talking wild and the Government has snapped at the chance to down the union. You know what our fellows are.'

'Yes. But I don't quite see what the Government's got to gain. Proclamations and military only make men worse, I think.'

'Sometimes they do and sometimes they don't,' answered Ned. 'A crowd that's doing no harm, only kicking up a bit of a row, will scatter like lambs sometimes if a single policeman collars one of them. Another time the same crowd will jump on a dozen policemen. The Government thinks the crowd'll scatter and I'm afraid the crowd'll jump.'

'Why afraid?' enquired Nellie, biting her lips.

'Because it has no chance,' answered Ned. 'These are all newspaper lies about them having arms and such nonsense. There aren't 500 guns in the whole Western country and half of them are old muzzle-loading shot guns. The kangarooers have got good rifles but nineteen men out of twenty no more carry one than they carry a house.'

'But the papers say they're getting them!'

'Where are they to get them from, supposing they want them and naturally the chaps want them when they hear of military coming to "shoot 'em down"? You can reckon that the Government isn't letting any be carried on the railways and, even if they did I don't believe you could buy 500 rifles in all Queensland at any one time.'

'Then it's all make-up that's in the papers? It certainly seemed to me that there was something in it.'

'That's just it, there is something in it. Just enough, I'm convinced, to give the Government an excuse for doing what they did during the maritime strike without any excuse and what the squatters have been planning for them to do all along.'

'One of the Queensland men who was here a week or two ago was telling me about the maritime strike business. It was the first I'd heard of that. Griffith didn't seem to be that way years ago,' said Nellie.

'Griffith is a fraud,' declared Ned, hotly. 'I'd sooner have one of the Pure Merinoes than Griffith. They do fight us out straight and fair, anyway, and don't cant much about knowing that things aren't right, with Elementary Property Bills and "Wealth and Want" and that sort of wordy tommy-rot. I like to know where to find a man and that trick of Griffith at the maritime strike in Brisbane showed where to find him right enough.'

'Was it Griffith?' asked Nellie.

'Of course it was Griffith. Who else would it be? The fellows in Brisbane feel sore over it, I tell you. When they'd been staying up nights and getting sick and preaching themselves hoarse, talking law and order to the chaps on strike and rounding on every man who even boo'd as though he were a blackleg, and when the streets were quieter with thousands of rough fellows about than they were ordinary times, those shop-keepers and wool-dealers and commission agents went off their heads and got the Government to swear in "specials" and order out mounted troopers and serve out ball cartridges. And all the time the police said it wasn't necessary, that the men on strike were perfectly orderly. Who'd ever do that but Griffith? And what can we expect from a government that did such a thing?'

'The Brisbane men do seem sore over that,' agreed Nellie. 'The man who told me vowed it would be a long time before he'd do policeman's work again. He said that for him Government might keep its own order and see how soon it got tired of it.'

'Well, it's the same thing going on now. I mean the Government and the squatters fixing up this military business between them just to dishearten our fellows. Besides, they've got it into their heads, somehow, that most men are only unionists through fear and that if they're sure of "protection" they'll blackleg in thousands.'

'That's a funny notion,' said Nellie. 'But all employers have it or pretend to have it. I fancy it comes through men, afraid of being victimised if they display independence, shifting the responsibility of their sticking up for rules upon the union and letting the boss think they don't approve of the rules but are afraid to break them, when they're really afraid to let him know they approve them.'

'That's about it, Nellie, but most people find it easy to believe what they want to believe. Anyway, I've got it straight from headquarters that the squatters expect to get blacklegs working under enough military protection to make blacklegging feel safe, as they look at it, and then they think our unions will break right down. And, of course, what maddens our crowd is that blacklegs are collected in another part of the world and shipped in under agreements which they can be sent to prison if they break, or think they can, which amounts to the same, and are kept guarded away from us, like convicts, so that we can't get to them to talk to them and win them over as is done in ordinary strikes in towns.'

'That's shameful!' said Nellie. 'The squatter governments have a lot to answer for.'

'And what can we do?' continued Ned. 'They won't let us have votes. There are 20,000 men in the back country altogether and I don't believe 5000 of them have votes and they're mostly squatters and their managers and "lifers" and the storekeepers and people who own land. I've no vote and can't get one. None of the fellows in my lot can get votes. We can't alter things in Parliament and the law and the government and the military and the police and the magistrates and everything that's got authority are trying to down us and we can't help ourselves. Do you wonder that our chaps get hot and talk wild and act a little wild now and then?'

Nellie pressed his arm answeringly.

'I feel myself a coward sometimes,' went on Ned. 'Last drought-time some of us were camped 'way back at a water-hole on a reserve where there was the only grass and water we could get for hundreds of miles. We had our horses and the squatter about wanted the grass for his horses and tried to starve us away by refusing to sell us stores. He wouldn't even sell us meat. He was a fool, for we took his mutton as we wanted it, night-times, and packed our stores from the nearest township, a hundred and eighty miles off. I used to think that the right thing to do was to take what we wanted off his run and from his store, in broad daylight, and pay him fair prices and blow the heads off anybody who went to stop us. For we'd a better right to the grass than he had. Only, you see, Nellie, it was easier to get even with him underhand and we seem to do always what's easiest.'

'They've always acted like that, those squatters, Ned,' said Nellie. 'Don't you recollect when they closed the road across Arranvale one drought 'cause the selectors were cutting it up a bit, drawing water from the reserve, and how everybody had to go seven miles further round for every drop of water? I've often wondered why the gates weren't lifted and the road used in spite of them.'

'They'd have sent for the police,' remarked Ned. 'Next year Arranvale shed was burned,' he added.

'It's always that way,' declared Nellie, angrily. 'For my part I'd sooner see the wildest, most hopeless outbreak, than that sort of thing.'

'So would the squatters, Nellie,' retorted Ned, grimly. 'I feel all you do,' he went on. 'But human nature is human nature and the squatters did their level best, ignorantly I admit, to make the men mere brutes, and the life alone has made hundreds mad, so we can't wonder if the result isn't altogether pleasant. They've made us hut in with Chinese and Malays. They've stuck up prices till flour that cost them tuppence a pound I've seen selling us for a shilling. They've cut wages down whenever they got a chance and are cutting them now, and they want to break up our unions with their miserable "freedom of contract" agreement. Before there were unions in the bush the only way to get even with a squatter was by some underhand trick and now we've got our unions and are ready to stand up manly and fight him fair he's coming the same dodge on us that the shipowners came on the seamen, only worse. Going to use contract labour from the South that we can't get near to talk to and that can't legally knock off if we did talk it over, and going to break up the camps and shoot down unarmed men just to stop the strike. How can you wonder if a few fires start or expect the chaps to be indignant if they do? Besides, half the fires that happen at times like this are old shanties of sheds that are insured above their value. It's convenient to be able to put everything down to unionists.'

'It worries me,' said Nellie, after a few minutes' silence.

'Me too,' said Ned. 'We've got such a good case if both sides could only be shown up. We've been willing to talk the whole thing over all along and we're willing yet or to arbitrate it either. We're right and lots of these fellows know it who abuse us. And if our chaps do talk a bit rough and get excited and even if they do occasionally carry on a bit, it's not a circumstance to the way the other side talk and get excited and carry on. Only all the law is against us and none against them. Our chaps are so hot that they don't go at it like lawyers but like a bull at a gate, when they talk or write. And so the Government gets a hold on us and can raise a dust and prevent people from seeing how things really are!'

'Ned,' she said, after a pause. 'Tell me honestly! Do you think there will be any trouble?'

'Honestly, I don't, Nellie. At least nothing serious. Some of the fellows may start to buck if the Government does try to break up the camps and it might spread a little, but there are no guns and so I don't see how it could. There seems to be a lot of talk everywhere but that's hard fact. Ten thousand bushmen with rifles wouldn't have much trouble with the Government and the Government wouldn't have much trouble with ten thousand bushmen without rifles. Besides, we're trying to do things peacefully and I don't see why we shouldn't win this round as things stand and get votes soon into the bargain!'

'But if there is trouble, Ned?' she persisted. 'Supposing it does start?'

'I shall go with the chaps, of course, if that's what you mean.'

'Knowing it's useless, just to throw your life away?' she asked, quietly, not protestingly, but as one seeking information.

'I've eaten their bread,' answered Ned. 'Whatever mad thing is done, however it's done, I'm with them. I should be a coward if I stood out of it because I didn't agree with it. Besides—'

'Besides what?'

'I believe in Fate somehow. Not as anything outside bossing us, you know, but as the whole heap of causes and conditions, of which we're a part ourselves. But I don't feel that there'll be any real trouble though some of us'll get into trouble just the same.'

'The Government will pick the big thistles, you mean.'

'Those they think the big thistles, I suppose. Of course the Government is only the squatters and the companies in another shape and they only want to break down the strike and are glad of any excuse that'll give them a slant at us. They have a silly idiotic notion that only a few men keep the unions going and that if they can get hold of a dozen or two the others will all go to work like lambs just as the squatter wants The fellows here have heard that the Government's getting ready to make a lot of arrests up there. I'm one.'

Nellie squeezed his arm again; 'I've heard that. I suppose they can do anything they like, Ned, but surely they won't dare to really enforce that old George the Fourth law they've resurrected?'

'Why not? They'll do anything, Nellie. They're frantic and think they must or the movement will flood them out. They'd like nothing better than a chance to shoot a mob of us down like wild turkeys. They have squatter magistrates and squatter judges—you know we've got some daisies up in Queensland—and they'll snap up all the best lawyers and pack the jury with a lot of shopkeepers who're just in a panic at the newspaper yarns. The worst interpretation'll be put on everything and every foolish word be magnified a thousand times. I know the gentry too well. They'll have us sure as fate and all I hope is that the boys won't be foolish enough to give them an excuse to massacre a few hundred. It'll be two or three years apiece, the Trades Hall people have heard. However, I suppose we can stand it. I don't care so long as the chaps stick to the union.'

'Do you think they will?' asked Nellie, after another pause.

'I'm sure they will. They can rake a hundred of us in for life and knock the union endways and in a year there'll be as much fight in the boys as there is now, and more bitter, too. Why they're raising money in Sydney for us already and I'm told that it was squeezed as dry as a bone over the maritime strike. The New South Wales fellows are all true blue and so they are down Adelaide way, as good as gold yet. The bosses don't know what a job they tackled when they started in to down unionism. They fancy that if they can only smash our fellows they'll have unionism smashed all over Australia. The fun will only just have started then.'

'What makes you so sure the men will stick, Ned?' enquired Nellie.

'Because they all know what the squatter was before the union and what he'll be the minute he gets another chance. The squatters will keep the unions going right enough. Besides everybody's on for a vote now in the bush and, of course, the Government is going to keep it from them as long as possible. Without unionism they'll never get votes and they know it.'

They had reached the path by Wooloomooloo Bay. Ned took off his hat and walked bareheaded. 'This is lovely!' he remarked, refreshed.

'What a fool Griffith is!' cried Nellie, suddenly.

'He's not as cunning as he ought to be,' assented Ned. 'But why?'

'Do you know what I'd do if I were him?' answered Nellie. 'I'd send all the military and all the police home and go up into the bush by myself and have a chat with the committee and the men at the camps and find out just how they looked at the thing and ask them to assist in keeping order and I'd see that they got justice if Parliament had to be called together specially to do it.'

'He's not smart enough to do that,' answered Ned. 'Besides, the squatters and the capitalistic set are the Parliament and wouldn't let him. I suppose he believes every lie they stuff him with and never gives a minute's thought to our having a side.'

'He didn't use to be a bad man, once,' persisted Nellie.

'I suppose he's not a bad man now,' cried Ned, boiling over. 'He's not on the make like most of them and he fancies he's very patriotic, I imagine, but what does he know of us or of the squatter? He sees us at our worst and the squatter at his best and we've got different ways of talking and when we get drunk on poisoned rum that the Government lets be sold we aren't as gentlemanly as those who get drunk on Hennessy and champagne. We don't curse in the same gentlemanly way and we splash out what we think and don't wear two faces like his set. And so he thinks we're ruffians and outlaws and he can't feel why the bushmen care for the unions. The squatter has taken up all the land and the squatter law has tied up what hasn't been taken and most of us are a lot of outcasts, without homes or wives or children or anything that a man should have barring our horses. We've got no votes and every law is set against us and we've no rights and the squatter'd like to throw us all out to make room for Chinese. There's nothing in front of the bushman now unless the union gets it for him and they're trying to break up our union, Griffith and his push, and, by God, they shan't do it. They haven't gaols enough to hold every good unionist, not if they hang a thousand of us to start with.'

'What does it matter, after all, Ned?' said Nellie, gently. 'The Cause itself gains by everything that makes men think. There'll never be peace until the squatter goes altogether and the banks and the whole system. And the squatter can't help it. I abuse him myself but I know he only does what most of our own class in his place would do.'

'Of course he can't help it, Nellie,' agreed Ned. 'They're mostly mortgaged up to the neck like the shopkeepers and squeeze us partly to keep afloat themselves. It's the system, not the squatters personally. A lot of them are decent enough, taking them off their runs and some are decent even on their runs. Even the squatters aren't all bad. I don't wish them any harm individually but just the same we're fighting them and they're fighting us and what I feel sorest about is that it's just because the New Unionism is teaching our chaps to think and to be better and to have ideas that they are trying so hard to down it.'

'They don't know any better,' repeated Nellie.

'That's what Geisner says, I recollect. I mind how he said they'd try sending us to prison here in Australia. They're beginning soon.'

They were right at the point now.

'There's only one thing I'd like to know first, Nellie.'

'What is it, Ned?' she asked, unconsciously, absorbed in her fear for him.

CHAPTER III

A WOMAN'S WHIM

'NELLIE!'

It was a husky whisper. His throat was parched, his lips dry, his mouth also. His heart thumped, thumped, thumped, so that it sickened him. He shook nervously. His face twitched. He felt burning hot; then deadly cold. He turned his hat slowly round and round in his trembling fingers.

It was as though he had turned woman. He did not even feel passion. He dared not look at her. He could feel her there. He did not desire as he had desired so often to snatch her to him, to crush her in his arms, to smother her with kisses, to master her. All his strength fled from him in an indescribable longing.

He had dreamed of this moment, often and often. He had rehearsed it in his mind a thousand times, when the reins dropped on his horse's neck, when he lay sleepless on the ground, even as he chatted to his mates. He had planned what to say, how to say it, purposing to break down her stubborn will with the passionate strength of his love for her, with mad strong words, with subtle arguments. He had seen her hesitating in his dreaming, had seen the flush come and go on her cheeks, her bosom heaving beneath the black dress he knew so well. He had made good his wooing with the tender violence that women forgive for love's sake, had caught her and kissed her till her kisses answered and till she yielded him her troth and pledged herself his wife. So he had dreamed in his folly. And now he stood there like a whipped child, pleading huskily:

'Nellie!'

He had not known himself. He had not known her. Even now he hardly understood that her glorious womanliness appealed to all that was highest in him, that in her presence he desired to be a Man and so seemed to himself weak and wicked. It was not her body only, it was her soul also that he craved, that pure, clear soul of hers which shone in every tone and every word and every look and every gesture. Beautiful she was, strong and lithe and bearing her head up always as if in stern defiance; beautiful in her cold virginity; beautiful in the latent passion that slumbered lightly underneath the pale, proud face. But most beautiful of all to him, most priceless, most longed for, was the personality in her, the individuality which would have brought him to her were she the opposite, physically, of all she was. He had wondered in reading sometimes of the Buddhist thoughts if it were indeed that she was his mate, that in re-incarnation after re-incarnation they had come together and found in each other the completed self. And then he had wondered if there were indeed in him such power and forcefulness as were in her and if he were to her anything more than a rough, simple, ignorant bush fellow, in whom she was interested a little for old acquaintance sake and because of the common Cause they served. For to himself, he had been still the same as before he ate from her hands the fruit of the Tree of Knowledge. Absorbed in his work, a zealot, a fanatic, conscious of all she had and of all he lacked, he had not noticed how his own mind had expanded, how broader ideas had come to him, how the confidence born of persistent thought gave force to his words and how the sincerity and passion that rang in his voice reached if but for a moment the hearts of men. When he thought of her mentality he doubted that she would be his, she seemed so high above him. It was when he thought of her solely as a Woman, when he remembered the smile of her parting, the hand-clinging that was almost a caress, the tender 'Come back to me again, Ned!' that he felt himself her equal in his Manhood and dreamed his dream of how he would woo and win her.

And now! Ah, now, he knew himself and knew her. He realised all that he was, all that he might have been. He would have wooed her and Nemesis struck him on the mouth, struck him dumb.

There come moments in our lives when we see ourselves. For years, for a generation, till dying often, we live our lives and do not know except by name the Ego that dwells within. We face death unflinchingly, as most men do, and it never speaks. We love and we hate, with a lightness that is held civilised, and it never stirs. We suffer and mourn and laugh and sneer and it lies hidden. Then something stirs us to the very base of our being and self-consciousness comes. And happy, thrice happy, in spite of all sorrow and pain, no matter what has been or what awaits him, is he to whom self-consciousness does not bring the self reproach that dieth not, the remorse that never is quite quenched. He would have wooed and he was dumb. For with a flash his life uprose before him. He saw himself naked and he was ashamed.

Tremblingly, shaken with anguish, he saw himself—unfit to look into the eyes of a woman such as this. Like loathsome images of a drunkard's nightmare scenes that were past came to him. Upon his lips were kisses that stung and festered, around his neck were the impress of arms that dragged him down, into his eyes stared other eyes taunting him with the evil glances that once seemed so dear. What had he of manhood to offer to this pure woman. It seemed to him a blasphemy even to stand there by her. His passion fled. He only felt a pitiful, gnawing, hopeless, indescribable longing.

What he had been! How he had drunk and drunk and drunk again of the filthy pools wherewith we civilised peoples still our yearnings for the crystal spring of Love, that the dragon of Social Injustice guards from us so well! His sins rose in front of him. They were sins now as they had never been before. The monogamy of his race triumphed in him. For men and for women alike he knew there was the same right and the same wrong.

His soul abhorred itself because of his unfitness to match with this ideal woman of his people. He could feel her purity, as he stood there by her.

He could feel that her lips still waited for the lover of her life, that round her waist the virgin zone still lay untied, that she could still give herself with all the strength of unsullied purity and unweakened passion. And he, who had thought in his miserable folly that at least he was as much Man as she was Woman? He could only give her the fragments of a life, the battered fragments of what once had been well worth the having.

He knew that now. He saw himself naked and he knew what he was and what he had been. He had feared comparison with her intellectually and he towered above her, even now; he knew it. He knew now that to him it had been given to sway the thoughts of men, to feel the pulse of the great world beat, to weld discontent into action, to have an idea and to dare and to give to others faith and hope. That came to him also, without conceit, without egotism—with a rush of still more bitter infinitely more unbearable, pain. For this, too, he had wasted, flung away, so it seemed to him in his agony of degradation: because he had not been true to his higher self, because he had not done as a true Man would. And so, he had been blind. He saw it plainly, now, the path he should have trod, trampling his weaknesses down, bending his whole life in one strong effort, living only for the work at hand. And to him it came that, perchance, on him was this great punishment that because of his unworthiness the Cause must wait longer and struggle more; that because he had not been strong little children would sob who might have laughed and men would long for death who might have joyed in living. And he knew, too, that had he but been what he might have been he would have stood fearlessly by her side at last and won her to cast in her lot with his. For there was a way out, indeed, a way out from the house of bondage, and none had been so near to it in all time as he had all his life, none had had their feet pointed so towards it, none had failed so strangely to pick up the track and follow it to the end. Years ago, as he thought, sleepless, under the stars, he had touched on it, Geisner had brought him near to it. And still he had not seen it, had not seen as he saw now that those who seek to change the world must first of all show the world that change is possible, must gather themselves together and go out into the desert to live their life in their own way as an example to all men. Who, could do this as the bushmen could, as he and his houseless, homeless, wandering mates could? If he only could lead them to it, Geisner helping him! If another chance might be his as the chance had been! Now, life seemed over. He had a prescience of misfortune. A Queensland gaol would swallow him up. That would be the end of it all.

He did not think that he was much the same as others, more forceful perhaps for evil as for good but still much the same. He did not think that social conditions had been against him, that Society had refused him the natural life which gives morality and forced upon him the unnatural life which fosters sin. What did that matter? The Puritan blood that flowed in his veins made him stern jury and harsh judge. He tried himself by his own ideal and he condemned himself. He was unworthy. He had condemned those who drank; he had condemned those who cursed and swore meaninglessly; he had looked upon smoking as a weakness, almost a fault. Now, he condemned himself, without reservation. He had sinned and his punishment had begun. He had lived in vain and he had lost his love. It never occurred to him that he might play a part before her—he was too manly. Yet his great longing grew greater as he realised everything. All the loneliness of his longing spoke in that hoarse whisper:

'Nellie?'

And Nellie? Nellie loved him.

She had held him as a brother for so long that this love for him had crept upon her, little by little, inch by inch, insidiously, unperceived. She remembered always with pleasure their school days together and their meetings since, that meeting here in Sydney two years before most of all. She had felt proud of him, of his strength and his fiery temper, of his determined will, of the strong mind which she could feel growing and broadening in the letters he had sent her of late. She could not but know that to him she was very much, that to her he owed largely the bent of his thinking, that to her he still looked as a monitress. But she lulled herself with the delusion that all this was brotherliness and that all her feelings were sisterliness. His coming that night, his gift of the rose, had filled her with a happiness that mingled strangely with the pain of her fears.

Coming along, arm in arm with him, she had been thinking of him, even while she spoke earnestly of other things. Would she ever see him again, she wondered with a sinking of the heart, would she ever see him again. Never had he thought or care for himself, never would he shrink from fear of consequences if it seemed to him that a certain course was 'straight.' She would not have him shrink, of course. He was dear to her because he was what he was, and yet, and yet, it pained her so to think that she nevermore might see him. Seldom she saw him it was true, only now and then, years between, but she always hoped to see him. What if the hope left her! What should she do if she should see him again nevermore?

The kaleidoscope of her memories showed to her one scene, one of the episodes that had gone to make up her character, to strengthen her devotion: the whirring of a sewing machine in a lamp-lit room and a life-romance told to the whirring, the fate of a woman as Geisner's was the fate of a man. A romance of magnificent fidelity, of heroic sacrifice illumined by a passionate love, of a husband followed to the land of his doom from that sad isle of the Atlantic seas, of prison bars worn away by the ceaseless labour of a devoted woman and of the cruel storm that beat the breath from her loved one as freed and unfettered he fled to liberty and her! She heard again the whirr of the machine, saw again the lamplight shine on the whitening head majestic still. For Ned, while he lived, no matter where, she would toil so. Though all the world should forget him she would not. But supposing, after all, she never saw him more. What should she do? What should she do? And yet, she did not know yet that she loved him.

They walked along, side by side, close together, through the dull weary streets, by barrack-rows of houses wrapped in slumber or showing an occasional light; through thoroughfares which the windows of the shops that thrive, owl-like, at night still made brilliant; down the long avenue of trim-clipped trees where under time-defying lovers still sat whispering;

past the long garden wall, startling as they crossed the road a troop of horses browsing for fallen figs; along the path that winds, water-lapped, under the hollowed rocks that shelter nightly forlorn outcasts of Sydney. She saw it all as they passed along and she did not see it. Afterwards she could recall every step they took, every figure they passed, every tree and seat and window and lamp-post on the way.

At one corner a group of men wrangled drunkenly outside a public-house. Down one deserted street another drunkard staggered, cursing with awful curses a slipshod woman who kept pace with him on the pavement and answered him with nerveless jeers. Just beyond a man overtook them, walking swiftly, his tread echoing as he went; he turned and looked at her as he passed; he had a short board and wore a 'hard hitter.' Then there was a girl plying her sorry trade, talking in the shadow with a young man, spruce and white-shirted. They had to wait at one street for a tram to rush past screeching and rattling. At one crossing Ned had seized her arm because a cab was coming carelessly. One of the lovers in the avenue was tracing lines on the ground with a stick, while her sweetheart leaned over her. Down under the rocks she saw the forms of sleepers here and there; from one clump of bushes came a sound of heavy snoring. She saw all this, everything, a thousand incidents, but she did not heed them. She was as one in a daze; or as one who moves and thinks and sees, sleep-walking.

So they reached the point by Lady Macquarie's Chair, paused for a moment at the turn, hesitated, then together, as of one accord, went down the grassy slope by the landing stairs and out upon the rough wave-eaten fringe of rock to the water's edge. They were alone together, alone in Paradise. There were none others in the whole world.

Above them, almost overhead, in the starry sky, the full round moon was sailing, her white glare failing upon a matchless scene of mingling land and water, sea and shore and sky. Like a lake the glorious harbour stretched before them and on either hand. In its bosom the moon sailed as in a mirror; on it great ships floated at anchor and islets nestled down; all round the sheltering hills verily clapped their hands. In the great dome of the universe there was not a cloud. Through the starless windows of that glorious dome they could see into the fathomless depths of Eternity. Under the magic of the moon not even the sordid work of man struck a discordant note. At their feet the faint ripplings of this crystal lake whispered their ceaseless lullaby and close behind them the trees rustled softly in the languid breathings of the sleeping sea. Of a truth it was Paradise, fit above all fitness to gladden the hearts of men, worthy to fill the soul to overflowing with the ecstasy of living, deserving to be enshrined as a temple of the Beautiful wherein all might worship together, each his own God.

The keen sense of its loveliness, its perfect beauty, its sublime simplicity, stole over Nellie as she stood silently by Ned's side in the full moonlight and gazed. Over her angry soul, tortured by the love she hardly knew, its pure languor crept, soothing, softening. She looked up at the silvery disc and involuntarily held out her hands to it, its radiance overpowering her. She wrenched her eyes away from it suddenly, a strange fearfulness leaping in her who knew no fear; the light at the South Heads flashed before her, the convent stood out in the far distance, a ferry-house shone white, the towers and roofs of Sydney showed against the sky, the lights on the shipping and on the further shore were as reflections of the stars above. And there in the water, as in a mirror, was that glowing moon. Startled, she found herself thinking that it would be heavenly to take Ned's hand and plunge underneath this crystal sheet that alone separated them from peace and happiness. She looked up again. There was the moon itself, swimming amid the twinkling stars, full and round and white and radiant. As its rays enwrapped her eyes, she heard the leaves rustling in melody and the wavelets rippling in tune.

All Nature lived to her then. There was life in the very rocks under her feet, language in the very shimmer of the waters, a music, as the ancients dreamed in the glittering spheres that circled there in space. The moon had something to say to her, something to tell her, something she longed to hear and shrank from hearing. She knew she was not herself somehow, not her old self, that it was as though she were being bewitched, mesmerised, drawn out of herself by some strange influence, sweet though fearful. Suddenly a distant clock struck and recalled her wandering thoughts.

'Half-past! Half-past eleven I suppose! I thought it was later, ever so much later. It has seemed like hours, it is so beautiful here, but we haven't been here many minutes,' she said. Adding incongruously: 'Let's go. It's getting very late.' She spoke decidedly. She felt that she dare not stay; why, she had not the least idea.

Then she heard Ned, who was standing there, rigid, except that he was twirling his soft straw hat round and round in his fingers, say in a low tremulous husky whisper:

'Nellie!'

Then she knew.

She was loved and she loved. That was what the stars sang and the little ripples and the leaves. That was what the hard rock knew and what the shimmer of the water laughed to think of and what the glowing moon had to tell her as it swam high in heaven, looking down into her heart and swelling its tumultuous tide. The moon knew, the full moon that ever made her pulse beat strong and her young life throb till its throbbing was a pain, the full white moon that, dethroned on earth, still governs from the skies the lives of women. She was loved. She was loved. And she, who had vowed herself to die unmarried, she loved, loved, loved.

She knew that those only laugh at Love to whom the fullness of living has been denied, in whose cold veins, adulterate with inherited disease, a stagnant liquid mocks the purpose of the rich red blood of a healthy race; that in that laugh of theirs is the, knell of them and of their people; that the nation which has ceased to love has almost ceased to live.

She knew that every breath she had ever drawn had been drawn that she might live for this moment; that every inch of her stature and every ounce of her muscle and every thought of her brain had built up slowly, surely, ultimately, this all-absorbing passion; that upon her was the hand of the Infinite driving her of her own nature to form a link in the great Life-chain that stretches from the Whence into the Whither, to lose herself in the appointed lot as the coral insect does whose tiny body makes a continent possible.

She knew that Love is from the beginning and to all time, knew that it comes to each as each is, to the strong in strength and to the weak in weakness. She knew that to her it had come with all the force of her grand physique and vigorous brain and dominant emotionality, that in her heart one man, one hero, one lover, was enshrined and that to him she would be loyal and true for ever and ever, choosing death rather than to fail him.

She knew that they do rightly and for themselves well who in Love's strength brush aside all worldly barriers and insensate prejudice. She knew that it is the one great Democrat strong as Death—when it comes, though sad to say in decaying states it comes too seldom; that its imperious mandate makes the king no higher than the beggar-girl and binds in sweet equality the child of fortune and the man of toil. She knew that the mysterious Power which orders all things has not trusted to a frail support in resting the conservation of the race upon the strength of loving.

All this she knew and more, knew as by instinct as her love flamed conscious in her.

She knew that there was one thing to which love like hers could not link itself and that was to dishonour, not the false dishonour of conventionalism but the real dishonour of proving untrue to herself. She know that when she ceased to respect herself, when she shrank from herself, then she would shrink before him whom she loved and who loved her. She knew that she could better bear to lose him, to go lonely and solitary along the future years, than shame that self-consciousness which ever she had held sacred but which was doubly sacred now he loved her.

How she loved him! For his soul, for his body, for his brain, for his rough tenderness, for his fiery tongue! She loved his broad shoulders and his broad mind. She loved his hearty laugh and his hearty hand-grip and his homely speech and his red-hot enthusiasm. She loved him because she felt that he dared and because she felt that he loved her. She loved him because she had learned to see in him her ideal. She loved him because he was in danger for the Cause and because he was going from her and because she had loved him for years had she but known. She loved him for a thousand things. And yet! Something held her back. It only needed a word but the word did not come. It was on her lips a dozen times, that one word 'Ned!' which meant all words, and she did not say it.

They stood there side by side, motionless, silent, waiting, Ned suffering anguish unspeakable, Nellie plunged in that great joy which comes so seldom that some say it only comes to herald deeper sadness. To him the glorious scene around spoke nothing, he hardly saw it; to her it was enchanted with a strange enchantment, never had it seemed so, all the times she had seen it. How beautiful life was! How sweet to exist! How glad the world!

'Nellie!' said Ned, at last, humbly, penitently, hopelessly. 'I'm not a good man. I haven't been just what you think I've been.' He stopped, then added, slowly and desperately as if on an afterthought: 'If—your own heart—won't plead—for—me—it's not a bit of use my saying anything.'

When one speaks as one feels one generally speaks to the point and this sudden despairing cry of Ned's was a better plea than any he could by long thinking have constructed. Wonderful are the intricacies of a man's mind, but still more intricate the mind of woman. Nellie at the moment did not care whether he had been saint or sinner. She felt that her love was vast enough to, wash him clean of all offending and make amend in him for all shortcoming. She could not bear to see him in pain thus when she was so happy; in uncertainty, in despair, when the measure of her love was not to be taken, so huge was it and all for him. If he had sinned, and how men sin there is little hid from the working girl, it was not from evil heart. If he had not been good he would be good. He would promise her.

'But you will be good now, will you not, Ned?' she asked, softly, not looking at him, dropping her hand against his, stealing her slender fingers into the fingers that nervously twirled the hat.

From bitter despondency Ned's thoughts changed to ecstatic hope. He swung round, his hand in Nellie's, his brain in a whirl. Was it a dream or was she really standing there in the strong moonshine, her lovelit eyes looking into his for a moment before the down-cast lids veiled them, her face flushed, her bosom heaving, her hand tenderly pressing his? He dropped his hat, careless, of the watery risk, and seizing her by both arms above the elbows, held her for a moment in front of him, striving to collect himself, vainly trying to subdue the excitement that made him think he was going to faint.

'Nellie!' he whispered, passionately, his craving finding utterance. 'Kiss me!' She lifted up the flushed face, with the veiled downcast eyes and soft quivering lips. He passed his hands under her arms and bent down. Then a white mist came over his eyes as he crushed her to him and felt on his parched lips the burning kiss of the woman he loved. For a moment she rested there, in his arms, her mouth pressed to his. The rose, shattered, threw its petals as an offering upon the altar of their joy.

The Future, what did it matter to him? The scaffold or the gaol might come or go, what did it matter to him? It flashed through his mind that Nellie could be his wife before he went and then all the governments in the world and all the military and all the gatling guns might do their worst. They could not take from him a happiness he had not deserved, but which had come to him as a free gift in despite of his unworthiness. And as he thought this, Nellie shook herself out of his arms, pushing him so violently that he staggered and almost fell on the uneven rocks.

'I cannot,' she cried, holding up her arms as if to ward him off. 'I cannot, Ned. You mustn't touch me. I cannot.'

'Nellie!' he replied, bewildered. 'What on earth is the matter?'

'I cannot,' she cried again. 'Ned, you know I can't.'

'Can't what?' he asked, gradually understanding.

'I can't marry. I shall never marry. It's cruel to you, contemptible of me, to be here. I forgot myself, Ned. Come along! It's madness to stay here.'

She turned on her heel and walked off sharply, taking the upper path. He picked up his hat and hastily followed. There was nothing else to be done. Overtaking her, he strode along by her side in a fury of mingled rage, sorrow, anger and disappointment.

She paused at the corner of her street. As she did so bells far and near began to strike midnight, the clock at the City Hall leading off with its quarters. They had been gone an hour and a quarter. To both of them it seemed like a year.

CHAPTER IV
THE WHY OF THE WHIM

NELLIE stopped at the corner of her street, under the lamp-post. Ned stopped by her side, fuming by now, biting his moustache, hardly able to hold his tongue. Nellie looked at him a moment, sadly and sorrowfully. The look of determination that made her mouth appear somewhat cruel was on her whole face; but with it all she looked heart-broken.

'Ned,' she begged. 'Don't be angry with me. I can't. Indeed, I can't.'

'Why not?' he demanded, boiling over. 'If you wouldn't have had me at first I wouldn't have blamed you. But you say you love me, or as good as say, and then you fly off. Nellie! Nellie, darling! If you only knew how for years I've dreamed of you. When I rode the horse's hoofs kept saying "Nellie". I used to watch the stars and think them like your eyes, and the tall blue gum and think it wasn't as full of grace as you. Down by the water just now I thought you wouldn't have me because I wasn't fit, and I'm not, Nellie, I'm not, but when I thought it I felt like a lost soul. And then, when I thought you loved me in spite of all, everything seemed changed. I seemed to feel that I was a man again, a good man, fit to live, and all that squatter government of ours could do, the worst they could do, seemed a bit of a joke while you loved me. And—'

'Ned! Ned!' begged Nellie, who had put her hands over her face while he was speaking. 'Have pity on me! Can't you see? I'm not iron and I'm not ice but I can't do as others do. I cannot. I will not.'

'Why not?' he answered. 'I will speak, Nellie. Do you—'

'Ned!' she interrupted, evidently forcing herself to speak. 'It's no use. I'll tell you why it's not.'

'There can be no reason.'

'There is a reason. Nobody knows but me. When I have said I would never marry people think it is a whim. Perhaps it is, but I have a reason that I thought never to tell anyone. I only tell you so that you may understand and we may still be friends, true friends.'

'Go on! I'll convince you that it doesn't mean what you think it does, this reason, whatever it is.'

'Ned! Be reasonable!' She hesitated. She looked up and down the street. Nothing moved. The moon was directly overhead. There were no shadows. It was like day. An engine whistle sounded like a long wail in the distance. In the silence that followed they could hear the rushing of a train. Ned waited, watching her pain-drawn face. A passionate fear assailed him, blotting out his wrath.

'You recollect my sister?' she asked, looking away from him.

He nodded.

'You heard she died? You spoke of her two years ago.'

He nodded again.

'I did not tell you the whole truth then ... I did not tell anybody ... I came down here so as not to tell ... I could not bear to go home, to chance any of them coming down to Brisbane and seeing me ... You know.' She stopped. He could see her hands wringing, a hunted look in the eyes that would not meet his.

'Never mind telling me, Nellie,' he said, a great pity moving him. 'I'm a brute. I didn't mean to be selfish but I love you so. It shall be as you say. I don't want to know anything that pains you to tell.'

'That is your own self again, Ned,' she answered, looking at him, smiling sadly, a love in her face that struck him with a bitter joy. 'But you have a right. I must tell you for my own sake. Only, I can't begin.' Her mouth trembled. Great tears gathered in her eyes and rolled down her cheeks. A lump rose in his throat. He seized her hands and lifted them reverently to his lips. He could not think of a word to say to comfort her.

'Ned!' she said, in a tone almost inaudible, looking at him through her tears. 'She died in the hospital but I didn't tell you how ... She died, oh, a terrible death ... She had gone ... down, Ned. Right down. Down to the streets, Ned.'

He pressed her hands, speechless. They stood thus facing one another, till down his face, too, the sad tears rained in sympathy, sad tears that mourned without reproach the poor dead sister whom the hard world had crushed and scorned, sad tears that fell on his passion like rain on fire and left in him only a yearning desire to be a comforter. Nellie, snatching her hands away, pressed them to her mouth to stifle the frantic sobs that began to shake her, long awful sobs that drew breath whistling through clenched fingers. And Ned, drawing her to him, laid her head on his shoulder, stroking her hair as a mother does, kissing her temple with loving, passionless kisses, striving to comfort her with tender brotherly words, to still her wild cries and frantic sobs in all unselfishness. There were none to see them in all this moonlit city. The wearied toilers, packed around them, slumbered or tossed unconsciously. Above them, serene and radiant, the full moon swam on amid the stars.

'She was so good, Ned,' cried Nellie, choking, with sobs, almost inarticulate, pouring out to him the pent-up thinking of long years. 'She was so good. And so kind. Don't you remember her, Ned? Such a sweet girl, she was. It killed her, Ned. This cruel, cruel life killed her. But before it killed her—oh!—oh!—oh!—oh! Why are we ever born? Why are we ever born?'

It was heart-rending, her terrible grief, her abandonment of anguish which she vainly endeavoured to thrust back into her throat. With all her capacity for passionate love she bewailed her sister's fate. Ned, striving to soothe her, all the while mingled his tears with hers. A profound sadness overshadowed him. He felt all his hopes numbed and palsied in the face of this omnipotent despair. This girl who was dead seemed for the time the symbol of what Life is. He had hated Society, hated it, but as its blackest abyss opened at his very feet his hate passed from him. He only felt an utter pity for all things, a desire to weep over the helpless hopelessness of the world.

Nellie quieted at last. Her sobs ceased to shake her, her tears dried on her pale face, but still she rested her head on Ned as if finding strength and comfort in him. Her eyelids were closed except for an occasional belated lingering sob she might have been asleep. Her grief had exhausted her. At last a coming footfall roused her. She raised her head, putting her hands instinctively to her hat and hair, pulling herself together with a strong breath.

'You are very kind to me, Ned,' she said, softly. 'I've been so silly but I'm better now. I don't often carry on like that.' She smiled faintly. 'Let's walk a bit! I shall feel better and I have such a lot to tell you. Don't interrupt! I want you to know all about it, Ned.' And so, walking backwards and forwards in the moonlit streets, deserted and empty, passing an occasional night prowler, watched with suspicious eyes by energetic members of the 'foorce' whose beats they invaded, stopping at corners or by dead-walls, then moving slowly on again, she told him.

*   *   *

'You know how things were at home on the Darling Downs, Ned. Father a "cooky", going shearing to make both ends meet, and things always going wrong, what with the drought and the wet and having no money to do things right and the mortgage never being cleared off. It wasn't particularly good land, either, you know. The squatters had taken all that and left only stony ridges for folks like ours. And we were all girls, six of us. Your father was sold up, and he had you boys to help him. Well, my father wasn't sold up but he might as well have been. He worked like a horse and so did mother, what with the cows and the fowls and looking after things when father was away, and we girls did what we could from the time we were little chits. Father used to get up at daybreak and work away after dark always when he was at home. On Sunday mornings after he'd seen to the things he used to lie on his back under that tree in front if it was fine or about the house if it was wet, just dead beat. He used to put a handkerchief over his face but he didn't sleep much. He just rested. In the afternoon he used to have a smoke and a read. Poor father! He was always thought queer, you recollect, because he didn't care for newspapers except to see about farming in and took his reading out of books of poetry that nobody else cared about. On Monday he'd start to work again, with only a few hours for sleep and meals, till Saturday night. Yet we had only just a living. Everything else went in interest on the mortgage. Twelve per cent. Mother used to cry about it sometimes but it had to be paid somehow.

'When Mary was fifteen and I was thirteen, you remember, she went to Toowoomba, to an uncle of ours, mother's brother, who had four boys and no girls and didn't know what to put the boys to. Father and mother thought this a splendid chance for Mary to learn a trade, there were so many of us at home, you know, and so they took one of my cousins and uncle took Mary and she started to learn dressmaking. Uncle was a small contractor, who had a hard time of it, and his wife was a woman who'd got frozen about the heart, although she was as good as gold when it melted a little. She was always preaching about the need for working and saving and the folly of wasting money in drink and ribbons and everything but what was ugly. She said that there was little pleasure in the world for those who had to work, so the sooner we made up our minds to do without pleasure the better we'd get on. Mary lived with them a couple of years, coming home once in a while. Then she got the chance of a place where she'd get her board and half-a-crown a week. She couldn't bear aunt and so she took it and I went to live at uncle's and to learn dressmaking, too. That was six months after you went off, Ned. I wasn't quite fifteen and you were eighteen, past. Seven years ago. I was so sorry when you went away, Ned.

'Aunt wasn't pleasant to live with. I used to try to get on with her and I think she liked me in her way but she made me miserable with her perpetual lecturing about the sin of liking to look nice and the wickedness of laughing and the virtue of scraping every ha'penny. I used to help in the house, of course, when I came from work and I was always getting into trouble for reading books, that I borrowed, at odd minutes when aunt thought I ought to be knitting or darning or slaving away somehow at keeping uncomfortable. I used to tell Mary and Mary used to wish that I could come to work where she did. We used to see each other every dinner hour and in the evening she'd come round and on Sundays we used to go to church together. She was so kind to me, and loving, looking after me like a little mother. She used to buy little things for me out of her halfcrown and say that when she was older aunt shouldn't make me miserable. Besides aunt, I didn't like working in a close shop, shut up. I didn't seem to be able to take a good breath. I used to think as I sat, tacking stuff together or unpicking threads that seemed to be endless, how it was out in the bush and who was riding old Bluey to get the cows in now I was gone and whether the hens laid in the same places and if it was as still and fresh as it used to be when we washed our faces and hands under the old lean-to before breakfast. And Toowoomba is fresher than Sydney. I don't know what I'd have thought of Sydney then. I used to tell Mary everything and she used to cheer me up. Poor Mary!

'For a long while she had the idea of going to Brisbane to work. She said there were chances to make big wages there, because forewomen and draping hands were wanted more and girls who had anything in them had a better show than in a little place. I used to remind her that it was said there were lots too many girls in Brisbane and that unless you had friends there you couldn't earn your bread. But she used to say that one must live everywhere and that things couldn't be worse than they were in Toowoomba. You see she was anxious to be able to earn enough to help with the mortgage. Father had been taken sick shearing: and had to knock off and so didn't earn what he expected and that year they'd got deeper into debt and things looked worse than ever. One day he came into Toowoomba with his cart, looking ten years older. Next day, Mary told me she didn't care what happened, she was going to Brisbane to see if she couldn't earn some money or else they'd lose the selection and that she'd spoken for her place for me and I was to have it. She'd been saving up for a good while what she could by shillings and sixpences and pennies, doing sewing work for anybody who'd pay her anything in her own time. She said that when she'd got a fivepound-a-week place she'd come back for a visit and bring me a new dress, and mother and father and the others all sorts of things and pay the interest all herself and that I should have the next best place in the shop and come to live with her. We talked about going into business together and whether it wouldn't be better for father to throw up the selection after a while and live with us in Brisbane. Ah! What simple fools we were! If we had but known!

'So Mary went to Brisbane, with just a few shillings beside her ticket and hardly knowing a soul in the big town. I went to the station with her in the middle of the night. She was going by the night train because then she'd get to Brisbane in the morning and have the day in front of her and she had nowhere to go if she got in at night. I recollect thinking how sweetly pretty she looked as she sat in the carriage all alone.

'You remember her, Ned? Well, she got prettier and prettier as she grew older, not tall and big and strong-looking like me but smaller than I was even then and with a fresh round face that always smiled at you. She had small feet and hands and hair that curled naturally and her skin was dark, not fair like mine. People in Toowoomba used to turn and look at her when she went out and everybody liked her. She was so kind to everybody. And she was full of courage though she did cry a little when she kissed me good-bye, because I cried so. I could never have stopped crying had I but known how I should see her again.

'She wrote in two or three days to say that she had got a place, just enough to pay her board, and expected to get a better one soon. She was always expecting something better when she wrote and my aunt when I saw her wagged her head and said that rolling stones gathered no moss. The interest-day came round and father just managed to scrape the money together. They'd got so poor and downhearted that I used to cry at night thinking of them and I used to tell Mary when I wrote. I used to blame myself for it once but I don't now. We all get to believe at last in what must be will be, Ned. And then I had a letter from Mary telling me she had a much better place and in two or three weeks mother wrote such a proud pleased letter to say that Mary had sent them a five-pound note. And for about a year Mary sent them two or three pounds every month and at Christmas five pounds again. Then her letters stopped altogether, both to them and to me. To me she had kept writing always the same, kind and chatty and about herself. She told me she had to save and scrape a little but that she had hope some day to be able to get me down. I never dreamed it was not so, not even when the letters stopped, though afterwards, when I went through them, I saw that the handwriting, in the later ones, was shaky a little.

'We waited and waited to hear from her but no letter came to anybody. There was a girl I knew whose father had been working in Toowoomba and who was in the same shop for a little while and her father was going to Brisbane to a job and they were all going. He was a carpenter. She and I had got to be friendly after Mary went away and she promised to find her but couldn't. You see we were bush folks still and didn't think anything of streets and addresses and thought the post office enough. And when two months passed and no letter came mother wrote half crazy, and I didn't know what to do, and I wrote to the girl I knew to ask her to get me work so that I could go to look for Mary. It just happened that they wanted a body hand in her shop and they promised me the place and I went the next day I heard. They wanted a week's notice where I was working and didn't want to give up my things without but aunt went and got them and gave me the money for my fare and told me if I wanted to come back to write to her and she'd find the money again. Poor old aunt! I shall never forget her. Her heart was all right if she had got hard and unhappy. That's how I got to Brisbane to look for Mary.

'I went to board with the girl I knew. I was earning ten shillings a week and paid that for my board and helped with the ironing for my washing. Her father had got out of work again for times were bad and they were glad to get my money. Lizzie got ten shillings a week and she had a brother about fourteen who earned five shillings. That was about all they had to live on often, nine in the family with me and the rent seven shillings for a shell of a place that was standing close up against other humpies in a sort of yard. There were four little rooms unceiled and Lizzie and I slept together in a sort of shelf bedstead, with two little sisters sleeping on the floor beside us. When it was cold we used to take them in with us and heap their bedclothes on top of us. The wind came through the walls everywhere. Out in the bush one doesn't mind that but in town, where you're cooped up all day, it doesn't seem the same thing. We had plenty of bread and meat and tea generally but the children didn't seem to thrive and got so thin and pale-looking that I thought they were going to be ill. Lizzie's father used to come home, after tramping about for work, looking as tired as my father did after his long day in the fields and her mother fretted and worried and you could see things getting shabbier and shabbier every week. I don't know what I should have done only Lizzie and I now and then got a dress to make for a neighbour or some sewing to do, night-times. Lizzie's mother had a machine and we used that and they always made me keep my half of what we got that way, no matter how hard up they were. They never thought of asking for interest for the use of the machine. And all the while I was looking for Mary.

'I used to stand watching as the troops of girls went by to work and from work, morning and evening, going to a new place every day so that I shouldn't miss her and in the dinner hours I used to go round the work rooms to see if she worked in one of them or if anybody knew her. At first, when I had a shilling to spare, I put an advertisement that she would understand in the paper, but I gave that up soon. I never dreamed of going to the police station, any more than we had dreamed of it in Toowoomba. I just looked and looked but I couldn't find her.

'I shall never forget the first time I got out of work. One Saturday, without a minute's warning, a lot of us were told that we wouldn't be wanted for a week or two. Lizzie and I were both told. She could hardly keep herself from crying but I couldn't cry. I was too wretched. I thought of everything and there seemed nothing to do anywhere. At home they couldn't help me. I shrank from asking aunt, for she'd only offered to help me to come back and what could I do in Toowoomba if I got there? And how could I find Mary? I had only ten shillings in the world and I owed it all for my board. I got to imagining where I should sleep and how long I could go without dying of hunger and I hated so to go into the house with Lizzie to tell them. Lizzie's mother cried when she heard it and Lizzie cried, but I went into the bedroom when I'd put my money on the table and began to put my things in my box. They called me to dinner and when I didn't come and they found out that I meant to go because I couldn't pay any more they were so angry. Lizzie's mother wanted to know if they looked altogether like heathens and then we three cried like babies and I felt better. I used to cry a good deal in those days, I think.

'Lizzie's father got a job next week a few miles out of Brisbane and went away to it and on the Monday I answered an advertisement for a woman to do sewing in the house and was the first and got it. She was quite young, the woman I worked for, and very nice. She got talking to me and I told her how I'd got out of work and about Mary. I suppose she was Socialist for she talked of what I didn't understand much then, of how we ought to have a union to get wages enough to keep us when work fell off and of the absurdity of men and women having to depend for work upon a few employers who only worked them when they could get profit. She thought I should go to the police-station about Mary but I said Mary wouldn't like that. What was more to me at the time, she paid me four shillings a day and found me work for two weeks, though I don't think she wanted it. There are kind people in the world, Ned.

'I got back to regular work again, not in the same shop but in another, and then Lizzie's folks moved out to where her father was working. I and another girl got a room that we paid five shillings a week for, furnished, with the use of the kitchen. It cost us about ten shillings a week between us for food, and I got raised to twelve-and-six a week because they wanted me back where I'd worked before. So we weren't so badly off, and we kept a week ahead. Of course we lived anyhow, on dry bread and tea very often, with cakes now and then as a treat, boiled eggs sometimes and a chop. There was this about it, we felt free. Sometimes we got sewing to do at night from people we got to hear of. So we managed to get stuff for our dresses and we kept altering our hats and we used to fix our boots up with waxed threads. And all the time I kept looking for Mary and couldn't see her or hear of her.

'I had got to understand how Mary might live for years in a place like Brisbane without being known by more than a very few, but I puzzled more and more as to how she'd got the money she'd sent home. The places where she might have earned enough seemed so few that everybody knew of them. In all dressmaking places the general run of girls didn't earn enough to keep themselves decently unless they lived at home as most did. Even then they had a struggle to dress neatly and looked ill-fed, for, you see, it isn't only not getting enough it's not getting enough of the right food and getting it regularly. Most of the girls brought their lunch with them in a little paper parcel, bread and butter, and in some places they made tea. Some had lots of things to eat and lots to wear and plenty of pocket money and didn't seem to have to work but they weren't my sort or Mary's.

'What made me think first how things might be was seeing a girl in the second place I worked at. She looked so like Mary, young and fresh and pretty and lively, always joking and laughing. She was very shabby and made-over when I saw her first, with darned gloves and stitched-up boots down at heel and bits of ribbon that she kept changing to bring the best side up. Then she got a new dress all at once and new boots and gloves and hat and seemed to have money to spend and the girls began to pass remarks about her when she wasn't bearing and sometimes to her face when they had words with her. I didn't believe anything bad at first but I knew she wasn't getting any more pay and then, all at once, I recollected being behind her one night when we came out of the shop and seeing a young fellow waiting in a door-way near. He was a good-looking young fellow, well-dressed and well to do, and as she passed with some other girls he dropped his stick out in front of her and spoke to her. She laughed and ran back to the shop when we'd gone on a little further and spoke to him for a second or two as she passed him. It was after that she was well dressed and I saw her out with him once or twice and and—I began to think of Mary. You see, I knew how hard the life was and how wearying it is to have to slave and half-starve all the time, and then Mary wanted money so to send home to help them. And when the girls talked at work they spoke of lots of things we never heard of in the bush and gradually I got to know what made me sick at heart.

'I was nearly mad when I thought of that about Mary, my sister Mary who was so good and so kind. I hated myself for dreaming of such a thing but it grew and grew on me and at last I couldn't rest till I found out. I didn't think it was so but it began to seem just possible, a wild possibility that I must satisfy to myself, the more I couldn't find her. I somehow felt she was in Brisbane somewhere and I learnt how easily one slips down to the bottom when one starts slipping and has no friends. So I used to go on Queen Street at night and look for her there. But I never saw her. I wanted to ask about her but I couldn't bear to. I thought of asking the Salvation Army people but when I went one night I couldn't.

'At last one night when we'd been working late at the shop, till eleven, as we did very often in busy times without getting any overtime pay though they turned us off as they pleased when work got slack, I saw a girl coming that I thought I'd ask. She was painted up and powdered and had flaring clothes but she looked kind. It was a quiet street where I met her and before I had time to change my mind she got to me and I stopped and asked her. I told her I'd lost my sister and did she know anything of her. She didn't laugh at me or say anything rude but talked nice and said she didn't think so and I mustn't think about that but if I liked she'd find out. I told her the name but she said that wasn't any good because girls always changed their name and she looked like crying when she said this. I had a photograph of Mary's that I always carried with me to show anybody who might have seen her without knowing her and the girl said if I'd trust her with it for a week she'd find Mary if she was in Brisbane and meet me. So I lent it to her. And we were just talking a bit and she was telling me that she was from London and that when she was a little girl a great book-writer used to pat her on the head and call her a pretty little thing and give her pennies and how she'd run away from home with a young officer, who got into trouble afterwards and came out to Australia without her and how she came out to find him and would some day, when a policeman came along and asked us what we were doing. She said we weren't doing anything and that he'd better mind his business and he said he knew her and she'd better keep a civil tongue in her head. Then he wanted to know what my name was and where I lived and the girl told me not to tell him or he'd play a trick on me and I didn't. But I told him I worked at dressmaking and roomed with another girl and he gave a kind of laugh and said he thought so and that if I didn't give him my name and address I'd have to come along with him. I began to cry and the girl told him he ought to be ashamed of himself ruining a poor hard-working girl who was looking for her sister and he only laughed again and said he knew all about that. I don't know what would have happened only just then an oldish man came along, wearing spectacles and with a kind sharp face, who stopped and asked what was the matter. The policeman was very civil to him and seemed to know him and told him that I wouldn't give him my address and that I was no good and that he was only doing his duty. The girl called the policeman names and told how it really was, only not my name, and the man looked at me and told the policeman I was shabby enough to be honest and that he'd answer for me and the policeman touched his hat and said 'good-night, sir,' and went on. Then the man told me I'd had a narrow escape and that it should be a lesson to me to keep out of bad company and I told him the girl had told the truth and he laughed, but not like the policeman, and said that was all the more reason to be careful because policemen could do what they liked with dressmakers who had no friends. Then be pulled out some money and told me to be a good girl and offered it to me, so kindly, but of course I didn't take it. Then he shook hands and walked off. There are kind people in the world, Ned, but we don't always meet them when we need them. I didn't know then how much he did for me or what cruel, wicked laws there are.

'Next week I met the girl again. I wanted so to find Mary I didn't care for all the policemen. I knew when I saw her coming that she'd found her. I didn't seem to care much, only as though something had snapped. It was only afterwards, when Mary was dead, that I used to get nearly crazy. I never told anybody, not even my room-mate, that I'd found her.

'She was in the hospital, dying, Mary was. I've heard since how that awful life kills the tender-hearted ones soon and Mary wasn't twenty-one. She was in a bleak, bare ward, with a screen round her, and near by you could hear other girls laughing and shouting. You wouldn't have known her. Only her eyes were the same, such loving, tender eyes, when she opened them and saw me. She looked up and saw me standing there by the bedside and before she could shrink away I put my arms round her neck and kissed her forehead, where I used to kiss her, because I was the tallest, just where the hair grew. And I told her that she mustn't mind me and that she was my dear, dear sister and that she should have let me known because it had taken me so long to find her. And she didn't say anything but clung tight to me as though she would never let me go and then all at once her arms dropped and when I lifted my head she had fainted and her eyelids were wet.

'She died three days after. I made some excuse to get away and saw her every day. She hardly spoke she was so weak but she liked to lie with my hand in hers and me fanning her. She said that first day, when she came to, that she thought I would come. But she wouldn't have written or spoken a word, Mary wouldn't. She didn't even ask after the folks at home or how I was getting on. She said once she was so tired waiting and I knew she meant waiting to die. She didn't want to live. The last day she lay with her eyes half-closed, looking at me, and all at once her lips moved. I bent down to her and heard her murmur: 'I did try, Nellie, I did try,' and I saw she was crying. I put my arms round her and kissed her on the forehead and told her that I knew she had, and then she smiled at me, such a sweet pitiful smile, and then she stopped breathing. That was the only change.

'I couldn't stay in Brisbane. I was afraid every minute of meeting somebody who'd known Mary and who might ask me about her, or of father or uncle or somebody coming down. I wrote home and said I'd found out that Mary had died in the hospital of fever and they never thought of wanting to know any more, they were so full of grief. And then I got wondering how I should get away, somewhere, where nobody would be likely to come to ask me about her, and I couldn't go because I had no money and I was just wishing one day that I could see you when who should I meet but that Long Jack. He gave me your address and I wrote to ask you to lend me thirty shillings, the fare to Sydney, and you sent me five pounds, Ned. That's how I came here. Mary wouldn't have anybody know if she could help it and I couldn't have stayed there to meet people who knew her and would have talked of her.'

CHAPTER V

AS THE MOON WANED

THE shadows were beginning to throw again as Nellie finished telling her story. The quarters had sounded as they walked backwards and forwards. It was past one when they stopped again under the lamp-post at the corner.

'You see, Ned,' she went on. 'Mary couldn't help it. It's easy enough to talk when one has everything one wants or pretty well everything but when one has nothing or pretty well nothing, it's different. I've been through it and know. The insults, the temptations, the constant steady pressure all the time. If you are poor you are thought by swagger people fair game. And, even workingmen, the young ones, who don't think themselves able to marry generally, help hunt down their working sisters. Women can't always earn enough to live decently and men can't always earn enough to marry on; and when well-to-do men get married they seem to get worse instead of better, generally. So upon the hungry, the weary, the hopeless, girls who have to patch their own boots and go threadbare and shabby while others have pretty things, and who are despised for their shabbiness by the very hypocrites who cant about love of dress, and who have folks at home whom they love, and who are penniless as well and in that abject misery which comes when there isn't any money to buy the little things, upon these is forced the opportunity to change all this if only for a little while. Besides, you know, women have the same instincts as men—why do we disguise these things and pretend they haven't and shouldn't when we know that it is right and healthy that they should?—and though it is natural for a woman to hate what is called

vice, because she is better than man—she is the mother-sex, you know—
yet the very instincts which if things were right would be for good and
happiness seem to make things worse when everything is wrong. Women
who work, growing girls as many are, have little pleasure in their lives,
less even than men. And wiseacres say we are light and frivolous and
chattering, because most women can only find relief in that and know of
nothing else, though all the time in the bottom of their hearts there are
deep wells of human passion and human love. If you heard sewing-room
talk you would call us parrots or worse. If you knew the sewing-room
lives you would feel as I do.'

He did not know what to say.

'For myself,' straightening herself with unconscious pride, 'it has not been
so much. I have been hungry and almost ragged, here in Sydney, wearing
another girls dress when I went to get slop-work, so as to look decent,
living on rye bread for days at a time, working for thirty-eight hours at a
stretch once so as to get the work done in time to get the money. That's
sweating, isn't it? Of course I'm all right now. I get thirty shillings a week
for draping and the wife of the boss wants to keep on friendly terms with
Mrs. Stratton and I'm a good hand, so I can organise without being
victimised for it. But even when I was hardest up it wasn't the same to me
as to most girls. As a last resort I used to think always of killing myself.
That would have been ever so much easier to me than the other thing. But
I am hard and strong. I've heard my mother say that her father was the
first of his people to wear boots. They went barefooted before then and
I'm barefooted in some things yet. Mary wasn't like me, but better, not so
hard or so selfish. And so, she couldn't help it, any more than I can.'

'Nellie,' he said, speaking the thought he had been thinking for an hour.
'What difference does all this make between you and me?'

'Don't you understand?' she cried. 'When people marry they have
children. And when my sister Mary ended so, who is safe? Nothing we
can do, no care we can take, can secure a child against misery while the
world is what it is. I try to alter things for that. I would do anything,
everything, no matter what, to make things so that little children would

have a chance to be good and happy. Because the unions go that way I am unionist and because Socialism means that I am Socialist and I love whatever strikes at things that are and I hate everything that helps maintain them. And that is how we all really feel who feel at all, it is the mother in us, the source of everything that is good, and mothers do not mind much how their children are bettered so long as they are bettered. No matter what the bushmen do up there in Queensland, my heart is with them, so long as they shake this hateful state of things. I can't remember when everybody round weren't slaving away and no good coming of it. My father has only a mortgaged farm to show for a life of toil. My sister, my own sister, who grew up like a flower in the Queensland bush and worked her fingers to the bone and should have been to-day a happy woman with happy children on her knee, they picked her up when she lay dying in the gutter like a dog and in their charity gave her a bed to die on when they wouldn't give her decent wages to live on. Everywhere I've been it's the same story, men out of work, women out of work, children who should be at school the only ones who can always get work. Everywhere men crawling for a job, sinking their manhood for the chance of work, cringing and sneaking and throat-cutting, even in their unionism. In every town an army of women like my Mary, women like ourselves, going down, down, down. Honesty and virtue and courage getting uncommon. We're all getting to steal and plunder when we get a chance, the work people do it, the employers do it, the politicians do it. I know. We all do it. Women actually don't understand that they're selling themselves often even when a priest does patter a few clap-trap phrases over them. Oppression on every hand and we dare not destroy it. We haven't courage enough. And things will never be any better while Society is as it is. So I hate what Society is. Oh! I hate it so. If word or will of mind could sweep it away to leave us free to do what our inner hearts, crushed by this industrialism that we have, tell us to do it should go. For we've good in our hearts, most of us. We like to do what's kind, when we've a chance. I've found it so, anyway. Only we're caught in this whirl that crushes us all, the poor in body and the rich in soul. But till it goes, if it ever goes, I'll not be guilty of bringing a child into such a hell as this is now. That to me would be a cruelty that no weakness of mine, no human longing, could excuse ever. For no fault of her own Mary's life was a curse to her in the end. And so it may be with any of us. I'll not have the sin of giving life on me.'

They stood face to face looking into each other's eyes. Unflinchingly she offered up her own heart and his on the altar of her ideal.

He read on her set lips the unalterability of her determination. It was on his tongue to suggest that it was easy to compromise, but there was that about her which checked him. Above all things there was a naturalness about her, an absence of artificiality, the emanation of a strong and vigorous womanliness. The very freedom of her speech was purity itself. The dark places of life had been bared to her and she did not conceal the fact or minimise it but she spoke of it as something outside of herself, as not affecting her excepting that it roused in her an intense sympathy. She was indeed the barefooted woman in her conception of morality, in her frankness and in her strong emotions untainted by the gangrene of a rotting civilisation. To suggest to her that fruitless love, that barren marriage, which destroys the soul of France and is spreading through Australia, would be to speak a strange language to her. He could say nothing. He was seized with a desire to get away from her.

'Good-bye!' he said, holding out his hand. She took it in both her own.

'Ned!' she cried. 'We part friends, don't we? If there is a man in the world who could make me change my mind, it's you. Wherever you go I shall be thinking of you and all life through I shall be the same. You have only to let me know and there's nothing possible I wouldn't do for you gladly. We are friends, are we not? Mates? Brother and sister?'

Brother and sister! The spirit moved in Ned's hot heart at the words. Geisner's words came to him, nerving him.

'No!' he answered. 'Friends? Yes. Mates? Yes. Brother and sister? No, never. I don't feel able to talk now. You're like a thorn bush in front of me that it's no use rushing at. But I'm not satisfied. You're wrong somewhere and I'm right and the right thing is to love when Love comes even if we're to die next minute. I'm going away and I may come back and I mayn't but if I do you'll see my way. I shall think it out and show you. Why, Nellie, I'm a different man already since you kissed me. You and I together, why, we'd straighten things out if they were a thousand times as crooked. What couldn't we do, you and me? And we'll do it yet, Nellie. When I come back you'll have me and we two will give things such a shaking that they'll never be the same again after we've got through with them. Now, goodbye! I'll come back if it's years and years, and you'll wait for me, I know. Good-bye, till then.'

She felt her feet leave the ground as he lifted her to him in a hug that made her ribs ache for a week, felt his willing lips on her passive ones, felt his long moustache, his warm breath, his reviving passion. Then she found herself standing alone, quivering and pulsating, watching him as he walked away with the waddling walk of the horseman.

In her heart, madly beating, two intense feelings fought and struggled. The dominant thought of years, to end with herself the life that seems a curse and not a blessing, to be always maid, to die in the forlorn hope and to leave none to sorrow through having lived by her, was shaken to its base by a new-born furious desire to yield herself utterly. It came to her to run after Ned, to go with him, to Queensland, to the bush, to prison, to the gallows if need be. An insane craving for him raged within her as her memory renewed his kisses on her lips, his crushing arm-clasp, the strength that wooed with delicious bruisings, the strong personality that smote against her own until she longed to stay the smiting. It flashed through her mind that crowning joy of all joys would be to have his child in her arms, to rear a little agitator to carry on his father's fight when Ned himself was gone for ever.

Then—she stamped her foot in self-contempt and walked resolutely to her door. When she got up to her room she went to the open window and, kneeling down there, watched with tearless eyes the full white moon that began to descend towards the roofs amid the gleaming stars of the cloudless sky.

The hours passed and she still knelt watching, tearless and sleepless, mind and body numbed and enwrapped by dull gnawing pain.

*   *   *

Pain is to fight one's self and to subdue one's self. Nellie fought with herself and conquered. A paradox this seems but is not, for in truth each individual is more than one, far more. Every living human is a bundle of faggot faculties, in which bundle every faculty is not an inert faggot but a living, breathing, conscious serpent. The weakling is he in whose forceless nature one serpent after another writhes its head up, dominant for a moment only, doomed to be thrust down by another fancy as fickle. The strong man is he whose forceful nature casts itself to subdue its own shifting desires by raising one supreme above the others and holding it there by identifying the dearest aspirations with its supremacy. And we call that man god-like whose heart yearns towards one little ideal, struggling for existence amid the tumultuous passions that clash in him around it, threatening to stifle it, and whose personality drives him to pick this ideal out and to lift it up and to hold it supreme lifelong. He himself is its bitterest enemy, its most hateful foe, its would-be murderer. He himself shrinks from and cowers at and abhors the choking for its sake of faculties that draw titanic strength from the innermost fibres of his own being. Yet he himself shelters and defends and battles for this intruder on his peace, this source of endless pain and brain-rending sorrow. A strength arises within him that tramples the other strength underfoot; he celebrates his victory with sighs and tears. So the New rises and rules until the Old is shattered and broken and fights the New no more; so Brutality goes and so Humanity comes.

Nellie fought with herself kneeling there at her window, watching the declining moon, staring at it with set eyes, grimly willing herself not to think because to think was to surrender. Into heart and ear and brain the serpents hissed words of love and thoughts of unspeakable joy. Upon her lips they pressed again Ned's hot kisses. Around her waist they threw again the clasping of his straining arms. 'Why not? Why not?' they asked her. 'Why not? Why not?' they cried and shouted. 'Why not? Oh, why not?' they moaned to her. And she stared at the radiant moon and clenched her fingers on the window sill and would not answer. Only to her lips rose a prayer for death that she disowned unuttered. Had she fallen so low as to seek refuge in superstition, she thought, and from that moment she bore her agony in her own way.

It did pass through her mind that the ideal she had installed in her passionate heart did not aid her, that it had shrunk back out of sight and left her alone to fight for it against herself, left her alone to keep her life for it free from the dominance of these mad passions that had lifted their heads within her and that every nerve in her fought and bled for. She crushed this back also. She would not think. Only she would be loyal to her conception of Right even though the agony of her loyalty drove her mad.

She knew what Pain meant, now. She drank to the very dregs the cup of human misery. To have one's desires within one's reach, to have one's whole being driving one to stretch out one's hand and satisfy the eternal instincts within, and to force one's self to an abnegation that one's heart revolts from, that indeed was Pain to her. She learnt the weakness of all the philosophies as in a flash of lightning one sees clearly. She could have laughed at the sophism that one chooses always that which pleases one most. She knew that there are unfathomed depths in being which open beneath us in great crises and swallow up the foundations on which we builded and thought sure. She paralysed her passion intuitively, waiting, as one holds breath in the water when a broken wave surges over.

Gradually she forgot, an aching pain in her body lulling the aching pain of her mind. Gradually the white disc of the moon expanded before her and blotted out all active consciousness. Slowly the fierce serpents withdrew their hissing heads again. Slowly the ideal she had fought for lifted itself again within her. She began to feel more like her old self, only strangely exhausted and sorrowful. She was old, so old; weary, so weary. Hours went by. She passed into abstraction.

The falling of the moon behind the roofs roused her. She gazed at its disappearing rim in bewilderment, for the moment not realising. Then the sense of bodily pain dawned on her and assured her of the Reality.

She stood up, feeling stiff and bruised, her back aching, her head swimming, all her desiring ebbing as the moon waned. Already the glimmer of dawn paled the moonshine. She could hear the crowing of the cocks, the occasional rumble of a cart, the indescribable murmur that betokens an awakening city. The night bad gone at last and the daylight had come and she had worn herself out and conquered. She thought this without joy; it was her fate not her heart. Nature itself had come to her rescue, the very Nature she had resisted and denied.

She struck a light and looked into the glass, curious to know if she were the same still. Dark circles surrounded her eyes, her nose was pinched, her cheeks wan, on her forehead between the brows were distinct wrinkles, from the corners of the mouth were chiselled deeply the lines of pain. She was years older. Could it be possible that only five hours ago she had flung herself into a lover's arm by the moonlit water, a passionate girl, in womanhood's first bloom? She had cast those days behind her for ever, she thought; she would serve the Cause alone, henceforth, while she lived. Rest, eternal rest, must come at last; she could only hope that it would come soon. At least, if she lived without joy, she would die without self-reproach.

Exhausted, she sank to sleep almost as her head touched the pillow. And in her sleep she lived again that night at the Strattons with Ned and heard Geisner profess God and condemn her hatred of maternity. 'You close the gates of Life,' he said. Taking her hand he led her to where a great gate stood, of iron, brass bound, and there behind it a great flood of little children pressed and struggled, dashing and crashing till the great gates shook and tottered.

'They will break the gates open,' she cried to him in anguish.

'Did you deem to alter the unalterable?' he asked. And his voice was Ned's voice and turning round she saw it was Ned who held her hand. They stood by the harbour side again and she loved him. Again her whole being melted into his as he kissed her. Again they were alone in the Universe, conscious only of an ineffable joy.

*   *   *

'Time to get up, Nellie!' called Mrs. Phillips, who was knocking at the door. Nellie's working day began again.

CHAPTER VI
UNEMPLOYED

AFTER ten minutes' walking Ned reached a broad thoroughfare. Hesitating for a moment, to get his bearings, he saw across the way one of the cheap restaurants of which 'all meals sixpence' is the symbol and which one sees open until all sorts of hours. The window was still lighted, so Ned, parched with thirst, entered to get a cup of coffee. It was a clean-looking place, enough. He saw on the wall the legend 'Clean beds' as he gulped down his coffee thirstily from the saucer.

'Can you put me up to-night?' he asked, overpowered with a drowsiness that dulled even his thoughts about Nellie and unwilling to walk on to his hotel.

'Yes, sir,' answered the waiter, a young man who was making preparations to close for the night. 'In half a minute.'

Soon a cabman had finished his late midnight meal and departed. But another passer-by dropped in, who was left over a plate of stew while the waiter led Ned to a narrow stair at the end of the room, passing round a screen behind which a stout, gray-haired man slumbered in an arm chair with all the appearance of being the proprietor. The waiter showed Ned the way with a lighted match, renewed when burnt out. Ned noticed that the papered walls and partitions of the stairway and upper floor were dirty, torn and giving way in patches. From the first landing a dark narrow passage led towards the front street while three or four ricketty, cracked doors were crowded at the stairhead. Snoring sounds came from all quarters. The waiter turned up a still narrower twisting stairway. As they neared the top Ned could see a dim light coming through an open doorway.

The room to which he was thus introduced was some fifteen feet long and as many broad, on the floor. Two gabled windows, back and front, made with the centre line of the low-sloping ceiling a Greek cross effect. A single candle, burning on a backless chair by one of the windows, threw its flickering light on the choked room-full of old-fashioned iron bedsteads, bedded in make-shift manner, six in all, four packed against the wall opposite the door at which the stairs ended and one on each side of the window whereby was the light. On one of these latter beds a bearded man lay stretched, only partly undressed; on its edge sat a youth in his shirt. Although it was so late they were talking.

'Not gone to bed yet?' asked the waiter.

'Hullo, Jack!' replied the youth. 'Aren't you coming to bed yet?'

'A gentleman of Jack's profession,' said the bearded man, whose liquorous voice proclaimed how he had put in his evening, 'doesn't require to go to bed at all. 'Gad, that's very good. You understand me?' He referred his wit to the youth. He spoke with the drawling hesitation of the English 'swell.'

'I understand you,' replied the youth, in a respectful voice that had acquired its tone in the English shires.

'I don't get much chance whether I require it or not,' remarked Jack, with an American accentuation, proceeding to make up the other bed by the light. There was nothing on the grimy mattress but a grimy blanket, so he brought a couple of fairly clean sheets from a bed in the opposite corner and spread them dexterously.

'Have we the pleasure of more company, Jack?' enquired the broken-down swell. 'You understand me?'

'I understand you,' said the English lad.

'This gentleman's going to stay,' replied Jack, putting the sheet over the caseless pillow.

'Glad to make your acquaintance, sir,' said the swell to Ned, upon this introduction. 'We can't offer you a chair but you're welcome to a seat on the bed. If you can't offer a man wine give him whisky, and if you haven't got whisky offer him the best you've got.' This last to the youth. 'You understand me?'

'I understand you,' said the youth. 'I understand you perfectly.'

'Thanks,' replied Ned. 'But it won't hurt to stand for a minute. There ain't much room to stand though, is there?'

His head nearly touched the ceiling in the highest part; on either side it sloped sharply, the slope only broken by the window gables, the stair casement being carried into the very centre of the room to get height for the door. The plaster on the ceiling had come off in patches, as if cannon-balled by unwary heads, showing the lath, and was also splashed by the smoke-wreaths of carelessly held candles; the papering was half torn from the shaky plastering of the wall; the flooring was time-eaten. A general impression of uncleanness was everywhere. On a ricketty little table behind the candle was a tin basin and a cracked earthenware pitcher. Excepting a limited supply of bedroom ware, which was very strongly in evidence, there was no other furniture. Looking round, Ned saw that on the bed opposite the door, hidden in the shadows, a man lay groaning and moaning. Through the windows could be seen the glorious moonlight.

'No. A man wants to be careful here,' said the waiter, throwing the blanket over the sheets and straightening it in a whisk. 'There,' he went on, 'will that suit you?'

'Anything'll suit me,' said Ned, pulling off his coat and hanging it over the head of the postless bed. 'I'm much obliged.'

'That's all right,' replied Jack, cheerfully. 'I'll be up to bed soon,' he informed the others and ran down stairs again. 'Will you have a cigarette?' asked the English lad, holding out a box.

'Thanks, but I don't smoke,' answered Ned, who had pulled off his boots and was wrestling with his shirt. Finally it came over his head. He lay down in his underclothing, having first gingerly turned back the blanket to the foot.

'I don't desire to be personal,' said the broken-down swell. 'You'll excuse me, but I must say you're a finely built man. You understand me? No offence!'

'He is big,' chipped in the youth.

'You don't offend a man much by telling him he's well built,' retorted Ned, with an attempt at mirth.

'Certainly. You understand me. It's not the size, my boy'—to the youth. 'Size is nothing. It's the proportion, the capacity for putting out strength. I've been an athlete myself and I'm no chicken yet. But our friend here ought to be a Hercules. Will you take a drink? You'll excuse the glass.' He offered Ned a flask half full of whisky.

'Thanks just the same but I never drink,' answered Ned, stretching himself carelessly. The lad refused also.

'You're wise, both of you,' commented the other, swallowing down a couple of mouthfuls of the undiluted liquor. 'If I'd never touched it I should have been a wealthy man to-day. But I shall be a wealthy man yet. You understand me?'

'Yes,' answered Ned, mechanically. He was looking at the frank, open, intelligent face and well-made limbs of the half-naked lad opposite and wondering what he was doing here with this grizzled drunkard. The said grizzled drunkard being the broken-down swell, whose highly-coloured face, swollen nose and slobbery eyes told a tale that his slop-made clothes would have concealed. 'How old are you?' he asked the lad, the drunkard having fallen asleep in the middle of a discourse concerning a great invention which would bring him millions.

'I'm nineteen.'

'You look older,' remarked Ned. 'Most people think I'm older,' replied the lad proudly.

'You're not a native.'

'No. I'm from the west of England.'

'Which county?'

'Devon.'

'My father's Devon,' said Ned, at which the poor lad looked up eagerly, as though in Ned he recognised an old friend.

'That's strange, isn't it? How you meet people!' he remarked.

'I've never been there, you know,' explained Ned. 'Fact is I don't think it would be well for me to go. If all my old dad used to say is true I'd soon get shipped out.'

'How's that?'

'Why, they transport a man for shooting a rabbit or a hare, don't they? My dad told me a friend of his was sent out for catching salmon and that his mother was frightened nearly to death when she knew he'd been off fishing one night. Of course, they don't transport to here any more. We wouldn't have it. But they do it to somewhere still, I suppose.'

'I don't know, I'm sure,' answered the lad. 'I never heard much about that. I came out when I was fourteen.'

'How was that?'

'Well, there was nothing to do in England that had anything in it and everybody was saying what a grand country Australia was and how everybody could get on and so I came out.'

'Your folks come?'

'My father was dead. I only had a stepfather.'

'And he wanted to get rid of you, eh?' enquired Ned, getting interested.

'I suppose he did, a little,' said the lad, colouring.

'You came out to Sydney?'

'No. To Brisbane. That didn't cost anything.'

'You hadn't any friends?'

'No. I got into a billet near Stanthorpe, but when I wanted a raise they sacked me and got another boy. Then I came across to New South Wales.

It wasn't any use staying in Queensland. I wish I'd stayed in England,' he added.

'How's that?'

'I can't get work. I wouldn't mind if I could get a job but it's pretty hard when you can't.'

'Can't you get work?'

'I haven't done a stroke for ten weeks.'

'Well, are you hard up?' enquired Ned, to whose bush experience ten weeks out-of-work meant nothing.

'Look here,' returned the lad, touching the front of his white shirt and the cuffs. Ned saw that what he had taken for white flannel in the dim candle-light was white linen, guileless of starch, evidently washed in a hand-basin at night and left to dry over a chair till morning. 'A man's pretty hard up—ain't he?—when he can't get his shirt laundried.'

'That's bad,' said Ned, sympathetically, determining to sympathise a pound-note. Starched shirts did not count to him personally but he understood that the town and the bush were very different.

'I've offered three times to-day to work for my board,' said the lad, not tremulously but in the matter-of-fact voice of one who had looked after himself for years.

'Where was that?' asked Ned, wide-awake at last, alarmed for the bushmen rapidly turning over in his mind the effect of strong young men being ready to work for their board.

'One place was down near the foot of Market Street, a produce merchant. He told me he couldn't, that it was as much as he could do to provide for his own family. Another place was at a wood and coal yard and the boss said I'd leave in a week at that price so it wasn't any good talking. The other was a drayman who has a couple of drays and he said he'd never pay under the going wage to anybody and gave me sixpence. He said it was all he could afford because times were so bad.'

'Are you stumped then?' asked Ned.

'I haven't a copper.'

Just then the broken-down swell woke up from his doze and demanded his flask. After some search it was found underneath him. Then, heedless of his interruptions, Ned continued the conversation.

'Do they take you here on tick?' he enquired.

'Tick! There's no tick here. That old man downstairs is as hard as nails. Why, if it hadn't been for this gentleman I'd have had to walk about all night or sleep in the Domain.'

'Fair dues, my boy, fair dues?' put in the broken-down swell, 'Never refer to private matters like that. You make me feel ashamed, my boy. I should never have mentioned that little accommodation. You understand me?'

'I understand you,' replied the lad. 'I understand you perfectly.'

'That's all right,' said Ned, suddenly feeling a respect for this grizzled drunkard. 'We must all help one another. How was it?'

'Well,' said the lad. 'I met a friend of mine and he gave me sixpence and this box of cigarettes. It was all he had. I've often slept here and so I came and asked the old man to trust me the other half. He wouldn't listen to it. I was going away when this gentleman came along. He only had threepence more than his own bed-money but he persuaded the old man to knock off threepence and he'd pay threepence. I thought I'd have had to go to the Domain.'

'But that's nothing,' said Ned. 'I'd just as soon sleep out as sleep in.'

'I've never come down to sleeping out yet,' returned the lad, simply. 'Perhaps your being a native makes a difference.' Ned was confronted again with the fact that the bushman and the townsman view the same thing from opposite sides. To this lad, struggling to keep his head up, to lie down nightly in the Domain meant the surrender of all self-respecting decency.

'I shouldn't have brought up the subject. You understand me?' said the drunkard. 'But now it's mentioned I'll ask if you noticed how I talked over that old scoundrel downstairs. You understand me? Where's that flask? My God! I am feeling bad,' he continued, sitting up on the bed.

'You're drinking too much,' remarked Ned.

The man did not reply, but, with a groan, pushed the lad aside, sprang from the bed, and began to retch prodigiously into the wash basin, after which he announced himself better, lay down and took another drink. Meanwhile the man in the far corner tossed and groaned as if he were dying.

'Your friend's still worse,' said the lad.

'He's just out of the hospital. I told him he shouldn't mix his drinks so soon but he would have his own way. He'll be all right when he's slept it off. A man's a fool who gets drunk. You understand me?'

'I understand you,' said the lad. 'I never want to get drunk. All I want is work.'

'Why don't you go up to Queensland?' asked the man, to Ned's hardly suppressed indignation. 'The pastoralists would be glad to get a smart-looking lad like you. Good pay, all expenses paid, and a six months' agreement! I believe that's the terms. You understand me?'

'I understand you,' said the English lad. 'I understand you perfectly. But that's blacklegging and I'd sooner starve than blackleg. I ain't so hard up yet that I'll do either.'

'Put it there, mate,' cried Ned, stretching his hand out. 'You're a square little chap.' His heart rose again at this proof that the union spirit was spreading.

'You're a good boy,' said the drunkard, slapping his shoulder. 'I'm not a unionist and I'm against the unions. You understand me? I am a gentleman—poor drunken broken-down swell—and a gentleman must stick to his own Order just as you stick to your Order. I'd like to see the working classes kept in their places, but I despise a traitor, my boy. You understand me?'

'I understand you perfectly,' said the lad.

'Yet you'd work for your board?' said Ned, enquiringly.

'I suppose I shouldn't,' said the lad. 'But one must live. I wouldn't cut a man out of a job by going under him when he was sticking up for what's right but where nobody's sticking up what's the use of one kicking. That's how I look at it. Of course, a lot don't.'

'They'll get a lot to go then?'

'I think they'll get a lot. Some fellows are so low down they'll do anything and a lot more don't understand. I didn't use to understand.'

'Would you go up with them for the union?' asked Ned, after a pause.

'You mean to come out again?'

'Yes, and to get as many to come out as you can by explaining things. It may mean three months' gaol so you want to make up your mind well.'

'I wouldn't mind going to gaol for a thing like that. It's not being in gaol but what you're in for that counts, isn't it?'

So they talked while the two drunkards groaned and tossed, the stench of this travellers' bedroom growing every moment more unbearable. Finally the waiter returned.

'Not gone to bed yet,' he exclaimed. 'Phew! This is a beauty to-night, a pair of beauties. Ain't it a wonder their insides don't poison 'em?'

'I thought I'd never get to bed,' he went on, coming to light his pipe at the candle and then returning to the bed he had taken Ned's sheets from. 'First one joker in, then another, and the old man 'ud stay open all night for a tanner. Past two! Jolly nice hour for a chap that's to be up at six, ain't it?'

He pulled off his boots and vest and threw himself down on the bare mattress in his trousers. 'Ain't you fellows going to bed to-night?' he enquired.

'It's about a fair thing,' said Ned, feeling nervous and exhausted with lack of sleep. So the young fellow blew the candle out and went over to the bed adjoining Jack's. As he lay down Jack picked up a boot and tapped the wall alongside him gently. 'I think I hear her,' he remarked. In a few moments there was an answering tap.

'Who's that?' asked Ned.

'The slavey next door,' answered Jack, upon which an interchange of experience took place between Jack and the young fellow in which gable windows and park seats and various other stage-settings had prominent parts.

At last they all slept but Ned. Drowsy as he was he could not sleep. It was not that he thought much of Nellie, at least he did not feel that he was thinking of her. He only wanted to sleep and forget and he could not sleep. The moonshine came through the curtainless window and lit up the room with a strange mysterious light. The snoring breathing that filled the room mingled with other snoring sounds that seemed to come up the stairway and through the walls. The stench of the room stifled him. The drunkards who tossed there, groaning; this unemployed lad who lay with his white limbs kicked free and bathed in the moonlight; the tired waiter who lay motionless, still dressed; were there with him. The clock-bells struck the quarters, then the hour.

Three o'clock.

He had never felt so uncomfortable, he thought, so uneasy. He twisted and squirmed and rubbed himself. Suddenly a thought struck him. He leaned up on his elbow for a moment, peering with his eyes in the scanty light, feeling about with his hand, then leaped clean out of the bed. It swarmed with vermin.

Like most bushmen, Ned, who was sublimely tolerant of ants, lizards and the pests of the wilds generally, shivered at the very thought of the parasites of the towns. To strip himself was the work of an instant, to carefully re-dress by the candle-end he lighted took longer; then he stepped to the English lad's side and woke him.

'Hello?' said the lad, rubbing his eyes in sleepy astonishment. 'What's the matter?'

'I can't sleep with bugs crawling over me,' said Ned. 'I'm going to camp out in the park. Here's a "note" to help you along and here's the address to go to if you conclude to go up to Queensland for the union. I'll see about it first thing in the morning so he'll expect you. The 'note's' yours whether you go or not.'

'I'm ever so much obliged,' said the lad, taking the money and the slip of paper. 'I'll go and I'll be square. You needn't be afraid of me and I'll pay it back, too, some day. Do you know the way out?'

'I'll find it all right,' replied Ned.

'Oh! I'll go down with you or you'd never find it. It's through the back at night.' So the good-hearted young fellow pulled on his trousers and conducted Ned down the creaking, stairway, through the kitchen and the narrow back yard to the bolted door that led to the alley behind.

'Shall I see you again?' asked the lad. Somehow everybody who met Ned wanted to see more of him.

'My name's Hawkins,' replied Ned. 'Ned Hawkins. Ask anybody in the Queensland bush about me, if you get there.'

'I suppose you're one of the bushmen,' remarked the lad, pausing. 'If they're all as big as you it ought to be bad for the blacklegs.'

'Why, I'm a small man up on the Diamantina,' said Ned laughing. 'Which is the way to the park?'

'Turn to your right at the end of the alley, then turn to the left. It's only five minutes' walk.'

'Thanks. Good-bye!' said Ned.

'It's thank you. Good-bye!' said the lad.

They shook hands and parted. In a few minutes Ned was in the park. He stepped over a low railing, found a branching tree and decided to camp under it. He pulled his boots off and his coat, loosened his belt, put boots and coat under big head for a pillow, stretched out full length on the earth and in ten seconds was in a deep slumber.

He was roused a moment after, it seemed to him; in reality it was nearly six hours after—by kicks on the ribs. He turned over and opened his eyes. As he did so another kick made him stagger to his feet gasping with pain. A gorilla-faced constable greeted him with a savage grin.

'Phwat d'ye mane, ye blayguard, indaycently exposing yersilf in this parrt av th' doomane? Oi've as good a moind as iver a man had in the wurrld to run yez in. Can't ye find anither place to unthdress yersilf in, ye low vaygrant?'

Ned did not answer. He buttoned up the neck of his shirt, which had opened in the night, tightened his belt again, drew on his boots and thrust his arms into his coat. While he did so the constable continued his abuse, proud to show his authority in the presence of the crowd that passed in a continuous stream along the pathway that cut through the carefully tended flower-bedded lawn-like park. It was one of Ned's strong points that he could control his passionate temper. Much as he longed to thrash this insolent brute he restrained himself. He desired most of all to get back to Queensland and knew that as no magistrate would take his word against a 'constable's' as to provocation received, to retaliate now would keep him in Sydney for a month at least, perhaps six. But his patience almost gave way when the constable followed as he walked away, still abusing him.

'You'd better not go too far,' warned Ned, turning round.

It suddenly dawned upon the constable that this was not the ordinary 'drunk' and that it was as well to be satisfied with the exhibition of authority already made. Ned walked off unmolested, chewing the cud of his thoughts.

This sentence of Geisner's rang in his ears:

'The slaves who "move on" at the bidding of a policeman.'

CHAPTER VII
'THE WORLD WANTS MASTERS'

'IT can't do any good. We have made up our minds that the matter might just as well be fought out now, no matter what it costs. We've made all our arrangements. There is nothing to discuss. We are simply going to do business in our own way.'

'It can't do any harm. There is always something to be said on the other side and I always find workingmen fairly reasonable if they're met fairly. At any rate, you might as well see how they look at it. The labour agitation itself can't be stifled. The great point, as I regard it, is to make the immediate relations of Capital and Labour as peaceable as possible. The two parties don't see enough of each other.'

'I think we see a great deal too much of them. It's a pretty condition of things when we can't go on with our businesses without being interfered with by mobs of ignorant fools incited by loud-tongued agitators. The fools have got to be taught a lesson some day and we might as well teach it to them now.'

'You know I'm no advocate of Communism or Socialism or any such nonsense. I look at the matter solely from a business standpoint. I am a loser by disturbances in trade, so I try to prevent disturbances. I've always been able to prevent them in my own business and I think they can always be prevented.'

'Well, Melsom, you may be right when it's a question of wages, but this is a question of principle. We're willing to confer if they'll admit "freedom of contract". That's all there is to say about it.'

'But what is "freedom of contract"? Besides, if it is questioned, there can't be much harm in understanding why. For my part, I find it an interminable point of discussion when it is raised and one of the questions that settles itself easily when it isn't.'

'It is the key of the whole position. If we haven't a right to employ whoever we like at any terms we may make with any individual we employ what rights have we?' 'Hear what they think of it, Strong! It can surely do no harm to find out what makes them fight so.'

And so on for half an hour.

'Well, I don't mind having a chat with one of them,' conceded Strong at last. 'It's only because you persist so, Melsom. I suppose this man you've been told is in town is an oily, ignorant fellow, who'll split words and wrangle up a cloud of dust until nobody can tell what we're talking about. I've heard these fellows.'

Thus it was that Ned, calling at the Trades Hall, after having washed and breakfasted at his hotel and seen to various items of union business about town, was greeted with the information that Mr. Melsom was looking for him.

'Who's Melsom?'

'Oh! A sort of four-leaved clover, a reasonable employer,' answered his genial informant. 'He's in a large way of business, interested in a good many concerns, and whenever he's got a finger in anything we can always get on with it. He's a great man for arbitration and conciliation and has managed to settle two or three disputes that I never thought would be arranged peaceably. He's a thoroughly decent fellow, I can assure you.'

'What does he want with me, I wonder?'

'He wants you to see Strong, just to talk matters over and let Strong know how you Queenslanders look at things.'

'Who's Strong?'

'Don't you know? He's managing director of the Great Southern Mortgage Agency. He's the man who's running the whole show on the other side and a clever man, too, don't you forget it.'

Ned recollected the man he had seen at the restaurant and what Nellie had said of him, two years ago.

'But I can't see him without instructions. I must wire up to know what they say about it,' said Ned.

'That's just what you mustn't do, old man. Strong won't consent to any formal interview, but told Melsom, that he'd be glad to see anybody who knew how the other side saw things, to chat the matter over as between one man and another. I told Melsom yesterday that you were in town till to-night and he came this morning to get you to see Strong at eleven. He'll be back before then. I told him I thought it would be all right.'

'I don't see how I can do that without instructions,' repeated Ned.

'If it were formal there could be only one possible instruction, surely,' urged the other. 'As it is absolutely informal and as all that Melsom hopes is that it may lead to a formal conference, I think you should go. You'd talk to anybody, wouldn't you? Besides, Melsom has his heart set on this. I don't believe it will lead to anything, mind you, but it will oblige him and he often does a good turn for us.'

'That settles it,' said Ned. 'Only I'll have to say I'm only giving my own opinion and I'll have to talk straight whether he likes it or not.'

'Of course. By the way, here are some wires that'll interest you, and I want to arrange about sending money up in case they proclaim the unions illegal. Heaven knows what they can't do now-a-days! Have you heard what they did here during the maritime strike?'

*   *   *

Shortly before eleven, Strong was closeted in his private office with a burly man of unmistakably bush appearance, modified both in voice and dress by considerable contact with the towns. Of sandy complexion, broad features and light-coloured eyes that did not look one full in the face, the man was of the type that attracts upon casual acquaintance but about which there is an indefinable something which, without actually repelling, effectually prevents any implicit confidence.

'You have been an officer of the shearers' union, you say?' enquired Strong, coldly.

'I've been an honorary officer, never a paid one,' answered the man, who held his hat on his knee.

'There's a man in Sydney now, named Hawkins. Do you know him?'

'Yes. I've shorn with him out at the—'

'What sort of a man is he?' interrupted Strong.

'He's a young fellow. There's not much in him. He talks wild.'

'Has he got much influence?'

'Only with his own set. Most of the men only want a start to break away from fellows like Hawkins. I'm confident the new union I was talking of, admitting "freedom of contract", would break the other up and that Hawkins and the rest of them couldn't stop it.'

'It seems feasible,' said Strong, sharply. 'At any rate, there's nothing lost by trying it. This is what we will do. We will pay you all expenses and six pounds a week from to-day to go up to Queensland, publicly denounce the union, support "freedom of contract" and try to start another union against the present one; generally to act as an agent of ours. Payment will be made after you come out. Until then you must pay your own expenses.'

'I think I should have expenses advanced,' said the man.

'We know nothing of you. You represent yourself as so-and-so and if you are genuine there is no injustice done by our offer. You must take or leave it.'

'I'll take it,' said the man, after a slight hesitation.

'There's another matter. Do you know the union officials in Brisbane?'

'I know all of them, intimately.'

'Then you may be able to do something with them. We are informed that they are implicated in all that's going on, the instigators of it. Bring us evidence criminally implicating them and we will pay well.'

'This is business,' said the man, a little shamefacedly. 'What will you pay?'

Strong jotted some figures on a slip of paper. 'If you are a friend of these men,' he said, passing the slip over, 'you will know their value apiece to you.' A sneer he could not quite conceal peeped from under his business tone.

'That concludes our business, I think,' he continued, tearing the slip up, having received it back. 'I will instruct our secretary and you can call on him this afternoon.'

He touched an electric bell-button on his desk. A clerk appeared at the door instantly.

'Show this man out by the back way,' ordered Strong, glancing at the clock. 'Good-day!'

The summarily dismissed visitor had hardly gone when another clerk announced Mr. Melsom.

'Anybody with him?'

'Yes, sir. A tall, bush-looking man.'

'Show them both in.'

'What sneaking brutes these fellows are!' Strong thought, contemptuously, jotting instructions on some letters he was glancing through, working away as one accustomed to making the most of spare minutes.

* * *

Mr. Melsom had left Ned and Strong together, having to attend to his own business which had already been sufficiently interfered with by his exertions on behalf of his pet theory of 'getting things talked over.' Ned had felt inwardly agitated as he walked under the great archway and up the broad iron stairway that led to the inner offices of this great fortress-like building, the centre of the southern money-power. He had noted the massive walls of hewn stone, the massive gates and the enormous bolts, chains and bars. In the outer office he had glanced a little nervously around the lofty, stuccoed, hall-like room, of which the wood-work was as massive in its way as were the stone walls without and of which the very glass of the partitions looked put in to stay, while the counters and desks, with their polished brass-work and great leathern-bound ledgers, seemed as solid as the floor itself; he wondered curiously what all these clerks did who leaned engrossed over their desks or flitted noiselessly here and there on the matting-covered flagstones of the flooring. Why he should be nervous he could not have explained. But he was cool enough when, after a minute's delay, a clerk led Melsom and himself through a smaller archway opening from this great office hall and up a carpetted stone stairway loading between two great bare walls and along a long lofty passage, wherein footfalls echoed softly on the carpetted stone floor. Finally they reached a polished, pannelled door which being opened showed Strong writing busily at a cabinet desk placed in the centre of the handsomely furnished office-room. The great financier greeted Melsom cordially, nodded civilly enough to Ned and agreed with the latter's immediate statement that he came, as a private individual solely, to see a private individual, at the request of Mr. Melsom.

'Now, where do we differ?' Strong asked, when Melsom had gone.

'We are you and me, of course,' said Ned, putting his hat on the floor.

Strong nodded.

'Well, you have sat down at your desk here and drawn up a statement as to how I shall work without asking me. I object. I say that, as I'm concerned, you and I together should sit down and arrange how I shall work for you since I must work for you.'

'In our agreement, that you refer to, we have tried to do what is fair,' replied Strong, looking sharply at Ned.

'Do you want me to talk straight?' asked Ned. 'Because, if you object to that, it's better for me to go now than waste words talking round the subject.'

'Certainly,' answered Strong. 'Straight talk never offends me.'

'Then how do I know you have tried to do fairly?' enquired Ned. 'Our experience with the pastoralists leads us to think the opposite.'

'There have been rabid pastoralists,' admitted Strong, after a moment's thought, 'just as there have been rabid men on the other side. I'll tell you this, that we have had great difficulty in getting some of the pastoralists to accept this agreement. We had to put considerable pressure on them before they would moderate their position to what we consider fair.'

Ned did not reply. He stowed Strong's statement away for future use.

'Besides,' remarked Strong, after a pause, during which he arranged the letters before him. 'There is no compulsion to accept the agreement. If you don't like it don't work under it, but let those who want to accept it.'

'I fancy that's more how it stands than by being fair,' commented Ned, bitterly.

'Well! Isn't that fair?' asked Strong, leaning back in his office chair.

'Is it fair?' returned Ned.

'Well! Why not?'

'How can it be fair? We have nothing and you have everything. All the leases and all the sheep and all the cattle and all the improvements belong to you. We've got to work to live and we can't work except for you. What's the sense of your saying that if we don't like the agreement we needn't take it? We must either break the agreement or take it. That's how we stand.'

'Well, what do you object to in it?'

'I don't know what the others object to in it. I know what I object to.'

'That's what I want to know.'

'Well, for one thing, when I've earned money it's mine. The minute I've shorn a sheep the price of shearing it belongs to me and not to the squatter. It's convenient to agree only to draw pay at certain times, but it's barefaced to deliberately withhold my money weeks after I've earned it, and it's thieving to forfeit wages in case a squatter and I differ as to whether the agreement's been broken or not.'

'There ought to be some security that a pastoralist won't be put to loss by his men leaving him at a moment's notice,' asserted Strong.

'You've got the law on your side,' answered Ned. 'You can send a man to prison, like a thief, if he has a row with a squatter after signing an agreement, but we can't send the squatter to prison if he's in fault. The Masters and Servants Act is all wrong and we'll alter it when we get a chance, I can assure you, but you're not content with the Masters and Servants Act. You want a private law all in your own hand.'

'We've had a very serious difficulty to meet,' said the other. 'Men go on strike on frivolous pretext and we must protect our interests. We've not cut down wages and we don't intend to.'

'You have cut down wages, labourers' wages,' retorted Ned.

'That has been charged,' replied Strong, lifting his eyebrows. 'But I can show you the list of wages paid on our stations during the last five years and you will see that the wages we now offer are fully up to the average.'

'That may be,' said Ned. 'But they are less than they were last year. I'm speaking now of what I know.'

'Oh! There may be a few instances in which the unions forced up wages unduly which have been rectified,' said Mr. Strong. 'But the general rate has not been touched.'

'The pastoralists wouldn't dare arbitrate on that,' answered Ned. 'In January, 1890, they tried to force down wages and we levelled them up. Now, they are forcing them down again. At least it seems that way to me.'

'That matter might be settled, I think,' said Strong, dismissing it. 'What other objections have you to the agreement?'

234

'As an agreement I object to the whole thing, the way it's being worked. If it were a proposal I should want to know how about the Eight Hours and the Chinese.'

'We don't wish to alter existing hours,' answered Strong.

'Then why not put it down?'

'And we don't wish to encourage aliens.'

'A good many pastoralists do and we are determined to try to stop them. It looks queer to us that nothing is said about it.'

'Some certainly did urge that Chinese should be allowed in tropical Queensland but our influence is against that and we hope to restrain the more impetuous and thus prevent friction.'

Ned shrugged his shoulders without answering.

'We hope—' began Strong. Then he broke off, saying instead: 'I do not see why the men should regard the pastoralists as necessarily inimical and as not desirous of doing what is fair.'

'Look here, Mr. Strong,' said Ned leaning forward, as was his habit when in earnest. 'We are beginning to understand things. We know that you people are after profits and nothing else, that to you we are like so many horses or sheep, only not so valuable because we're harder to break in and our carcasses aren't worth anything. We know that you don't care a curse whether we live or die and that you'd fill the bush with Chinese to-morrow if you could see your way to making an extra one per cent. by it.'

'You haven't much confidence in us, at any rate,' returned Strong, coolly. 'But if we look carefully after profits you must recollect that a great deal of capital is trust funds. The widow and the orphan invest their little fortunes in our hands. Surely you wouldn't injure them?'

'I thought we were talking straight to one another,' said Ned. 'You will excuse me, Mr. Strong, for thinking that to talk "widow and orphan" isn't worthy of a man like you unless you've got a very small opinion of me. When you think about our widows and orphans we'll think about your widows and orphans. That's only clap-trap. It doesn't alter the hard fact that you're only after profit and don't care what happens to us so long as you get it.'

The financier bit his lips, flushing. He took up a letter and glanced over it before replying.

'Do you care what happens to us?'

'As things are, no. How can we? The worst that could happen to one of you would leave you as well off as the most fortunate of us. There is war between us, only I think it possible to be a little civilised and not to fight each other like savages as we are doing.'

'I am glad you admit that some of your methods are savage.'

'Of course I admit it,' answered Ned. 'That is my opinion of the way both sides fight now. Instead of conferring and arbitrating on immediate questions and leaving future questions to be talked over and understood and thoroughly threshed out in free discussion, we strike, you lockout, you victimise wholesale and, naturally, we retaliate in our own ways.'

'You prefer to be left uninterrupted to preach this new socialistic nonsense?'

'Why not, if it is sound? And if it isn't sound, why not? Surely your side isn't afraid of discussion if it knows it's right.'

'Do you really think that we should leave our individual rights to be decided upon by an ignorant mob?'

'My individual rights are at the mercy of ignorant individuals at present,' said Ned. 'I am not allowed to work if I happen to have given offence to a handful of squatters.'

'I think you exaggerate,' answered Strong. 'I know that some pastoralists are very vindictive but I regard most of them as honourable men incapable of a contemptible action.'

'Of course they are,' said Ned. 'The only thing is what do they call contemptible? You and I are very friendly, just now, Mr. Strong. You're not small enough to feel any hatred just because I talk a bit straight but you know very well that you'd regard it as quite square to freeze me out because I do talk straight.'

The two men looked into each other's eyes. Strong began to respect this outspoken bushman.

'I think that one of the most fundamental of all rights in any civilised society is the right of a man to employ whom he likes at any terms and under any conditions that he can get men to enter his employment. It seems to me that without this right the very right to private property itself is disputed for in civilisation private property does not mean only a hoard, stored up for future use, but savings accumulated to carry on the industrial operations of civilisation. These savings have been prompted by the assurance that society will protect the man who saves in making, with the man who has not saved, the contracts necessary to carry on industry, unhampered by the interference of outsiders. That seems to me, I repeat, a fundamental right essential to the very existence of society. The man who disputes it seems to me an enemy of society. Whether he is right or wrong, or whether society itself is right or wrong, is another question with which, as it is a mere theory, practical men have nothing to do.' Strong had only been fencing in his talk before. Now that he was ready he stated his position, quite coolly, with a quiet emphasis that made his line of argument clear as day.

'Then why confer at all, under any conditions, oven if unionists admitted all this?' asked Ned.

'Simply for convenience. Some of our members object to any conference but the general opinion is that it does not involve a sacrifice of principle to discuss details provided principles are admitted. In the same way, some favoured the employment of men at any wage arranged between the individual man and his employer, but the general opinion was that it is advisable and convenient for pastoralists in the same district to pay the same wages.'

'Then the pastoralists may combine but the bushmen mayn't.'

'We don't object to the bushmen forming unions. We claim the right to employ men without asking whether they are unionist or non-unionist.'

'Which means,' said Ned, 'the right to victimise unionists.'

'How is that?' asked Strong.

'We know how. Do you suppose for a moment, Mr. Strong, that ideas spring up with nothing behind them? All those who are acquainted with the history of unionism know that "close unionism", the refusal to work with non-unionists, arose from the persistent preference given by employers to non-unionists, which was a victimising of unionists.'

'That may have been once, but things are different now,' answered Strong.

'They are not different now. Wherever employers have an opportunity they have a tendency to weed out unionists. I could give you scores of instances of it being done. The black list is bad enough now. It would be a regular terrorism if there was nothing to restrain the employer. Then down would come wages, up would go hours and in would come the Chinese. If it is a principle with you, it is existence itself with us.'

'I think the pastoralists would agree not to victimise, as you call it,' said Strong, after thinking a minute.

'Who is to say? How are we to know?' answered Ned. 'Supposing, Mr. Strong, you and I had a dispute in which we both believed ourselves right would you regard it as a fair settlement to submit the whole thing, without any exception, to an arbiter whom we both chose and both believed to be fair?'

'Certainly I should,' said Strong.

'The whole dispute, no matter what it was? You'd think it fair to leave it all to the arbiter?'

'Certainly.'

'Then why not leave "freedom of contract" to arbitration?' demanded Ned. 'You say you are right. We say we are right. We have offered to go to arbitration on the whole dispute, keeping nothing back. We have pledged ourselves to stand by the arbitration. Isn't that honest and fair? What could be fairer? It may be that we have taken a wrong method against victimising in close unionism. But it cannot be that we should not have some defence against victimising, and close unionism is the only defence we have as yet, that any union has had, anywhere, except in Sheffield and I don't suppose you want rattening to start here. Why not arbitrate?'

'It is a question of principle,' answered Strong, looking Ned in the face.

'That means you'll fight it out,' commented Ned, rising and picking up his hat. Then he put his foot on his chair and, leaning on his knee, thus expressed his inward thoughts: 'You can fight if you like but when it's all over you'll remember what I say and know it's the straight wire. You've been swallowing the fairy tales about ours being a union of pressed men but you will see your mistake, believe me. You may whip us; you've got the Government and the police and the P.M.'s and the money and the military but how much nearer the end will you be when you have whipped us? You'll know by then that the chaps up North, like men everywhere else, will go down fighting and will come up smiling to fight again when you begin to take it out of them because they're down. And in the end you'll arbitrate. You'll have no way out of it. Its fair and because it's fair and because we all know it's fair we'll win that or—' Ned paused.

'I'm sorry you look at the matter so,' said Strong, arranging his papers.

'How else should we look at it? If we pretend to give in as you want us to do, it'll only be as a trick to gain time, as a ruse to put you off until we're readier. We won't do that. For my part, and for the part of the men I know, the union is a thing which mustn't get a bad name. We may lie individually but the union's word must be as good as gold no matter what it says. If the union says the sheep are wet, they're wet, and if it says they're dry, they are dry—if the water's dripping off 'em,' added Ned, with a twinkle in his eye. 'I mean, Mr. Strong, that we're trying to be better men in our rough way and the union is what's making us better and some of us would die for it. But we'd sooner see it die than see it do what's cowardly.'

'I am sorry that men like you are so deceived as to what is right,' said Strong.

'Perhaps we're all deceived. Perhaps you're deceived. Perhaps the whole of life is a humbug.' So Ned said, with careless fatalism. 'Only, if your mates were in trouble you'd be a cur if you didn't stand by them, wouldn't you? That's the difference between you and me, Mr. Strong. You don't believe that we're all mates or that the crowd has any particular troubles and I do. And as long as one believes it, well, it doesn't matter to him whether he's deceived or not, I think. I won't detain you any longer. Its no use our talking, I can see.'

Strong got up and walked towards the door.

'I think not,' he said. 'But I am glad to have met you, Mr. Hawkins, and I can't help feeling that you're throwing great abilities away. You'll get no thanks and do no good and you'll live to regret it. It's all very well to talk lightly of the outlook in Queensland but when you have become implicated in lawlessness and are suffering for it the whole affair will look different. Don't misunderstand me! You are a young man, capable, earnest. There is no position you might not aspire to. Be warned in time. Let me help you. I shall be only too glad. You will never repent it for I ask nothing dishonourable.'

'I don't quite understand,' said Ned, sternly, his brow knitting.

'I'm not offering a bribe,' continued Strong, meeting Ned's gaze unflinchingly. 'That's not necessary. You know very well that you will hang yourself with very little more rope. I am talking as between one man and another. I meet only too few manly men to let one go to destruction without trying to save him. The world doesn't need saviours; it needs masters. You can be one of them. Think well of it: Not one in a million has the chance.'

'You mean that you'll help me to get rich?'

'Rich!' sneered Strong. 'What is rich? It is Power that is worth having and to have power one must control capital. In your wildest ranting of the power of the capitalist you have hardly touched the fringe of the power he has. Only there are very few who are able to use it. I offer you the opportunity to become one of the few. I never make a mistake in men. If you try you can be. There is the offer, take it or leave it.'

For an instant Ned dreamed of accepting it, of throwing over everything to become a great capitalist, as Strong said so confidently he could be, and then, after long years, to pour his wealth into the treasuries of the movement, now often checked for lack of funds. Then he thought of Nellie and of Geisner, what they would say, still hesitating. Then he thought of his mates expecting him, waiting for him, and he decided.

'I was thinking,' he said, straightforwardly, 'whether I wouldn't like to make a pile so as to give it to the movement. But, you see, Mr. Strong, the chaps are expecting me and that settles it. I am much obliged but it would be dishonourable in me.'

'You know what is in front?' asked Strong, calmly, making a last effort.

'I think so. I'm told I'm one of those to be locked up. What does that matter? That won't lose me any friends.'

'A stubborn man will have his way,' remarked Strong. Adding, at a venture: 'Particularly when there is a woman in it.'

'There is a woman in it,' answered Ned, flushing a little; 'a woman who won't have me.'

Strong opened the door. 'I've done my best for you,' he said. 'Don't blame me whatever happens. You, at least, had your choice of peace or war, of more than peace.'

'I understand. Personally, I shan't blame you,' said Ned. 'I choose war, more than war,' and he set his mouth doggedly.

'War, at any rate,' answered Strong, holding out his hand, his face as grave as Ned's. The two men gripped hands tightly, like duellists crossing swords. Without another word they shook hands heartily and separated.

Strong closed the door and walked up and down his room, hurriedly, deep in thought, pulling his lip. He sat down at his desk, took up his pen, got up and paced the room again. He went to the window and looked out into the well that admitted light to the centre of the great fortress-building. Then walked back to his desk and wrote.

'He is a dangerous man,' he murmured, as if excusing himself. 'He is a most dangerous man.'

A youth answered a touch of the button. Strong sent for his confidential clerk.

'Send this at once to Queensland in cipher,' he instructed, in a business tone, when the man appeared; 'this' being:

> *Prominent bush unionist named Hawkins leaves Sydney to-night by train for Central Queensland via Brisbane. Have him arrested immediately. Most important.*

CHAPTER VIII
THE REPUBLICAN KISS

'I'VE never felt so before,' said Ned. 'For about ten minutes I wanted to go back and kill him.'

'Why?'

'Because he is like a wall of iron in front of one. If he were a fat hulking brute, as some of them are, I wouldn't have minded. I could have pitied him and felt that he wasn't a fair specimen of Humanity. But this man is a fair specimen in a way. He looks like a man and he talks like a man and you feel him a man, only he's absolutely unable to understand that the crowd are the same flesh and blood as he is and you know that he'd wipe us down like ninepins if he could see he'd gain by it. He's all brains and any heart he's got is only for his own friends. He is Capitalism personified. He made me feel sick at heart at the hopelessness of fighting such men in the old ways. I felt for a little while that the only thing to do was to clear them out of the way as they'd clear us if they were in our shoes.'

'You've got over it soon.'

'Of course,' admitted Ned, with a laugh. 'He can live for ever, for me, now. It was a fool's thought. It's the system we're fighting, not the products of it, and he's only a product just like the fat beasts we abuse and the ignorant drunken bushmen he despises. I was worrying, as you call it, or I shouldn't have even thought of it.'

Ned was talking to Connie. After having had dinner at a restaurant with his Trades Hall friend, to whom he related part of his morning's interview, he had found himself with two or three hours on his hands. So he had turned his steps towards the Strattons, longing for sympathy and comfort, being strangely depressed and miserable without being able to think out just how he felt.

He found Mrs. Stratton writing in her snug parlour. The rooms had the same general appearance that they had two years before. The house, seen by daylight for the first time, was embowered in trees and fringed back and front with pretty flower beds and miniature lawns. Connie herself was fair and fresh as ever and wore a loose robe of daintily flowered stuff; the years had passed lightly over her, adding to rather than detracting from the charms of her presence. She welcomed him warmly and with her inimitable tact, seeing his trouble, told him how they all were, including that Josie had married and had a beautiful baby, adding with a flush that she herself had set Josie a bad example and bringing in the example for Ned to admire. The other children were boating with George and Josie, she explained, George not having yet escaped from that horrible night-work.

Harry was well and would be home after a while. He was painting a series of scenes from city life, the sketches of which she showed him. Arty was married to a very nice girl, who knew all his poetry, every line, by heart. Ford was well, only more bitter than ever. When Ned asked after Geisner, she said he had not been back since and she had only heard once, indirectly, that he was well. Thus she led him to talk and he told her partly what took place between Strong and himself. Strong's offer he could not tell to anyone.

'You didn't get on with Nellie last night?' she asked, alluding to his 'worrying.' Having taken the baby out she had sat down on the stool by the open piano.

Ned looked up. 'How do you know? Has she been here?'

'No. She hasn't been here, but I can tell. You men always carry your hearts on your sleeve, when you think you aren't. You asked her to marry you, I suppose, and she said "No". Isn't that it?'

'I can't tell you all about it, Mrs. Stratton,' answered Ned, frankly. 'That's about it. But she did quite right. She thought she shouldn't and when Nellie thinks anything she tries to do it. That's what should be.'

Mrs. Stratton strummed a few notes. 'I'll show you something,' she said, finally, getting up. 'It passes the time to show old curiosities.'

She left the room, returning in a few minutes with a quaint box of dark wood, bound with chased iron work and inlaid with some semi-transparent substance in the pattern of a coat-of-arms. She opened it with a little key that hung on her watch chain. Inside were a number of compartments, covered with little lids. She lifted them all, together, exposing under the tray a deeper recess. From this she took a miniature case.

'Look at it!' she said, smiling. 'I ought to charge you sixpence but I won't.'

Ned pressed the spring, the lid of the case flew up, and there, in water-colour, was the head and bust of a girl. The face was a delicate oval, the mouth soft and sweet, the eyes bright with youth and health, the whole appearance telling of winning grace and cultured beauty. The fullness of the brows betrayed the artist instinct. The hair was drawn to the top of the head in a strange foreign fashion. The softly curving lines of face and figure showed womanhood begun.

'She is very beautiful,' commented Ned. Then, looking at it more closely: 'Do you know that somehow, although it's not like her, this reminds me of Nellie?'

'I knew you'd say that,' remarked Connie, swinging round on the music stool so as to reach the keys again and striking a note or two softly. 'It has got Nellie's presentment, whatever you call it. I noticed it the first time I saw Nellie. That was how we happened to speak first. Harry noticed it, too, without my having said a word to him. They might be sisters, only Nellie's naturally more self-reliant and determined and has had a hard life of it, while she'—nodding at the miniature—'had been nursed in rose-leaves up to the time it was taken.'

'I don't see just where the likeness comes in,' said Ned, trying to analyse the portrait.

'It's about the eyes and the mouth particularly, as well as a general similitude,' explained Connie.

'As I tell Nellie, she's got a vicious way of setting her lips, so,' and Mrs. Stratton, mimicking, drew the corners of her mouth down in Nellie's style. 'Then she draws her brows down till altogether she looks as though the burden of the whole world was on her. But underneath she has the same gentle mouth and open eyes and artist forehead as the picture and one feels it. It's very strange, don't you know, that Geisner never seemed to notice it and yet he generally notices everything. After all, I don't know that it is so strange. It's human nature.'

'Geisner?' said Ned, clumsily, having nothing particular to say. 'Has he seen it?'

'Once or twice,' observed Connie. 'It belongs to him. He leaves it with me. That's how Harry's seen it and you. It's the only thing he values so he takes care of it by never having it about him, you know,' she added, in the flippant way that hid her feelings.

'I suppose it is—that it's—it's the girl he—' stumbled Ned, beginning to understand suddenly.

'That's her,' said Connie, strumming some louder notes. 'She died. They had been married a few days. She was taken ill, very ill. He left her, when her life was despaired of. She would have him go, too. She got better a little but losing him killed her.'

Ned gazed at the portrait, speechless. What were his troubles, his grief, his sorrows, beside those of the man who had loved and lost so! Nellie at least lived. At least he had still the hope that in the years to come he and she might mate together. His thoughts flew back to Geisner's talk on Love on the garden terrace, in the bright afternoon sunshine. Truly Geisner's had been the Love that elevated not the Lust that pulled down. The example nerved him like fresh air. The pain that had dumbed his thoughts of Nellie passed from him.

'He is a man!' cried Ned.

'That wasn't all,' went on Connie, taking the case from his hands and officiously dusting it with her handkerchief. 'When she was pining for him, dying of grief, because she had lost her strength in her illness, they offered him his liberty if he would deny the Cause, if he would recant, if he would say he had been fooled and misled and desired to redeem his position. They let him hear all about her and then they tempted him. They wanted to disgust the people with their leaders. But it wasn't right to do that. It was shameful. It makes me wild to think of it yet. The way it was done! To torture a man so through his love! Oh, the wretches! The miserable dogs! I'd—' Connie broke off suddenly to put the handkerchief to her indignant eyes. The thunderstorm of her anger burst in rain. She was a thorough woman. 'I suppose they didn't know any better, as he always says of everybody that's mean. It's some consolation to think that they overshot the mark, though,' she concluded, tearfully.

'How?'

'How! Why if they had let Geisner go and everybody else, there'd be no martyrs to keep the Cause going. Even Geisner, if his wife had lived, poor girl, and if children had grown up, could hardly be quite the same, don't you know. As it is he only lives for the Cause. He has nothing else to live for. They crushed his weakness out of him and fitted him to turn round and crush them.'

'It's time he began,' remarked Ned, thoughtfully.

'He has begun.'

'Where?'

'Everywhere. In you, in me, in Nellie, in men like Ford and George and Harry, in places you never dream of, in ways nobody knows but himself. He is moulding the world as a potter moulds clay. It frightens me, sometimes. I open a new book and there are Geisner's very ideas. I see a picture, an illustrated paper, and there is Geisner's hand passed to another. I was at a new opera the other night and I could hardly believe my ears; it seemed as though Geisner was playing. From some out of the way corner of the earth comes news of a great strike; then, on top of it, from another corner, the bubbling of a gathering rising; and I can feel that Geisner is guiding countless millions to some unseen goal, safe in his work because none know him. He is a man! He seeks no reward, despises fame, instils no evil, claims no leadership. Only he burns his thoughts into men's hearts, the god-like thoughts that in his misery have come to him, and every true man who hears him from that moment has no way but Geisner's way. A word from him and the whole world would rock with Revolution. Only he does not say it. He thinks of the to-morrow. We all suffer, and he has passed through such suffering that he is branded with it, body and soul. But he has faced it and conquered it and he understands that we all must face it and conquer it before those who follow after us can be freed from it. "We must first show that Socialism is possible", he said to me two years ago. And I think he hoped, Ned, that some day you would show it.'

'You talk like Geisner,' said Ned, watching her animated face. He had come to her for comfort and upon his sad heart her words were like balm. Afterwards, they strengthened the life purpose that came to him.

'Of course. So do you when you think of him. So does everybody. His wonderful power all lies in his impressing his ideas on everybody he meets. Strong is a baby beside him when you consider the difference in their means.'

'I wish Strong was on our side, just the same.'

'Why? The Strongs find the flint on which the Geisners strike the steel. Do you think for a single moment that the average rich man has courage enough or brains enough to drive the people to despair as this Strong will do?'

'Yes, monopoly will either kill or cure.'

'It will cure. This Strong is annihilating the squatters as fast as he's trying to annihilate the unions. I hear them talking sometimes, or their wives, which is the same thing. They fairly hate him. He's doing more than any man to kill the old employer and to turn the owners of capital into mere idle butterflies, or, if you like it better, into swine wallowing in luxury, living on dividends. Not that they hate that,' went on Connie, contemptuously. 'They're an idle, vicious set, taken all round, at the best. But he's ruining a lot of the old landocrats and naturally they don't like it. Of course, very few of them like his style or his wife's.'

'Too quiet? Nellie was telling me something of him once.'

'Yes. He's very quiet at home. So is his wife. He reads considerably. She is musical. They have their own set, quite a pleasant one. And fashionable society can rave and splutter but is kept carefully outside their door. They don't razzle-dazzle, at any rate.'

'Don't what?' asked Ned, puzzled.

'Don't razzle-dazzle!' repeated Connie, laughing. 'Don't dance on champagne, like many of the society gems?'

'The men, you mean.'

'The men! My dear Ned, you ought to know a little more about high life and then you'd appreciate the Strongs. I've seen a dozen fashionable women, young and old, perfectly intoxicated at a single fashionable ball. As for the men, most of them haven't any higher idea of happiness than a drunken debauch. While as for fashionable morality the less you say about it the better. And the worst of the lot are among the canting ones. The Strongs and their set at least are decent people. Wealth and poverty both seem to degrade most of us.'

'Ah, well, it can't last so very much longer,' remarked Ned.

'It could if it weren't for the way both sides are being driven,' answered Connie. 'These fat wine-soaked capitalists would give in whenever the workmen showed a bold front if cast-iron capitalists like Strong didn't force them into the fight and keep them fighting. And you know yourself that while workmen get a little what they want they never dream of objecting to greater injustices. And if it weren't for the new ideas workmen would go on soaking themselves with drink and vice and become as unable to make a change as the depraved wealthy are to resist a change. Everything helps to make up the movement.'

'I know I'm inconsistent,' she went on. 'I talk angrily myself often but it's not right to feel hard against anybody. These other people can't help it, any more than a thief can help it or a poor girl on the streets. They're not happy as they might be, either. And if they were, I think it's better to suffer for the Cause than to have an easy time by opposing it. I'd sooner be Geisner than Strong.'

'What a comparison!' cried Ned.

'Of one thing I'm sure,' continued Connie, 'that it is noble to go to prison in resisting injustice, that suffering itself becomes a glory if one bears it bravely for others. For I have heard Geisner say, often, that when penalties cease to intimidate and when men generally rise superior to unjust laws those special injustices are as good as overthrown. We must all do our best to prevent anything being done which is unmanly in itself. If we try to do that prison is no disgrace and death itself isn't very terrible.'

'I know you mean this for me,' said Ned, smiling. 'I didn't mind much, you know, before. I was ready for the medicine. But, somehow, since I've been here, I've got to feel quite eager to be locked up. I shall be disappointed if it doesn't come off.' He laughed cheerfully.

'Well, you might as well take it that way,' laughed Connie. 'I can't bear people who take everything seriously.'

'There was one thing I wanted you to do,' said Ned, after a while. 'Nellie promised me years ago to tell me if ever she was hard up. I've got a few pounds ahead and what my horses are worth. If anything happens can I have it sent down to you so that you can give it to her if she needs it?'

Connie thought for a moment, 'You'd better not,' she answered. 'We'll see that Nellie's all right. I think she'd starve rather than touch what you'll need afterwards.'

'Perhaps so,' said Ned. 'You know best about that. I must go now,' rising.

'Can't you wait for dinner?' asked Counie. 'Harry will be here then and you'd have time to catch the train.'

'I've a little business to do before,' said Ned. 'I promised one of our fellows to see his brother, who lives near the station.'

'Oh! You must have something to eat first,' insisted Connie. 'You'll miss your dinner probably. That won't do.' So he waited.

They had finished the hurriedly prepared meal, which she ate with him so that he might feel at home, when Stratton came in.

'He's always just in time,' explained Connie, when the greetings were over. 'He gives me the cold shivers whenever we're going to catch a train. Say "good-bye" to Ned now, and don't delay him! I'll tell you all he said, all but the secrets. He's going to Queensland to-night and hasn't a minute to spare.'

'I'm sorry you can't stay overnight,' said Harry, heartily. 'I'd like to have a long talk but I suppose my fine society lady here hasn't wasted time.'

'I've talked enough for two, you may depend upon it,' announced Connie, as they went to the front door together, chatting.

'Well, good-bye, if you must go,' said Harry, holding Ned by both hands. 'And remember, whatever happens, you've got good friends here, not fair-weather friends either.'

'He must go, Harry,' cried Connie. 'I've kept him just to see you. You'll make him miss the next boat. Come, Ned! Good-bye!'

Ned turned to her, holding out his hand.

'Bend down!' she said, suddenly, her lips smiling, her eyes filling. 'You're so tall.'

He bent to her mechanically, not understanding. She took his head between her hands and kissed him on both cheeks.

'The republican kiss!' she cried, trying to laugh, offering her own cheek to him as he stood flushed and confused. Something choked him as he stooped to her again, touching the fair face with his lips, reverentially.

'Good-bye!' she exclaimed, her mouth working, grasping his hands. 'Our hearts are with you all up there, but, oh, don't let your good heart destroy you for no use!' Then she burst into tears and, turning to her husband, flung herself into the loving arms that opened for her. 'It's beginning again, Harry. It's beginning again. Will it never end, I wonder? And it's always the best it takes from us, Harry, the bravest and the best.' And she sobbed in his arms, quietly, resignedly, as she had sobbed, Ned recollected, when Geisner thundered forth that triumphant Marseillaise.

Her vivid imagination showed her friends and husband and sons going to prison and to death as friends and father and brother had gone to prison and to death in the days gone by. She knew the Cause so well—had it not suckled her and reared her?—with all the depth of the nature that her lightness of manner only veiled as the frothy spray of the flooded Barron veils the swell of the cataract beneath, with all the capacity for understanding that made her easily the equal of brilliant men. It was a Moloch, a Juggernaut, a Kronos that devoured its own children, a madness driving men to fill with their hopes and lives the chasm that lies between what is and what should be. It had lulled a little around her of late years, the fight that can only end one way because generation after generation carries it on, civilisation after civilisation, age after age. Now its bugle notes were swelling again and those she cared for would be called, sooner or later, one by one. Husband and children and friends, all must go as this bushman was going, going with his noble thoughts and pure instincts and generous manhood and eager brain. At least, it seemed to her that they must. And so she bewailed them, as women will even when their hearts are brave and when their devotion is untarnished and undimmed. She yearned for the dawning of the Day of Peace, of the Reign of Love, but her courage did not falter. Still amid her tears she clung to the idea that those whom the Cause calls must obey.

'Ned'll be late, Harry,' she whispered. 'He must go.' So Ned went, having grasped Harry's hand again, silently, a great lump in his throat and a dimness in his eyes but, nevertheless, strangely comforted.

He was just stepping on board the ferry steamer when Harry raced down, a little roll of paper in his hand. 'Connie forgot to give you this,' was all he had time to say. 'It's the only one she has.'

Ned opened the little roll to find it a pot-shot photograph of Nellie, taken in profile as she stood, with her hands clasped, gazing intently before her, her face sad and stern and beautiful, her figure full of womanly strength and grace. He lovered [sic] it, overjoyed, until the boat reached the Circular Quay. He kept taking it out and stealing sly peeps at it as the bus rolled up George-street, Redfern way.

CHAPTER IX

NED GOES TO HIS FATE

AT the station some of the Sydney unionists wore waiting to see Ned off. As they loaded him with friendly counsel and encouraged him with fraternal promises of assistance and compared the threats made in Sydney during the maritime strike with the expected action of the Government in Queensland, a newspaper boy came up to them, crowded at the carriage door.

'Hello, sonny! Whose rose is that?' asked one of the group, for the little lad carried a rose, red and blowing.

'It's Mr. Hawkinses rose,' answered the boy.

'For me!' exclaimed Ned, holding out his hand. 'Who is it from?'

'I'm not to say,' answered the urchin, slipping away.

The other men laughed. 'There must be a young lady interested in you, Hawkins,' said one jocularly; 'our Sydney girls always have good eyes for the right sort of a man.' 'I wondered why you stayed over last night, Hawkins,' remarked another. 'Trust a Queenslander to make himself at home everywhere,' contributed a third. Ned did not answer. He did not hear them. He knew who sent it.

Then the guard's whistle blew; another moment and the train started, slowly at first, gradually faster, amid a pattering of good-byes.

'Give him a cheer, lads!' cried one of his friends. 'Hip-hip-hurrah!'

'And one for his red rose!' shouted another. 'Hip-hip-hurrah!'

'And another for the Queensland bush men! Hip-hip-hurrah!'

Ned leaned over the door as the train drew away, laughing genially at the cheering and waving his hand to his friends. His eyes, meanwhile, eagerly searched the platform for a tall, black-clad figure.

He saw her as he was about to abandon hope; she was half concealed by a pillar, watching him intently. As his eyes drank her in, with a last fond look that absorbed every line of her face and figure, every shade of her, even to the flush that told she had heard the cheer for 'his red rose,' she waved her handkerchief to him. With eager hands he tore the fastening of a fantastically-shaped little nugget that hung on his watch-chain and flung it towards her. He saw her stoop to pick it up. Then the train swept on past a switch-house and he saw her no more, save in the picture gallery of his memory stored with priceless paintings of the face he loved; and in the little photo that he conned till his fellow-passengers nudged each other.

*   *   *

At Newcastle he left the train to stretch himself and get a cup of tea. As he stepped from the carriage a man came along who peered inquisitively at the travellers. He was a medium-sized man, with a trimmed beard, wearing a peaked cap pulled over his forehead. This inquisitive man looked at Ned closely, then followed him past the throng to the end of the platform. There, finding the bushman alone, he stepped up and, clapping his hand on Ned's shoulder, said quietly in his ear:

'In the Queen's name!'

Ned swung round on his heel, his heart palpitating, his nerves shaken, but his face as serene as ever. It had come, then. After all, what did it matter? He would have preferred to have reached his comrades but at least they would know he had tried. And no man should have reason to say that he had not taken whatever happened like a man. At the time he did not think it strange that he was not allowed to reach the border. The squatters could do what they liked he thought. If they wanted to hang men what was to stop them? So he swung round on his heel, convinced of the worst, calm outwardly, feverish inwardly, to enquire in a voice that did not shake:

'What little game are you up to, mister?'

The inquisitive man looked at him keenly.

'Is your name Hawkins?' he asked.

'Suppose it is! What does that matter to you?' demanded Ned, mechanically guarding his speech for future contingencies.

'It's all right, my friend,' replied the other, with a chuckle. 'I'm no policeman. If you're Hawkins, I've a message for you. Show me your credentials and I'll give it.'

'Who're you, anyway?' asked Ned. 'How do I know who you are?'

The inquisitive man stopped a uniformed porter who was passing. 'Here, Tom,' he said, 'this gentleman wants to know if I'm a union man. Am I?'

'Go along with your larks!' retorted the man in uniform. 'Why don't you ask me if you're alive?' and he passed on with a laugh as though he had heard an excellent joke.

'Hang it!' said the inquisitive man. 'That's what it is to be too well known. Let's see the engine-driver. He'll answer for me.'

'The other's good enough,' answered Ned, making up his mind, as was his habit, from the little things. 'Here's my credentials!' He pulled out his pocket-book and taking out a paper unfolded it for the inquisitive man to read.

'That's good enough, too,' was the stranger's comment. 'You answer the description but it's best to be sure. Now'—lowering his voice and moving still further from the peopled part of the platform—'here's the message. "Dangerous to try going through Brisbane. Police expecting him that way. Must go overland from Downs." Do you understand it?'

'I understand,' said Ned, arranging his plans quickly. 'It means they're after me and I'm to dodge them. I suppose I can leave my portmanteau with you?'

'I'm here to help you,' answered the man.

'Well, I'll take my blankets and leave everything else. I'm a Darling Downs boy and can easily get a horse there. And when I'm across a horse in the bush they'll find it tough work to stop me going through.'

'You'd better take some money,' remarked the man, after Ned had handed out his portmanteau. 'You may have to buy horses.'

'Not when I'm once among the camps,' said Ned. 'I can get relays there every few miles. I've got plenty to do me till then. How do you fellows here feel about things?'

'Our fellows are as sound as a bell. If everybody does as much as the miners will you'll have plenty of help. We don't believe everything the papers say. You seem a cool one and if the others will only keep cool you'll give the squatters a big wrestle yet.'

So they talked on till the train was about to start again.

'Take my advice,' said the man, drawing back further out of hearing and putting the portmanteau down between them, 'and get a cipher for messages. We had to arrange one with Sydney during the end of the maritime strike and that's what they've used to-night to get the tip to you. If it wasn't for that the other side would know what was said just as well as we do. Now, good-bye! Take care of yourself! And good luck to you!'

'Good-bye, and thanks!' said Ned, shaking hands as he jumped into his carriage. 'You've done us a good turn. We won't forget the South up in Queensland. You didn't tell me your name,' he added, as the train moved.

The man answered something that was lost in the jarring. Ned saw him wave his hand and walk away with the portmanteau. The train sped on, past sheds and side-tracked carriages, past steaming engines and switch-houses and great banked stacks of coal, out over the bridge into the open country beyond, speeding ever Queenslandwards.

Ned, leaning over the window, watched the sheen of the electric lights on the wharves, watched the shimmering of the river, watched the glower that hung over the city as if over a great bush fire, watched the glorious cloudless star-strewn sky and the splendid moon that lit the opening country as it had lit the water front of Sydney last night, as it would light for him the backtracks of the mazy bush when he forced his horses on, from camp to camp, six score miles and more a day. It was a traveller's moon, he thought with joy; let him once get into the saddle with relays ahead and let the rain hold off for four or five days more, then they could arrest him if they liked; at least he would have got back to his mates.

Newcastle faded away. He took his precious photo out again and held it in his hand after studying its outlines for the hundredth time; unobserved he pressed the red rose to his lips.

His heart filled with joy as he listened to the rumbling of the wheels, to the puffing of the engine, to the rubble-double-double of the train. Every mile it covered was a mile northward; every hour was a good day's journeying; every post it flew by was a post the less to pass of the hundred-thousand that lay between him and his goal. He would get back somehow. Where 'the chaps' were he would be, whatever happened. And when he got back he could tell them, at least, that the South would pour its willing levies to help them fight in Queensland the common enemy of all. It never struck him that he was getting further and further from Nellie. In his innermost soul he knew that he was travelling to her.

What good fellows they were down South here, he thought, with a gush of feeling. Wherever he went there were friends, cheering him, watching over him, caring for him, their purses open to him, because he was a Queensland bushman and because his union was in sore trouble and because they would not see brother unionists fall into a trap and perish there unaided. From the Barrier to Newcastle the brave miners, veterans of the Labour war, were standing by. In Adelaide and Sydney alike the town unions were voting aid and sympathy. The southern bushmen, threatened themselves, were sending to Queensland the hard cash that turns doubtful battles. If Melbourne was cool yet, it was only because she did not understand; she would swing in before it was over, he knew it. The consciousness of a continent throbbing in sympathy, despite the frowns and lies and evil speakings of governments and press and capitalistic organisations and of those whom these influence, dawned upon him. All the world over it was the same, two great ideas were crystallising, two great parties were forming, the lists were being cleared by combats such as this for the ultimate death-struggle between two great principles which could not always exist side by side. The robbed were beginning to understand the robbery; the workers were beginning to turn upon the drones; the dominance of the squatter, the mine-owner, the ship-owner, the land-owner, the shareholder, was being challenged; this was not the end, but surely it was the beginning of the end.

'Curse them!' muttered Ned, grinding his teeth, as he gazed out upon the moonlit country-side. 'What's the good of that?' he thought. 'As Geisner says, they don't know any better. A man ought to pity them, for they're no worse than the rest of us. They're no better and no worse than we'd be in their places. They can't help it any more than we can.'

A great love for all mankind stole over him, a yearning to be at fellowship with all. What fools men are to waste Life in making each other miserable, he thought! Why should not men like Strong and Geisner join hands? Why should not the republican kiss pass from one to another till loving kindness reigned all the world round? Men were rough and hasty and rash of tongue and apt to think ill too readily. But they were good at heart, the men he knew, and surely the men he did not know were the same. Perhaps some day— He built divine castles in the air as he twisted Nellie's rose between his fingers. Suddenly a great wonder seized him—he realised that he felt happy.

Happy! When he should be most miserable. Nellie would not be his wife and his union was in danger and prison gates yawned in front and already he was being hunted like an outlaw. Yet he was happy. He had never been so happy before. He was so happy that, he desired no change for himself. He would not have changed of his free will one step of his allotted path. He hated nobody. He loved everybody. He understood Life somewhat as he had never understood before. A great calm was upon him, a lulling between the tempest that had passed and the tempests that were coming, a forecast of the serenity to which Humanity is reaching by Pain.

'What does it matter, after all?' he murmured to himself. 'There is nothing worth worrying over so long as one does one's best. Things are coming along all right. We may be only stumbling towards the light but we're getting there just the same. So long as we know that what does the rest matter?'

'What am I?' he thought, looking up at the stars, which shone the brighter because the moon was now hidden behind the train. 'I am what I am, as the, old Jew God was, as we all are. We think we can change everything and we can change nothing. Our very thoughts and motives and ideals are only bits of the Eternal Force that holds the stars balanced in the skies and keeps the earth for a moment solid to our feet. I cannot move it. I cannot affect it. I cannot shake it. It alone is.'

'No more,' he thought on, 'can Eternal Force outside of me move me, affect me, shake me. The force in me is as eternal, as indestructible, as infinite, as the whole universal force. What it is I am too. The unknown Law that gives trend to Force is manifest in me as much as it is in the whole universe beside, yet no more than it is in the smallest atom that floats in the air, in the smallest living thing that swims in a drop of water. I am a part of that which is infinite and eternal and which working through Man has made him conscious and given him a sense of things and filled him with grand ideals sublime as the universe itself. None of us can escape the Law even if we would because we are part of the Law and because every act and every thought and every desire follows along in us to that which has gone before and to the influences around, just as the flight of a bullet is according to the weight of the bullet, and its shape, and the pressure, and the direction it was fired, and the wind.'

'It is as easy,' he dreamed on, 'for the stars to rebel and start playing nine-pins with one another, as it is for any man to swerve one hair's breadth from that which is natural for him to do, he being what he is and influences at any given time being what they are. None of us can help anything. We are all poor devils, within whom the human desire to love one another struggles with the brute desire to survive one another. And the brute desire is being beaten down by the very Pain we cry out against and the human desire is being fostered in us all by the very hatreds that seem to oppose it. And some day we shall all love one another and till then, I suppose, we must suffer for the Cause a little so that men may see by our suffering that, however unworthy we are, the Cause can give us courage to endure.'

'I must think that out when I have time,' he concluded, as the train slowed down at a stopping-place where his last fellow-passenger got out. 'I'll probably have plenty of time soon,' he added, mentally, chuckling good-humouredly at his grim joke. 'It's a pity, though, one doesn't feel good always. When a fellow gets into the thick of it, he gets hot and says things that he shouldn't and does things, too, I reckon.'

He had not heeded the other passengers but now that he found himself alone in the carriage he got down his blankets and made his bed. He took off his boots and coat as he had done in the park, stretched himself out on the seat, and slept at once the sleep of contentment. For the first time in his life the jarring of the train did not make his head ache nor its perpetual rubble-double irritate and unnerve him. He slept like a child as the train bore him onward, passing into sleep like a child, full of tenderness and love, slept dreamlessly and heavily, undisturbed, with the photo against his heart and the rose in his fingers and about his hands the hand-clasp of friends and on his cheeks the republican kiss as though his long-dead mother had pressed her lips there.

*   *   *

In Queensland the chain was prepared already whereto he was to be fastened like a dog, wherewith he was to be driven in gang like a bullock because his comrades trusted him. Yet he smiled in his sleep as the train sped on and as the moon stole round and shone in on him.

Over the wide continent the moon shone, the ever-renewing moon that had seen Life dawn in the distant Past and had seen Humanity falter up and had witnessed strange things and would witness stranger. It shone on towns restless in their slumbering; and on the countryside that dreamed of what was in the womb of Time; and on the gathering camps of the North; and on the Old Order bracing itself to stamp out the new thoughts; and on the New Order uplifting men and women to suffer and be strong. Did it laugh to think that in Australia men had forgotten how social injustice broods social wrongs and how social wrongs breed social conflicts, here as in all other lands? Did it weep to think that in Australia men are being crushed and women made weary and little children born to sorrow and shame because the lesson of the ages is not yet learned, because Humanity has not yet suffered enough, because we dare not yet to trust each other and be free? Or did it joy to know that there is no peace and no contentment so long as the fetters of tyranny and injustice gall our limbs, that whether we will or not the lash of ill-conditions drives us ever to struggle up to better things? Or did it simply not know and not care, but move ever to its unknown destiny as All does, shedding its glorious light, attracting and repelling, ceaseless obeying the Law that needs no policeman to maintain it?

The moon shone down, knowing nothing, and the moon sank down and the sun rose and still Ned slept. But over him and over the world, in moonlight and in darkness and in sunlight, sleeping or waking, in town and country, by land and sea, wherever men suffer and hope, wherever women weep, wherever little children wonder in dumb anguish, a great Thought stretched its sheltering folds, brooding godlike, pregnant, inspiring, a Thought mightier than the Universe, a Thought so sublime that we can trust like children in the Purpose of the forces that give it birth.

To you and to me this Thought speaks and pleads, wherever we are, whoever we are, weakening our will when we do wrong, strengthening our weakness when we would do right. And while we hear it and listen to it we are indeed as gods are, knowing good from evil.

It is ours, this Thought, because sinful men as we all are have shed their blood for it in their sinfulness, have lived for it in their earnest weakness, have felt their hearts grow tender despite themselves and have done unwittingly deeds that have met them in the path, deeds that shine as brightly to our mental eyes as do the seen and unseen stars that strew the firmament of heaven.

The brute-mother who would not be comforted because her young was taken gave birth in the end to the Christs who have surrendered all because the world sorrows. And we, in our yearnings and our aspirations, in our longings and our strugglings and our miseries, may engender even in these later days a Christ whom the world will not crucify, a Hero Leader whose genius will humanise the grown strength of this supreme and sublime Thought.

Let us not be deceived! It is in ourselves that the weakness is. It is in ourselves that the real fight must take place between the Old and the New. It is because we ourselves value our miserable lives, because we ourselves cling to the old fears and kneel still before the old idols, that the Thought still remains a thought only, that it does not create the New Order which will make of this weary world a Paradise indeed.

Neither ballots nor bullets will avail us unless we strive of ourselves to be men, to be worthier to be the dwelling houses of this Thought of which even the dream is filling the world with madness divine. To curb our own tongues, to soften our own hearts, to be sober ourselves, to be virtuous ourselves, to trust each other—at least to try—this we must do before we can justly expect of others that they should do it. Without hypocrisy, knowing how we all fall far short of the ideal, we must ourselves first cease to be utterly slaves of our own weaknesses.

JOHN MILLER.

About the Author

William Lane, of Irish-English parentage, was the eldest of five sons and one daughter. After his education at Bristol Grammar School, Lane worked his passage to Canada in 1867. He had various jobs before becoming a compositor, then reporter in Detroit during the 1880s. The American experience developed his radical thinking and he was influenced by the socialists Henry George and Edward Bellamy. Lane married Anne Mary McQuire in 1883. The couple sailed with their daughter for England in 1885. They stayed there briefly before travelling to Brisbane, Queensland, to join Lane's brothers who had preceded him to Australia. He worked as a journalist for *Figaro, the Telegraph, the Courier* and *the Observer*. He wrote under various pseudonyms including 'Sketcher' and 'Bystander'. The one mostly used, 'John Miller', came from the first chapter of the Marxist romance, *A Dream of John Ball* by William Morris (1887).

Lane and a compositor friend Alfred Walker established *The Boomerang* in 1887 and it was from his reporting on labour issues that he became an active participant in Queensland's trade union movement. Lane was at the forefront of the Queensland Australian Labour Federation (ALF), which established a new paper, *The Worker* (1890), that Lane edited, supporting the strikes of 1890 and 1891. His first novel, *White or Yellow? A Story of the Race War of A.D. 1908*, was serialised in the *Boomerang* in twelve episodes in 1888 under the pseudonym of 'Sketcher', but Lane's best-known work is *The Workingman's Paradise*, written to raise funds for the families of unionists jailed for conspiracy during those strikes and to explain socialism to the world.

Lane was familiar with utopian communities in North America and founded the New Australia Co-operative Settlement Association in the early 1890s. In 1893 more than 200 colonists travelled with Lane to Paraguay where he established a settlement. Disappointed by the refusal of members to adhere to his strict social rules, Lane migrated to New Zealand in 1899. There he wrote for Auckland's conservative *New Zealand Herald*. With the pseudonym of 'Tohunga' (the Maori word for prophet) Lane reversed his radical thought and denounced many of the causes he had championed while in Australia..

Lane has been featured in various other works, including *Hail Tomorrow* (1947), a play by Vance Palmer about the shearers' strike of 1891.

Other Titles in the Australian Classics Library Series

Jessica Anderson, *The Commandant,* ISBN 9781920898946

Barbara Baynton, *Bush Studies,* ISBN 9781920898953

Martin Boyd, *A Difficult Young Man,* ISBN 9781920898960

Rosa Cappiello, *Oh Lucky Country,* ISBN 9781920898977

C.J. Dennis, *The Moods of Ginger Mick,* ISBN 9781920898984

Ernest Favenc, *Tales of the Austral Tropics,* ISBN 9781920898991

Henry Lawson, *Joe Wilson and His Mates,* ISBN 9781920899011

Gerald Murnane, *Inland,* ISBN 9781920899028

A.B. Paterson, *The Man from Snowy River and Other Verses,* ISBN 9781920899035

Henry Handel Richardson, *Maurice Guest,* ISBN 9781920899042

Price Warung, *Tales of the Early Days,* ISBN 9781920899059

For further information and a complete list of books published by Sydney University Press please see our website at www.sup.usyd.edu.au